American Indian Literature and Critical Studies Series
Gerald Vizenor, General Editor

A Pipe for February

A Pipe for February

A Novel

CHARLES H. RED CORN

UNIVERSITY OF OKLAHOMA PRESS : NORMAN

This is a work of fiction. Names, characters, places, and incidents are either the product of the author's imagination or are used fictitiously, and any resemblance to actual events, locales, or persons, living or dead, is entirely coincidental.

Library of Congress Cataloging-in-Publication Data

Red Corn, Charles H. (Charles Harold), 1936–
    A pipe for February: a novel / Charles H. Red Corn.
        p. cm. — (American Indian literature and critical
    studies series; v. 44)
        ISBN 978–0–8061–3454–3 (cloth)
        ISBN 978–0–8061–3726–2 (paper)
        1. Osage Indians—Fiction. 2. Petroleum industry and
    trade—Fiction. 3. Oklahoma—Fiction. I. Title. II. Series.

    PS3618.E426P57 2002
    813'.6—dc21

                                            2002020036

A Pipe for February: A Novel is Volume 44 in the American Indian Literature and Critical Studies Series.

The paper in this book meets the guidelines for permanence and durability of the Committee on Production Guidelines for Book Longevity of the Council on Library Resources, Inc. ∞

dedicated to
my parents

Emma Louise Gray Red Corn
Pah-hui-le-zeh
of the Deer Clan

Harold A. Red Corn
Ki-he-un-tah
of the Peace Clan

Osages were warriors and were able negotiators. Those two interwoven characteristics helped our people to hang on to our old customs and there was strength in those old ways.

Our ancient culture was on a collision course with both good and evil forces of economics that would occur early in the nineteen hundreds when oil was discovered on our reservation.

Some of our people abandoned the ancient teachings and some went a little crazy with wealth. Some of our people stood back and watched and tried to make sense of it in the context of the old culture.

A Pipe for February

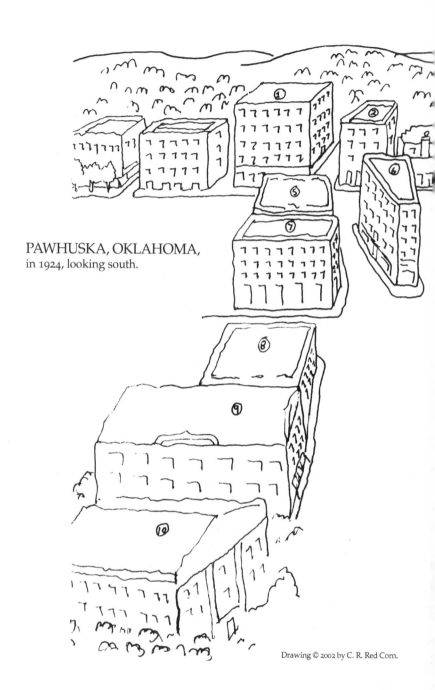

PAWHUSKA, OKLAHOMA,
in 1924, looking south.

Drawing © 2002 by C. R. Red Corn.

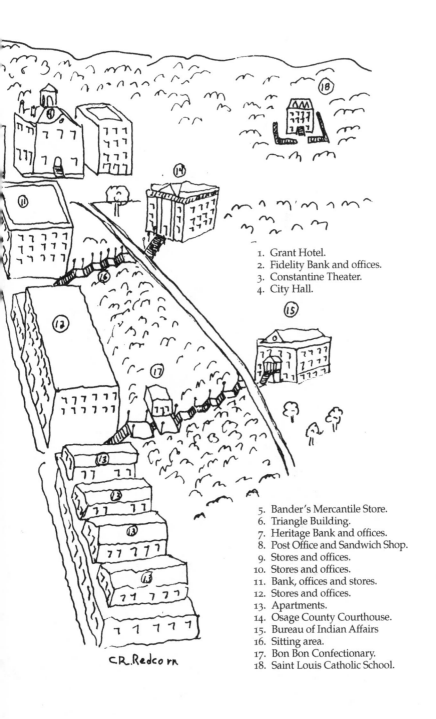

1. Grant Hotel.
2. Fidelity Bank and offices.
3. Constantine Theater.
4. City Hall.
5. Bander's Mercantile Store.
6. Triangle Building.
7. Heritage Bank and offices.
8. Post Office and Sandwich Shop.
9. Stores and offices.
10. Stores and offices.
11. Bank, offices and stores.
12. Stores and offices.
13. Apartments.
14. Osage County Courthouse.
15. Bureau of Indian Affairs
16. Sitting area.
17. Bon Bon Confectionary.
18. Saint Louis Catholic School.

C.R.Redcorn

PROLOGUE

November 1904

I was only five years old but I remember those four days. Dad and Grandpa were riding ahead on horses and we were traveling in a wagon to a camp where the families were planning to bury a pipe. It was an important Sacred Pipe.

My cousins and I were outside and crowded up close in the darkness to the lodge made of bark. Inside, the old men sat in a circle and a small fire flamed in the center of the lodge, and the women sat in an outer circle next to the walls of the lodge. The Non-hon-zhin-ga who led the meeting spoke and we could hear him.

"Tomorrow we will bury this one. This Pipe Person. When we needed courage this one gave us courage. Courage to face our enemies and courage to face the challenges of nature. This Pipe spoke for us. This one has been our messenger to Wah-kon-tah.

"This world has changed. It is time for us to bury this Pipe with dignity and to put away its teachings. There are other Pipes and we may bury them also. We will see. For now we will bury this Pipe.

"Those children who are outside listening, they will learn another language. They will be taught by white people. They will learn new ways and will not know our ways."

The old man stopped and looked thoughtful for a moment, then he continued.

"Tomorrow when Grandfather Sun is overhead we will bury this Sacred Pipe. We have agreed to do this, and it is hard to put aside things this sacred. Still, tomorrow we will bury this Pipe."

A woman held the Pipe wrapped in its woven cover. Her husband was the Keeper of the Pipe for his clan and as his wife her position was to look after the Pipe. She held it cradled in her arms and close to her breasts and in her grief she rocked the Pipe as she would rock an infant and when the woman could no longer restrain herself she began wailing a prayer song for one who has died.

CHAPTER

1

February 1924

It seems we were living the past and we were living the future. The past was deep and meaningful and we had clan names and a belief in Wah-kon-tah. In the future each Osage was wealthy and things moved faster than I thought possible.

On that day in February Grandpa and his friend Mi-keh-wa-ti-an-kah sat in the backseat of the long and luxurious Pierce Arrow and I drove. I was with Grandpa when he purchased the car. The salesman kept repeating that it was a luxurious car. It was as long and as large as any car Grandpa looked at, so he bought it. Grandpa always sat in the backseat and I would drive. Sometimes Tom would drive.

Many times Grandpa explained that Mi-keh-wa-ti-an-kah was a Sun Carrier. Some time in the far distant past the Sun Carrier Clan took its name from that force, that power, that makes things stay there in the sky. Things like the Sun and the Moon and the Stars. Even smoke must have some force to keep it up there. So it is they are the Sun Carriers, a war clan.

Grandpa and Mi-keh-wa-ti-an-kah are what their clans say they are. They have those qualities and traits of their clan symbols. I asked Grandpa when does an Osage become what his clan is. *"It takes time,"* he said. *"An Osage is born into a clan so you know who you will be and then you receive your clan name. That is when you become a person. About a year."*

We were going to cut cedar wood for the stem of a pipe.

On the drive to Mi-keh-wa-ti-an-kah's home, Grandpa explained the several ways to describe the months of the year, generally called moons. One of the phrases describing February may be interpreted as "Don't let it fool you." In other words it is not always what it seems to be, so do not get caught out away from shelter during February because the weather may change and you could be in danger.

By the turn of the century it was known that the oil on the old reservation was a high-grade petroleum and there was a lot of it. It is also important to know that the old clan system that guided the tribe always had a balance built into its organization. So, in 1906 when we divided up the oil income, each man, woman, and child received an equal amount of income. A child was financially equal with established leaders under the new law. Women were financially equal with men. Equal in land and in oil income.

I think Grandpa and Mi-keh-wa-ti-an-kah do not think of themselves as being wealthy. They seem to regard their position of wealth as a natural occurrence. I suppose, all things considered, their acquisition of wealth was as much a natural occurrence as it was planned.

The day had a chill in the air and the sun was bright. There were clouds in the northwest but the rest of the sky was clear.

Grandpa and Mi-keh-wa-ti-an-kah dressed alike. They wore buckskin leggings with cloth shirts, and moccasins. They had blankets wrapped around their waists. Mi-keh-wa-ti-an-kah wore his hair in two braids. Grandpa wore his hair in a strip from the top of his head to the back of his lower neck.

They sat in the backseat and at times like this I would drive and listen. I did not always hear anything because they often communicated in the sign language they knew as people who relied on hunting for food and who moved and worked quietly because they were warriors. I would hear nothing for a while and then they would laugh.

We drove north of the town to a place near Cedar Creek where we left the highway on the ridge of a hill and followed a trail along the ridge for about two hundred yards. We then went downhill and crossed the creek about one hundred yards downstream from where Grandpa had raised his family.

In what I suppose you could call more recent times my father and I had often fished that beautiful stream.

The cedar tree had been struck by lightning and was well seasoned and still standing. The limbs were close to the ground and the green leafy parts had fallen to the damp ground.

Grandpa pointed to the branch he wanted and as they watched I cut some small branches so I could get to the one they wanted. I then cut the branch they selected and carried it to them. I handed Grandpa the cedar and I asked in Osage, *"Is this good?"*

"It is good," he said.

"Grandpa, what kind of pipe is this going to be?"

"I will tell you about it later. I want to tell you the full story at one time."

I went to the edge of the water and rubbed clay into each end of the cedar so the wood would continue to season slowly and would not crack. I wrapped the wood with cloth and carefully placed the wood into the trunk of the car.

When I returned they were walking toward Grandpa's old camp. I told them I could drive through the woods to the camp but they chose to walk. It was mostly a tree-covered area with undergrowth of brush and some grass with dead leaves. They left their blankets in the car and I walked with them. They walked slowly and the dry leaves made almost no rustling sound. They stopped and talked and they would point in the direction of some happening they remembered and we would walk on. There was a buffalo hunt they discussed. A prominent man had apparently died during the hunt because of a horse falling.

"You always miss a man like him," Mi-keh-wa-ti-an-kah said.

Grandpa pointed to walnuts and pecans on the ground and to wild grapevines where my grandmother had harvested those foods. *"She was a good woman,"* he said.

It was a short distance but it was near midday when we reached the campsite and the sun shone through the leafless trees, and the air seemed colder.

The campsite is on a level clearing between huge boulders that form a wall that runs parallel with the creek bank. It is a natural campsite. Grandpa showed me the precise spot where my father and my uncle were born and the spot where Grandmother died. The fireplace was a small indentation in the ground with one side of the cook pit still showing the burnt and baked clay wall of the pit where my grandmother cooked.

Grandpa pointed to a crevice in the rock wall and said, *"Over there between those rocks, I would hide things there when we went to hunt buffalo. We would be gone longer than a moon."*

A large cedar tree partially hid the crevice. He said, *"That cedar tree. It was small. I tied a leather strap to it and pulled it over to hide our belongings."*

As near as I can tell Grandpa lived at the camp from 1873 until 1905 when he built the rock house over the hill. The stream was running and the water was clear. Near the base of the boulders an artesian spring gave them cooking and drinking water. I held the evergreen sapling back and Grandpa and Mi-keh-wa-ti-an-kah walked near and looked at the spring. He called it Ni-ni Mi-ka-sabe, Black Man Springs. He said he did not know why they called it that. The spring was full of water and had leaves and twigs in it and needed cleaning.

The chill I felt in the air earlier now felt like a strong cold front moving in. I have never worried much about Grandpa in cold weather. As a child I saw Grandpa and Dad swim the stream during winter when the water was near freezing, but that was several years ago.

I told Grandpa that I would come back soon and clean the spring. He thought a moment then said, *"That is good."*

While I walked toward the car to get their blankets, the front blew in hard and the wind was freezing and fast-moving clouds covered the sky and a loud crack of thunder shook the air and roared away from us and it was several seconds before we no longer could hear the thunder. A heavy rain hit suddenly and the rain fell just briefly, then I could hear sleet hitting the trees just north of us and I was wet but the sleet that moved in was better than the rain. I ran through the woods to the car and I could hear sleet hitting the trees that were around me.

The rain turning to sleet was good because the sleet would not soak into the ground and make it soft. I reached the car and navigated the trees and brush and the tall, thick grass that covered part of the ground helped to keep the tires from sinking on soft ground.

The wind and sleet swirled through the low area below the boulders. Grandpa and Mi-keh-wa-ti-an-kah stood between a cedar tree and the boulders and they were wet and still talking. I parked as near as I could and ran to them and handed them the blankets and they wrapped themselves in the blankets and slowly walked to the car and climbed into the backseat. They continued discussing a time when they butchered a buffalo they ran off the boulders and they said cattle are easy to butcher compared to a buffalo. They said they seldom had the chance to get a buffalo that way. They laughed about when my grandmother told them she did not want more buffalo falling into her camp.

Mi-keh-wa-ti-an-kah seemed to be okay, but Grandpa was starting to sneeze on the way home. I had never seen Grandpa sneeze. They talked about how funny they must have looked hurrying in the freezing rain. They laughed about February fooling them but Grandpa kept sneezing.

CHAPTER

2

No matter how formally he carried himself to me he was Grandpa and in two hours we would bury him. He was born in 1848 and lived the life of an Osage. He hunted buffalo on horseback with a bow and built his home from willow branches, bark, and buffalo hides. He fought the enemy, hand to hand, and he knew the rituals of the clans and on his chest were tattooed symbols of our clan, Tzi-zhu-wah-shta-gi, the Peace Clan.

I was sad and feeling alone, but I also knew that Grandpa had prepared me for that moment and I would face that moment.

Townspeople, government people, and Grandpa's attorney were there, but mostly it was our family and clansmen and members of the tribe. The main living room and the sunroom were filled with guests and more people waited outside in the cold.

Six years ago he had his burial clothes made. Now he was dressed in those buckskin leggings and blue shirt and blanket.

I stood by the heavy oak casket in Grandpa's living room, looking at him for the last time. Several people have told me they saw Grandpa shoot an arrow into a knot in a rope while riding at full speed on horseback.

The plastered walls of the living room were hand finished in what the architect called Florentine finish. The drapery was imported from Italy and the glass panel doors were made by a man from Kansas

City who stayed several days until the job was done. One day the man saw me drawing a picture of a horse and he stopped what he was doing and we discussed the art of drawing.

A crystal chandelier hung from the center of the living room ceiling and four smaller crystal chandeliers lit the rest of the room. During construction Grandpa would turn the lights on and watch the chandeliers sparkle. Then he would turn the lights off and look at another part of the house and then return to his little rock house out back.

Grandpa's war club hung over the fireplace. Once he had slain seven of the enemy with the club in one afternoon. The handle was made of willow wood and was covered with dark blue trade cloth. He told me not to bury the club with him because I may need it. I thought he was joking but he did not laugh.

Outside in the cold air the smoke from the summer kitchen and smokehouse gave the clear winter day a smell of food cooking and hickory burning. I tried to keep all of those senses in my memory as if the memories would be gone when we buried Grandpa.

I thought of Grandpa giving me my first horse and teaching me to ride. After my parents died, Grandpa did all he could to make up for me not having parents and I appreciated his trying as much as the things he did for me.

The hearse carrying Grandpa drove through the town of Paw-huska as he requested. We drove past the Triangle Building, which is the center of the town. The streets were crowded with people from all parts of the country who were buying and selling oil and the equipment to drill for oil. People on the street removed their hats and stood facing the long line of black cars.

Grandpa requested we take this route because he was intrigued that people could build large buildings. The red-brick buildings stood side by side on Main Street and on Kihekah Avenue. Grandpa financed the building where Harry Kirk the tailor rents space. When Harry heard Grandpa had died, he worked late so I could have a new suit for the funeral. Harry tells me I get a good price for tailoring, but the bill goes directly to the Agency so I really don't know.

The arrangement with Harry Kirk was set up when I was probably fifteen or sixteen.

I loaned the funds to build the Grand Hotel, but I knew nothing about it. I was told I had loaned the money and that I held a mortgage on the hotel. It is a fine, large hotel.

On the sidewalks cowboys and ranchers were mixed in with the men who wore dark suits. A crew of oil field workers turned to watch. Grandpa was not well known outside of the tribe and few people knew whose funeral it was. Stopping to pay respect is a custom afforded anyone whose time on earth has come to an end.

We drove north on Kihekah Avenue where the red-brick street climbs to the next level of the hill overlooking the valley and town. We drove past the Osage Agency employee homes and the homes of the townspeople. It is a short drive to the cemetery.

My parents' funeral was also in February and when we carried Grandpa from the hearse to the grave site the crunching of frozen grass was familiar and made me feel sad and cheated.

Henry Bigcreek held a small bucket of food covered with a cloth and placed the food at the head of Grandpa's grave. The food was part of the feast that would take place after the funeral and the spirit within the food would sustain Grandpa until he reached his destination.

Father Olfengaille, the young Catholic priest, in full vestments sang his formal Latin prayer as he swung the incense smoke over and around the casket to bless the soul of my grandfather and in his prayers the young priest asked the Creator to take Grandpa into his paradise.

Whitedeer wore white buckskin leggings and he was wrapped in a dark blanket. His head was covered with an otter skin bandeau and the braids of his hair were wrapped with otter fur. He is one of the leaders of the Deer Clan and he is tall and straight and old and he was a striking figure.

Standing near Whitedeer, dressed in traditional Osage clothing, was the hereditary Chief of the Osages. He, of course, would never allow our eyes to meet but his expression carried a message of compassion that I somehow felt. Whitedeer prayed in the smooth easy cadence of the formal Osage language, which is somewhat different from conversational Osage. Whitedeer's prayer was a formal prayer learned when he first began steps to be a Non-hon-zhin-ga.

The prayer was the only sound in the cold clear air, and his voice would rise to a high pitch and then his voice would lower and the cadence of the prayer continued for several minutes. He seemed to concentrate as he moved his eagle tail fan for expression.

When Grandfather Sun was directly overhead, Whitedeer's prayer ended and he remained still. Several women began wailing their prayer songs of mourning. At that moment Grandpa was lowered into the earth and began his journey with Grandfather Sun as Grandfather Sun passed above us.

CHAPTER

3

After the burial, Cousin Molly rode with me back to Grandpa's home near Cedar Creek. I am a year older than Molly and we were raised together and we are close friends. Her mother was my mother's sister. Molly looked warm wrapped in her fur with a matching fur hat.

Long cars were parked randomly on the grounds of Grandpa's home. Older people were wrapped in their blankets and younger people were dressed in the latest fashions. They seemed to walk slowly toward the summerhouse where dinner would be served and the smoke from the cooks' fires drifted low in the cold late winter air.

Getting out of the car I told Molly, "I'm going to see Tom and thank the cooks."

"I'm cold. I think I'll go on in the summerhouse," Molly answered. Her collar was turned up so that only the upper part of her face was exposed to the cold. "See ya inside."

Henry, or Hank, was tending the fire. The Bigcreeks are Cherokee and they had helped us during the four days since Grandpa died.

"Doin' okay, John?"

"I'm doing pretty good, Hank. The fire feels good." And I warmed my hands to the fire.

Aunt Mary always wears Osage clothing and on that cold day she covered her head with a scarf and wore a blanket. I suppose in

European terms Aunt Mary and Grandpa were first cousins. She is getting old and physically she is slowing down, but Aunt Mary keeps moving steadily and accomplishes a lot.

It was late winter but Aunt Mary had a good supply of dried foods to prepare a feast. I thought we should have had someone outside the family oversee the twenty or so cooks and servers and firetenders, but Aunt Mary wanted to do it. She was persuasive in her argument, she said she was going to do it.

While standing by the fire, I watched the cooks turning the fry bread in three brass kettles over the fire. Aunt Mary insists that the bread be served hot.

"You go in there and sit down," Aunt Mary told me. "They'll be waitin for you there in the summerhouse." I know that some day I will be an adult in Aunt Mary's eyes.

Aunt Mary uses English when she speaks to my cousins and me because she believes our lives will be easier if we speak only English. She and Grandpa silently disagreed on that point.

"I will go on over," and I walked to the summerhouse and waited in line to use the cedar smoke and water and then went inside. The food was on the tables and people were being seated.

Cousin Molly was waiting for me. "How are you holding up?"

"I'm doing well," I said. "I am tired and none of this seems like reality."

"Eat and you will feel better. Reality will set in soon enough." She poured me a bowl of coffee from the pot on the table. The heat from the bowl felt good and drinking the coffee made me warm and relaxed and I was hungry for the first time in several days.

Whitedeer again gave a traditional prayer. It is a prayer that has many verses and it took a few minutes to complete. Everyone was attentive and the servers stopped their movements and the room was quiet except for the voice of Whitedeer. Earlier the prayers were for Grandpa and his journey and this prayer was for those of us left behind.

The prayer ended and two hundred or so friends and family ate. It was a feast with all the traditional Osage foods. I ate the steam-fried meat gravy and hominy made from corn that was boiled with the ashes from the cooks' fire and the dried berries and squash. Those foods made me think of Grandpa. Molly was right, when I began eating I felt better.

Cousin Ted Bearsky and Roper were sitting across the table from me.

I noticed Harry the tailor was leaving and I wanted to thank him for making the suit and I caught up with him. "Here, Harry. Take this with you."

"No, no," Harry said. "I no take food with me. You are good customer Johnny."

"Harry, my aunt will be offended if you do not take this food with you. It is a custom of ours. We call it *o-lo-shka*."

"Carrying food away from your house is your custom?"

"Yes. An old custom."

Harry began to smile and to shake my hand. "I see, John, a custom. I will be glad to take your food home with me, if it is your custom."

"It is our custom and I want to thank you again for making the suit for me."

"For you John, I will make suit anytime."

I suppose we would have gone on thanking each other had Mr. Alan S. Sanders not been waiting for me. Mr. Sanders is always there when our family has a need and I did not want to keep him waiting. He wore a brown suit and a heavy overcoat that he did not remove when he came inside and he carried his brown hat. Mr. Sanders handled legal work for Grandpa and for my father.

Mr. Sanders has something of a slump in his posture. It is the posture of a man who has spent too many years bending over a desk working with papers. His hair has more gray than most fifty-year-old men, and in his view a funeral may be the only time when a person should not discuss business. Mr. Sanders shook my hand and patted me heavily on the shoulder with his other hand.

"How are you feeling, John?" Sanders adjusted his glasses. "I want you to know that I spoke with the superintendent about handling your grandfather's estate. You know I advised your grandfather on his will. Now, I know this is not the time to discuss business, but I want to see you when you are rested. Take your time and when you feel like it, come in and see me."

"I appreciate your help, sir, and I will drop by your office as soon as I am rested. Shouldn't be that long."

"That will be fine, John. Just fine." He looked around the room as if he wanted to say more, or maybe speak with someone else, but he did neither of those things. Rather, he buttoned the heavy overcoat and put on his hat and went outside.

Mr. Henry Hugel the superintendent of the Agency wore a dark suit and he wished me well. "Would you come by and see me in a few days, John? There is nothing urgent, but I think it would be good to talk about your grandfather's estate."

"Of course. I will come by next week. I will make an appointment."

He patted me on the shoulder, "Just anytime, John. Whenever you are rested I will see you there in my office."

I saw distant relatives I seldom see and people who knew Grandpa and my parents. It was a good time for me and I spoke with everyone there.

The guests said their farewells and the cooks and servers and firetenders enjoyed eating and telling stories and they laughed a lot. They had worked hard.

I dressed so that I would be warm and I walked to the top of the hill east of the house and stood near a rock that is about as high as my waist and looked out over the hills and at the leafless trees along the creek and the blackjacks standing against the winter cold on the ridge of the hill to the north.

This walk up the hill was not a deep and somber moment that would dictate the direction of my life. Rather, it was a few minutes to be alone for the first time in several days. The ritual of the funeral had taken care of my emotional needs as it was designed to do by those old Osages.

There was a cold wind. The birds and other earth creatures made no noises and the earth was silent, except for the wind.

A mature bald eagle sailed across the sky soaring westward, following the sun I thought. A bald eagle is a beautiful creature and in the complex tribal makeup it is one of the symbols of the Sky People and it gave my blood a small rush.

As the sun dropped lower toward the horizon the air became very cold and I felt strong and prepared to face whatever was ahead of me.

Grandfather Sun turned the sky and clouds a brilliant series of colors as he followed his winter path carrying Grandpa on his journey, and I watched as the intense orange color slowly turned a brilliant red, then he disappeared beyond the horizon. It was at that moment standing alone on that cold hilltop I said goodbye to Grandpa.

CHAPTER

4

During the week following the funeral the frigid cold moved on out of the old reservation and the ice and snow began melting and soaking the ground. The warm sun felt good.

I stood on the porch watching a coyote in the tall grass halfway down the hillside and he seemed to be watching the house. While watching the coyote I heard Aunt Mary's car enter the gate and at the sound of the car the coyote turned and trotted over the ridge of the hill. He stopped once and looked back. I had never seen a coyote act that way.

Inside I sat in the living room with Aunt Mary and Molly and I waited until Aunt Mary drank coffee and was comfortable with what she wanted to say. *"Grandson. I think it would be good if you took a trip. I have asked your sister to come with me to tell you this."*

I am certain that Aunt Mary was speaking in Osage because Grandpa always spoke to me in Osage and it was a concession she was making to his memory. It was a concession I appreciated.

We boarded the train at midday and I sat in the drawing room next to a window and I had planned to read. Molly and Ted went to the dining car and later said several Osages were on the train. Among them Whitedeer's oldest daughter and her husband and children were on board. Sonny Adams's cousin, Luke Adams, and his parents were in the next car. They said Sonny had planned to come with them but decided at the last minute not to come. I would see all of them and others before we reached Colorado Springs.

The next morning I watched the prairie of western Kansas go by. The scattered patches of snow looked cold and I thought of Grandpa hunting buffalo on those plains. The buffalo are gone but the buffalo wallows are still on the plains. Grandpa told me about buffalo wallows where the buffalo would roll and wallow in the dirt and kick up the dust or would roll and wallow in the mud. Grandpa told me so much about the buffalo hunts that I could picture them in my mind's eye and that was the first time I relaxed and enjoyed the journey.

Grandpa told me a story about himself and a friend who were on horseback in this part of the country. It was very cold and they built a fire on a large flat rock overlooking a stream. They cooked some meat and made coffee then pushed the embers away and made their beds on the rock. Sometime during the night Grandpa's friend died. Grandpa did what he needed to do in the way of prayers and put the man on his horse and took him back to the camp. It was a long ride. Grandpa told me that story many times and always warned me about sleeping on a warm rock.

I wanted to rent a cabin in the mountains but Molly and Ted call that roughing it so we stayed at the Antlers Hotel. That was not roughing it. The music was good, mostly ragtime. Molly likes music probably more than Ted and I do. The food at the Antlers was excellent. All of our rooms were on the west side and gave a good view of Pike's Peak.

A snowstorm moved in the first day and the hotel offered just about anything we would want and there was no good reason for Molly and Ted to leave the hotel. I went for long walks and spent time outdoors walking or sitting and looking at the Rocky Mountains. The streets and roads were snow packed and rough, but one day I hired a touring car to drive into the mountains and we made it as far as the Garden of the Gods, to a little café called Joe's that was open. The driver and I had lunch there. Joe is an Italian who in the off-season does the waiting and cashiering as well as the cooking.

I had eaten there many times before and he remembered one day when he took my dad into the kitchen and taught him how to make Joe's special salad. The memory of traveling with my parents was good, and it was dark when I returned to the hotel. March would normally be a little early in the season to go to the mountains, but Aunt Mary's idea to take a trip came at a good time in my healing. My cousins and I are close enough that we did not feel a need to entertain each other. We had been there several days when the sun came out and I talked them into hiring the touring car to drive up into the mountains to the Garden of the Gods. We had our picture taken near a large boulder where we took our picture with our parents when I was six years old. I went back the next day and picked up the picture that was then on a post card and I mailed the card to Barbara Williams in Kentucky. She and I had not communicated in a while.

Ted spent one afternoon conversing about different wines with a gentleman in the lobby of the hotel. I went shopping with Molly and carried her packages. When we visit the Springs during warm weather we spend a lot of time at the arcades and at the skating rink, but they were closed because of weather.

On the last day I took the touring car back to Joe's and ate. That evening we had a big dinner in the main dining room of the hotel and on the next morning when the day was warm and the sun bright we boarded the train for the trip home.

I knew things would be different but I was anxious to get home and get started. Getting started on what exactly, I did not know. I thought of painting and even thought of sculpture. I thought of trying a business of some sort. Whatever it would be, I was anxious to get started.

Tom was chopping wood when I drove through the driveway and he stopped and walked toward the garage. Tom was wearing his red plaid hunting cap tilted to the left and forward and he needed a shave. "Hi, Johnny. How was the trip?" He pulled the white tobacco bag from his shirt pocket.

"It was a good trip, Tom. Good to see you."

"Doris got supper ready. She's had supper ready all week."

I was seven the first time I saw Tom. Mom told me Dad would be coming home from a horse race in Arkansas that afternoon. I sat on the rock gate entrance to our home and waited for two hours, maybe three. It was not long because I was waiting for my dad. At first Cousin Molly sat with me but she tired and went inside to visit with my mother. She probably sat on the kitchen counter and talked while my mother cooked and listened.

About four o'clock, I saw his car come up out of the valley followed by two trucks. He slowed down to turn into the driveway and Dad stopped, and I rode with him on to the stables.

"I want you to meet someone," Dad said. "This is Tom Woodson. Tom is going to stay with us for a while." He was the smallest man I had ever seen and he shook my hand.

"Your Dad told me a lot about you."

"Glad to meet you, Tom," I said, and except for two years Tom spent in Europe fighting the war he has been with our family since that day. Like all jockeys Tom is a small wiry man. Tom told me once that he is just one of those people who is more comfortable around Indians than around white people.

During the war Tom inhaled poison gas and suffered lung damage that causes him to cough. He talks about a pension from the War Department and I have written several letters for him but they want details about France. We wrote back that it was at Ishytale but that is wrong and he has no records.

Tom keeps three months ahead on wood cutting so the cooking and heating wood is well seasoned and burns hot and clean. We have a truck and a tractor, but Tom prefers to hitch the horses to the wagon and haul the wood back to the house the same way he did it when I was a child and would sometimes help him.

Later that evening when we were eating Tom said he went looking for a horse to work with and may have found one.

"There's one thing that did happen while you was gone that you oughta know about. I was up on the hill yesterday, goin to get a load of wood, and it looks like somebody has been camped out up there. I think he's been watchin the house. He didn't build no fire or nothin. Looks like he's been up there night and day. Smoked a lotta smokes and he made a bed. Now that I know he's up there, I'll catch him. At least I'll see who he is.

"Johnny, I got a feelin that old boy mighta been pokin around in the barn, too. Don't know exactly why, but I just got that feelin." He took a draw of the tobacco and said, "I told Doris so she'd know."

Doris was interested but said nothing.

"Any idea who it might be?"

"Nope. Thought I might take my squirrel gun and sneak up there some night and see if I can catch him." Tom took a deep drag from his cigarette. "I don't want to put no lead in him I just wanna find out what he's up to."

That night Tom circled the hill and watched the hiding place but whoever had been there did not show up. Tom said he would keep an eye on the hill.

CHAPTER

5

The morning following our return from Colorado, Roper called on the telephone. He wanted to meet for lunch at the Santa Fe Railroad Depot to wait for a telegraph message that would confirm the shipment of cattle from Kansas City. Roper has been a good friend since grade school. He says his Indian blood only shows in his nose. His skin is that of a white man and his hair is blond, but he has a nose like the Indian on the nickel.

Roper's great-grandfather was an Osage and his other seven great-grandparents were French and Irish. That would make him one-eighth Osage blood. In the fourth grade an Osage boy transferred to Indian Camp School and the first day there he called Roper E'n-shta-keh. Roper knew enough Osage to know he had been called a white boy. Roper thought a moment then he charged the new arrival and they rolled around on the ground grunting and throwing an occasional punch. Roper managed to tear the shirt off the other boy before Mrs. Perkaiser stopped them. He had a similar fight in the seventh grade and I think that was his last fight, but I have known since then Roper will fight.

After high school Roper attended the Oklahoma Agriculture and Mechanical College to study ranching. He did well for three years but did not return for his senior year. Roper says he just became more interested in ranching than in the study of ranching. It was during this time that Roper tried using his real name of Williard Watson for awhile.

Roper is in good physical shape and he is a pretty good cowboy, but I do not know how capable a rancher he might be. I would say he is generally regarded as a better rancher than I am regarded as an artist.

Anyway, in addition to oil royalties each Osage received six hundred fifty-eight acres of land. Roper's land is out on the western side of the old reservation on the prairie and like most Osage families Roper and his family members took their land in the same general area. When several family members put their land together they can create a profitable ranching operation.

He leases grazing land from other Osages. Being Osage gives Roper an edge in that important aspect of ranching. Dad said there are two parts to a ranch, cattle and land, and you can buy the cattle anywhere. Acquiring land is competitive and I doubt that Roper has the drive in his spirit to build a large ranch. Each morning he drives to town and buys two newspapers and finds a place to drink coffee and read. We tease him about being a gentleman rancher and he takes teasing well.

Molly's cousin Evelyn Thunder and Roper spend a lot of time together. They argue a lot, but the arguing is teasing. The last time I was with them Evelyn accused Roper of going out with her so he can lease her land. Roper laughed and spent the evening talking about ways he could get her land.

We arrived at the depot at the same time. The rail yard is six tracks wide and a long train had pulled into the station. I watched the workers busy with their wagons and black trucks and teams of horses and tractors unloading pipe and timbers and huge spools of cable and machinery and steel tanks. Some day, that would make a good painting, but I have many things to paint before I paint the rail yard, like the painting of the cathedral I have been putting off for almost a year.

Roper asked about the trip and I told him it was good.

"John, there is something I need to tell you. I drove over to the sale at Dewey with Martha and Evelyn, we went to that little rodeo over near Copan."

"I've been to that Copan rodeo. Good little rodeo."

"Anyway, John, when we got back to Grayhorse and drove up to the house there was a man standing in that little corner where the fireplace sticks out from the house.

"Well, anyway, I hollered at him and asked him what he wanted and he did not move. So, we drove to Fairfax and got the sheriff's deputy and we all went back out there and looked around, but the guy was gone. The girls didn't find anything missing. They stayed at their parents' house that night and the next day I went with them and they bought a gun, but I don't know that they would use it. Evelyn might. She might blow somebody up," and Roper smiled about that.

"Did you get a look at him?"

"No, it was too dark. We couldn't see anything, except that he was all dressed in dark clothes."

"You know, Roper, Tom thinks someone has been snooping around our place."

"Think it could be the same guy?"

"Could be. I'll let you know if I learn anything."

Just as we finished talking Molly drove into the rail station.

CHAPTER
6

The waitress in the restaurant of the Santa Fe Railroad Depot brought our drinks. "Molly, here's your tea, hot as you ordered. Roper and John, here's your coffee.

"Ted, here's your big tonic water with very little ice." She smiled, "Your food will be ready in just a little while."

"Okay, two questions, you guys," Molly said. "Do you like my hair short like this, and do you like it parted on one side like it is?"

I believe Roper had been thinking about the cattle, but he took Molly's question seriously and turned his attention to her. "I think it looks good. It matches the way you dress, too."

"Good," she said. "I like it. I just wondered how it looks to other people."

Ted stirred the drink and asked me, "Have you been back to see Mr. Sanders? He told me you and him had a good talk."

"We had a meeting, but I haven't decided on Grandpa's estate."

"You oughta deal with him. If you hire Sanders you don't have to talk to Herbert and Bartholomew at the Agency. Sanders will do that for you, and he'll get you money when you want it."

"Mr. Sanders is pretty good," Molly said. "I have one hundred thirty-six cows. I will get a balance sheet next week that will tell me what they're worth."

The waitress brought the food. Ted was sipping his drink and watching the train come into the station. "You can talk to Sanders in a minute. He's getting off the train."

Mr. Alan S. Sanders stepped onto the dock from the train. He wore a suit and hat and was carrying a briefcase, and he waved to us. Molly waved and Ted raised his glass to Sanders.

"Ted. Quit that," Molly said. "He's a nice man."

"He deserves a good toast. He's my guardian."

Sanders saw Ted's toast and he smiled.

Ted took another drink, "Oh, hell, he's coming in here."

"Now, Ted, you behave when he gets here," Molly said.

"I'll behave. I'm always have." That is a line Ted has used since grade school.

Mr. Sanders entered the cafe and came to our table. I stood to shake his hand. "Keep your seat, John. You too, Roper. Ted." He nodded to Ted. "Miss Molly, how are you?"

"I am fine, Mr. Sanders. Roper is coming out day after tomorrow to look at my cattle. I don't know much about cattle."

"That's good, Roper." He held his thumb in his vest pocket and adjusted his glasses.

"John, you need to stop by the office and visit with me. I have been working on that plan I told you about. I think that plan will make you a wealthy young man."

I nodded, "I'll stop by in a day or two."

"Good, John, good. You all enjoy your lunch and, John, I'll see you in a day or two." He took the watch from his vest pocket and looked at it. He more or less cupped the watch in his hand and I could not see it. "I must run along now," and he left.

Molly said, "A wealthy young man, huh?"

Ted was still looking out the window, watching a young lady getting off the same car as Alan Sanders. She was attractive with light red hair and wore a long brown coat with a fur collar that was a little warm for the day, but she was traveling and she carried a parasol. She gave the Negro porter instructions for placing her luggage onto a cart. The young lady looked in our direction and smiled at Ted and went on with her business of instructing the porter.

"Do you know her?" Molly asked.

"Nope. Wish I did."

"You should invite her to your party," I said. "A young girl away from home, no friends. You should make her feel welcome and at home."

Roper added, "If you were away from home you'd want to go to her party."

"You know," Ted said. "She oughta be at my party."

The young lady came into the café and paused a moment. The porter was young and tall and he waited while she repaired what Molly called the spit curls of her hair and adjusted her hat to fit just right. She pointed to the table next to us and told the porter, "Just put my bags over there by that table."

She tipped the porter and he thanked her, and the young lady turned to us and asked, "Do you all know Mister Otis Davis?"

"Not me," Roper said.

"Was he supposed to meet you?" Molly asked. She was genuinely concerned.

"Well, I am not sure. You see, he's my uncle and I thought he'd be here to meet me. He's the nicest man in the world and I know if he got my letter he'd be here."

"Does he live in Pawhuska?"

"On Eighth Street. I know he's pretty busy with all of the wells they're drilling."

"He drills wells?" Ted asked.

"Well, not exactly. He sets up the derricks and gets them ready for somebody else to drill."

"Well then, don't bother him," Ted said. "We need all the wells we can get."

She laughed and extended her hand to Molly. "My name is Mavis Davis."

We each introduced ourselves to Mavis Davis. "Would you like to join us while you wait for your uncle?" Molly asked.

"Yes, ma'am. I would," Mavis said. "I love your outfit, Molly. It's so chic."

"Thank you, Mavis," and Molly smiled.

A taxi driver entered the restaurant, looked around to our table. "Miss Davis?"

"Yes. That's me."

"Your Uncle Otis sent me to pick you up."

"That's thoughtful of him." She turned to us. "It's been good meetin' you all." She looked at Ted and said, "I hope we can see more of each other."

"I'll get the tea," Ted said.

She adjusted her hair just a little and smiled. "Thank you, Ted."

Ted stood holding his glass. "If you're gonna be in town maybe you can come to my party. Saturday night April the third."

"I would love to come. Is the party at your place? I guess what I mean is, where is the party and what should I wear?"

"It's at my place a few miles north and west of town. People will be dressed about any way you can imagine. Bob Wills is playin for the dance and we'll have lots of food and stuff to drink," Ted said. "Ever hear of Bob Wills?"

"I think I've heard of him, but I can't say I know anything about him, but he sounds sensational. Just drop the invitation by the Grand Hotel. I'll pick it up." With that Miss Mavis Davis walked to the door and turned and waved to us, focusing her smile on Ted. "Nice to meet y'all," and she left the station.

Molly said, "Pretty good, Ted."

Roper added, "Proud of you, Ted."

"I bet she comes," I added.

"Of course she will come," Molly said. "She likes to watch big Indian men drool."

We were eating when the station agent came to our table and informed Roper his cattle would arrive the next morning at six o'clock at the Onapah stock pens north of town. He handed the telegram to Roper. Roper looked at the telegram, folded it, and put it into his shirt pocket.

Molly was watching Ted and she was smiling. Molly has a nice genuine smile. She was humming the tune and singing softly. "Five foot two, eyes of blue,"

Ted looked at her. "What are you saying?"

"I'm five foot two," she smiled again, "and I was singing about myself, Ted. Of course, my eyes are not blue, but I am five foot two."

Outside Ted swept his finger over the hood of the yellow Stutz Bearcat convertible to see if it had collected any dust.

Molly told Ted, "I would have the car cleaned and swept out before I went looking for Mavis Davis."

"Who said anything about Mavis Davis?"

"No one. You just remember Aunt Mary's meeting next week."

"I bet I wrote it down before you did." Ted did not say where he was going, he just backed the car away from the curb and spun his wheels a little as he drove away, throwing gravel and creating a little cloud of dust.

"You know," Molly said, "I worry about Ted driving so fast."

"There are several things about Ted worth worrying about, and I suppose his driving is one of them."

CHAPTER

7

That evening I went into the room next to the living room that the architect called the sunroom. The natural light is good for painting and I had started calling the room my studio. Books and sketch pads were stacked and leaning against the walls and on the bookshelves and the smell of oil paint made it seem like a studio.

During my college days I was excited about Van Gogh and Renoir and just about all of the impressionist painters. I thought I understood what they were doing and I once spent four weeks in Paris to soak up the atmosphere. From there I went to Rome and to more remote places in Italy and viewed magnificent paintings and sculpture and architecture. After traveling Europe I knew I would put great works of art on my canvas when I got back to Osage country, but that night I sat staring at the canvas wondering how the cathedral fit onto that blank white space. I had no idea, and I was glad Ted called, wanting to meet at the restaurant in the Grand Hotel.

"Sit down, Cuz," Ted said. "You look tired. Better eat."

"I ate at home, but I'll have a soda. What are you up to?"

"Nothing, just bored. Thought we might do something."

"I thought you would have found Miss Mavis Davis by now."

"I thought I might bump into her here at the hotel."

"Let's go upstairs to that speakeasy. I think they have a band up there."

"You know, Cuz, I bet there's another room like that speakeasy in the hotel that they don't tell everybody about."

"Could be."

"You own this place, why don't you ask the manager?"

"I don't own this place. I just loaned Mr. Baskins the money to build it. I've never known anything about the hotel."

"Well, you have a stake in it. Why don't you ask that Baskins guy?" Ted's thought was interrupted by the people at a table across the room. "Hey, Cuz, look over there."

"What is it?"

"I think it's Rosa Hoots. You know, the Osage lady with the race-horse that might run in the Kentucky Derby."

"Okay. Give me a minute and I'll look." I waited a moment and got up and walked to the cash register and picked up a toothpick. That was a pretty weak reason, but I got to look. Mrs. Hoots wore a large white hat with a big red bow in the back. Her hat was a part of the outfit, as Molly would call it, and she was telling a story to the several people at her table.

"You're right, Ted, that's her. Dad introduced me to her once. They talked about buying a horse together. You know both of them owning it, but Dad said it would never have worked out."

"If your dad introduced you to her, you can introduce me."

"Okay, come on."

So, I introduced them. Mrs. Hoots is a friendly and gracious woman as well as being outspoken. She remembered me and asked us to sit down. She had learned earlier in the day that Black Gold would compete in the Kentucky Derby and she and her group of friends were starting a celebration.

Mrs. Hoots invited us to Louisville for the Derby and we agreed we would be there if we could. She said a good number of Osages were going. She and Ted had a small disagreement about who would pick up whose check. I was proud of Ted, he won. That is not easy with a woman like Rosa Hoots.

Upstairs the room was smoky and crowded and there was a rag-time band and it was loud.

"What d'ya need, honey?" It was the barmaid with the raspy voice who people call Sam. I don't know her real name. It may be Sam.

"Just a soda."

"Soda? Got a hangover?"

"No. Just don't feel like drinking."

"I was gonna say," Sam said, "that if you gotta hangover you need a drink."

"I feel like drinking," Ted said. "The other night you had something a guy from Kansas City had brought down. English or Irish."

"Irish whiskey?"

"Yeah. I bet that's it. Bring me one."

"Okay. Is that about it, honey?"

"That's it," Ted said.

When Sam went to get our drinks, she spoke to two women who were sitting at the bar. They were dressed in what Cousin Molly calls flapper dresses and they turned and looked in our direction and Ted did not see them look at us. They walked to our table and one of them said. "Care if we join you boys?"

"Not at all," Ted said. "Tell Sam what you want to drink."

We talked to the girls. They were from Tulsa and were thinking about moving to Pawhuska. Ted danced with them and did not seem to be bored, but he kept looking around the room.

I knew I had to sleep if I was to be at Onapah by six, so I went home and went to bed and, eventually, I slept. The last thought I had before falling to sleep was to wonder if Ted ever found Mavis Davis.

CHAPTER
8

At four o'clock I awoke to the strong aroma of Tom's coffee. He had a fire going in the kitchen and he had breakfast ready. I have always thought Tom's cooking is like that of a chuck wagon cook on a cattle drive. I had several biscuits and three eggs that were fried in bacon grease and some bacon that, as Ted once said, had the hell fried out of it. I put three biscuits in my coat pocket and we left.

I opened the barn door to the familiar smell of animals and hay and straw and the horses snorted and I heard them moving in the darkness toward the feed boxes in the corners of the stalls. My Dad was a horseman and designed the layout of the barn.

Tom hung the lantern on a post. He knows the barn well and did not need much light to bring a bucket of oats to each of the horses. It was a routine that Tom and the horses knew well.

I waited in the tack room for a few minutes while the horses ate the oats. The smell of leather reminds me of good and pleasant times. I carried the blankets, saddles, and bridles out to the wide main aisle of the barn where the lantern hung and we saddled the horses. Seneca is a pinto and Choctaw a big bay. Osage was the first horse Dad named after a tribe. Osage died several years ago.

Tom and I started west in the early morning darkness. Tom's black and brown hound that he calls Wolf followed. Wolf and Tom are every bit as close as Tom and I. We crossed the creek and followed the trail over the hill to Onapah. Tom and Seneca knew the trail and rode ahead of me. The moon gave some light and the pre-dawn sounds made a good ride to the loading pens. Choctaw is a big gentle horse and I enjoy riding him.

From the top of the hill looking down to the rail line we saw a lantern light and a campfire at Onapah. The lantern hung on a pole by the loading chute and lit a sign on the loading pens that identified Onapah to the train engineers.

The still darkness had a definite chill, and riding down the hill I saw Cloud squat near the fire and pour coffee, and another cup of coffee seemed like a good idea. Slowly and with some effort Cloud got back to his feet.

Cloud's full name is Jackson White Cloud, but everyone around Osage Country calls him Cloud. He is a Sioux, so that makes him a cousin of sorts to Osages. Cloud is a good cowboy who competes in rodeos when he needs the prize money. He would be a big help in moving the herd over to Roper's place. I knew for sure he would be more help than I would be. Like many people who have made a living around horses, Cloud had broken several bones, and the bones may have mended but the ache is still there on a chilly morning.

Cloud is older than us, early forties I would bet. He lives hard and is lean and has a strong Sioux accent. The worn broad-brimmed hat and his strong Sioux features show a lot of wear. Those features were highlighted by the moving flames and somehow gave me some confidence in what we were undertaking.

We reached them and Roper was telling Cloud the story about when he was called E'n-shta-keh and had settled it with a fight. Cloud smiled and looked at Roper, and Cloud's expression told me nothing of what he thought about Roper's story.

We stood near the fire and sipped the coffee and talked, mostly about working and shipping cattle. At five minutes before six we heard the train coming from the north. It was still two or three miles up the line when the train engineer blew the whistle.

"Why in hell is he blowing that damned whistle?" Roper asked. He gets irritable when he has not had enough sleep.

"I suppose to let the cattle know it's time for them to get off the train," I said.

"Yeah. Never thought of that." It was still a little early for much humor.

"Have more coffee," Cloud said, and he poured more coffee.

We could see the light in the distance and we could hear the train noises as it began to stop. The engineer gave the whistle two more toots.

"Them heifers oughta be ready to get off now," Roper said.

We all seemed to move at once. Tom poured the coffee out onto the fire and replaced the old coffeepot upside down over the tall skinny pole and he kicked dirt over the smoking ashes until there was no more smoke.

Cloud reassured the horses with his hands and a low voice and when the horses were okay he joined us at the loading chute.

I checked the pen for places the heifers might get out. "Cloud already done that," Roper told me over his shoulder. He was holding his paper up to the lantern to read it.

"It's a little late for that too," I told him.

"You just count the cows," Roper told me. "Make sure there are eighty of them."

The train slowly came to a stop. A brakeman stepped from the train at the loading chute. The brakeman's lantern gave enough light to see more or less what was going on.

Within a few minutes the doors to the stock cars were open and we were unloading the cattle. What had been a still, quiet morning was full of the noises of the train hissing, cattle bawling, and Roper and Cloud cursing, and the sounds of cattle hitting and kicking the stock cars and the loading chute and pens, and Wolf barking. Tom kept the little cigarette in his mouth while he pushed and grunted at the heifers. Soon he lost the cigarette and was able to curse the heifers out loud.

In about twenty minutes things settled down. The cattle were out of the two cars and into the pens. It took about as long to unload as we had thought. Roper signed the papers that accepted the shipment and the engineer started stoking up the engine and slowly leaving.

"Did you count eighty of em?" Roper asked me.

"It was kinda dark, but I'd say there were about eighty."

"Damn," Roper said. He still was not ready for humor.

Cloud hooked a bell to the rope on the neck of the gentle lead cow. The idea is that the heifers will follow the bell cow. These were young cattle and we were not certain they would follow the bell cow. Cloud rode an Appaloosa he brought down from up north. His saddle was well worn and I could tell Cloud kept good care of it.

Roper was familiar with the trail that led to his ranch. Tom was on the left of the herd and Cloud on the right. I brought up the tail. It was getting light in the east when we crossed the highway that was next to the loading pens and headed west down a dirt road for a quarter of a mile where we entered Grandpa's pasture. In a half hour the sun would break.

We crossed the creek without any problems and headed up a long hill. When we reached the top of the hill Roper reined in the horse he calls Crow and held his hand in the air as a signal to stop. When Roper stopped the bell cow stopped and so did the heifers. There were buffalo wallows on the top of the hill. Except for the wallows the grass was good on top of the hill. There was some new bluestem grass in the brown grass left from winter. The heifers began grazing and we were silent.

Roper dismounted. He held the reins in his left hand and motioned with his right hand for us to move forward and join him. I quietly walked forward and waited near Roper. We both looked down into the valley. In the valley an older Osage man and woman walked toward the east. Their hair was hanging loose and the woman wore a cloth dress. The man was dressed in buckskin leggings and a breech-cloth that covered his lower body and legs. He was bare above the waist. They must have heard the bell cow in the distance, but they gave no indication they were aware of our presence.

Roper took the bell from the cow's neck and we stood on the edge of the flat-topped hill, holding the reins of the horses. We waited and watched. Tom dropped the reins of Seneca and the horse stood. Cloud hung onto the reins of his horse.

The older man's name is Hum-pa-hu, a member of the Night Clan. His name means "day arrives," or "dawn." His wife's name is E-ne-op-pe, and it has something to do with being a protector. It is an ancient name and I am not certain of the full meaning. She is a member of our clan, the Peace Clan. I know she is a relative but I do not know exactly how we are related. They have been married over fifty years.

The prairie land we were crossing was her land and had not been pastured and the new grass was tall as was the brown and bronze grasses of late winter. She took allotment very near to Grandpa and Dad and our family, including my allotment. There was no fence between our lands. They own a home in town but spend most of their time out here in their small house.

In a few moments the sun would break over the hill. They were preparing to offer their morning prayer chant to Wah-kon-tah, the Creator, the Mystery.

Because we were on the hilltop the sun's rays reached us first and the first warm rays of the day felt good. We waited.

Just before the rays of the sun reached the two worshipers waiting in the valley, their prayers began and the prayers lasted several minutes and their voices were clear and strong. The other sounds of morning quietened and the valley and the hills were still except for the prayers making their way to the sun and to Wah-kon-tah.

Grandpa was one of the people in the tribe who still prayed that way. My parents did sometimes but not often. My parents had pretty much followed most of the tribe and moved toward Moon Head, the Caddo prophet who brought the teachings of Jesus to the Osages through Grandfather Peyote.

When Hum-pa-hu and E-ne-op-pe had completed their prayer the sun was fully up and the earth was alive and the sounds of the animals continued. The couple turned and walked toward their home beyond a stand of blackjack trees.

Roper blew out the small flame of the lantern. I took off my coat and tied it to the back of the saddle and Tom rolled a cigarette and lit it but no one spoke.

When we were sure they were back to their home we started again to move the cattle. Roper did not tie the bell back onto the cow and it did not seem to make any difference, the heifers followed Roper and the cow.

Tom rode on ahead to open the gate that led to Roper's pasture. When I was in the Tuscany region of Italy I thought the land looked so much like Osage country and I thought of that when we were riding across Roper's grandfather's land.

Cloud said, "I haven't seen that in a while. Reminded me of home, and I guess the Cheyenne and the Crows, them that ain't rodeoing or too busy doing something else. Like me, I guess." Cloud added, "I think all tribes gave up a lot."

During the next hour and a half we crossed another creek and the cattle and horses drank. Tom rode ahead to open the gate to Roper's land. We lost forty-five minutes when three of the cattle broke from the herd and ended up in thick brush. Tom and I got them out of the brush while Cloud and Roper kept the herd. There are few things more frustrating than getting cattle out of brush when they don't want out.

At close to noon we reached Roper's place and drove the cattle into his corral next to the barn. He wanted to look the cattle over. "To see what I bought," he said.

After lunch Tom and I began riding toward home and I thought about what Cloud said about Indian People giving up a lot. Grandpa expressed that same thought about giving up the tribe's rituals and the clans in order to survive.

I remembered when I was very young and my mother was dressing me for the *I'n-lon-shka* dance. She seldom spoke Osage to me but on that occasion she did. *"Wah-ni-un-tah, enjoy this dance while you can. It is like the old way, and it is good. But I do not think you will have this dance when you are old."*

She had seen a lot and it bothered her that so few of our people prayed the old way like Hum-pa-hu and E-ne-op-pe. I have
often thought about that and I hope my mother was wrong about
the dance.

CHAPTER

9

The evening following the cattle drive my physical tiredness was good. On that morning when we were driving cattle across the grass-covered Osage hills I thought of my trip to Europe. I had traveled in the Tuscany region of Italy and it reminded me of Osage country. Tuscany made me feel artistic just as the Osage hills make me feel artistic and the land looked so much like Osage country that it eased a case of homesickness that had bothered me.

There are times when I am conversing with people and I act casual about traveling in Europe and I talk like something of a world traveler, but that is far from a true picture. I was unsure and nervous when I started the trip from France. I would be a better traveler now. I would certainly know more.

I always listened to Grandpa and Dad and Mom and had accepted the concept of Wah-kon-tah and the concept of Jesus, but I had never tried to understand religion. However, when I saw those magnificent cathedrals of Europe, I realized those people must have had a deep commitment to their religion.

It has been almost a year since I spent those two days sketching the cathedral in Orvieto that was off the beaten path and was unbelievably beautiful. When I was there I could feel the sweat and work and dedication those people must have felt during their entire lives, building such a structure, never to see the finished product but knowing their lives were well spent. When I began to sketch, I relaxed and was too engrossed with the cathedral to think of my uncertainty as a world traveler.

While staying at an inn in Orvieto, I became acquainted with the family that owned the inn. It was during the fall of the year and I am sure the family felt sorry for me when they asked me to come with them to the vineyards to harvest grapes and to make wine. There were many families of the community involved in the harvest and wine making. The families working together reminded me of when we were children and we would go to Aunt Mary's or to Molly's parents' or they would come to our house and it would take four days for us to gather and dry the corn. The family atmosphere in Tuscany made me homesick again and I was not a good traveler for at least a week.

From Orvieto I moved on to Assisi where the very tiny and dim and dark cathedral of Saint Francis moved me to stay another three days sketching and feeling for three days what I thought those people felt for a lifetime. The outside front of the cathedral was rather plain and beautifully aged. The inside of the cathedral was magnificent and the brothers as a favor provided a brighter light so I could better see the small basement basilica. That, somehow, was the most important day of the five months I traveled in Europe.

While traveling I struggled to compare the rituals and teachings of the Catholic Church with the rituals and teachings of the Osage clan system. That was the first time I thought somehow I could paint such a concept.

Since I had no one to intelligently discuss the subject with I decided I would wait until I returned home where I posed the question to Grandpa.

I remember that day when I approached Grandpa with my question. He was sitting on the platform outside of his little rock house and he had his small drum and he was singing a song about the time several Osages traveled a great distance on horseback to the west. They saw some red cliffs and one of the men made a song about those red cliffs and their experiences on that trip. The song has a fast beat and Grandpa sang it well and I waited until he was through singing and I walked to the platform and stood so he could see me.

"Grandson, I did not see you standing there. I have not seen you since that day you said you wanted to talk to me. Sit down. Tell me what you want to talk about."

I explained my question and Grandpa said, *"I think the priest teaches a life that is built on a man named Jesus. Jesus comes from the one who created us and the earth. Jesus is a mystery like Wah-kon-tah. I have wondered if Jesus and Wah-kon-tah may be the same.*

"Grandson, I think the teachings of Wah-kon-tah are from nature. Those old People, those Osages, they took the stars and the sun and the lightning and animals and they took the trees and water and the birds and learned how to live on this earth. I thought you would learn about Jesus from your church and your school. I thought you would learn from the House of Jesus in that place in Italy you are going to paint. I thought after you learned that you would come and see me and we would sit down and you would tell me if they are the same. I do not know, Grandson."

"Grandfather, I do not know when I will learn about Jesus and Wah-kon-tah. I think about it often."

Neither of us spoke for a few moments and I said, *"Grandfather, that song you were singing, do you know when the Osages took that trip to the west?"*

"I think it was eight generations. I do not know what year. Do you know that song?"

"I think I do. It is a fast song and I like to dance on the song."

"I wonder how long we can keep the songs. No one works at learning them. Those old people, they worked at things like that, Grandson."

I left and Grandpa started singing another song about a war party that more or less patrolled the river between the Osages and the Pawnees in more recent times. I was still wondering how long it would be until we forget the songs. Grandpa had mentioned that before and I think he wanted me to start learning the songs. I remember thinking that was a good idea but Grandpa did not know how busy I was in those days.

CHAPTER

10

While looking at the Agency grounds I thought the tall stone buildings with steep gabled roofs would make a good painting. I will come back next winter after the first snow and study the scene again.

Inside, Mr. Henry Hugel was expecting me and he was smiling. He has a harsh German accent that becomes a friendly harsh German accent when you get to know him.

He extended his arm as a gesture. "How have you been?"

"I have been fine, sir."

I explained to Mr. Hugel that I thought myself capable of managing my own affairs. I told him Grandfather's estate should be probated with the use of an attorney but without the use of a legal guardian for me. He was attentive and stared out the window while I explained my point of view. I had rehearsed my words on the drive into town and they came out better than I expected. At one point he thoughtfully tilted his head slightly and once he frowned just a little. Several times he adjusted his eyeglasses while continuing to look out the window.

When I was through speaking Mr. Hugel smiled. We agreed he would discuss the matter with the lawyer Mr. Bartholomew, who handles guardianships and estates. I then thanked him for considering my request. When I left Mr. Hugel's office I met the lawyer Mr. Bartholomew at the door. He is a very tall man with a dark brown beard and a full head of hair. Certainly his eyebrows are full. He nodded to me and I left the Agency to walk down the steps to the Bon Bon.

Molly's plan was for me to walk back up the stairs with her to inform Mr. Hugel she would be withdrawing funds for a trip to Colorado Springs. Later in the day Alan Sanders would advance the funds to Molly. I wonder if all governments function that way, but I have no way of knowing.

Monsieur and Madame Richarde who operate the Bon Bon are nice people. They take pride in their pastries and teas and coffees and in their service. They treat their regulars well. During the winter months the Richardes return to France and on the first day of March they are back in Pawhuska and open for business.

Roper was sitting at a table under a large umbrella and Molly was with him and it was apparent Molly had been crying.

"What's wrong?"

"Cousin Martha died," Molly said.

"Your cousin Martha died?"

"Yes."

"How did she die? What happened? When did she die?"

"I don't know. Sonny came by the house and he said she was dead."

I looked at Roper. "I haven't heard a thing," Roper said.

"What else did Sonny tell you?" I asked Molly.

"He was on his way to Grayhorse, and in a hurry." She waited as if trying to remember. "All he said was one of the Grayhorse boys came by his house and said Martha was dead. I think that was all he knew about it."

Mrs. Richarde came to the table. "Are you all right, Molly?" Madame Richarde was sincerely concerned about Molly and her French accent conveyed the feeling well.

"Yes, Madame Richarde. I will be fine. I just heard some bad news."

"I will get something special for you, Molly." During the war Madame Richarde endured some difficult and dangerous circumstances in France and her facial expressions are troubled and she is always ready to help a person in need.

"When did it happen?" I asked.

"Sometime last night, I think," Molly said.

Looking down and toward the street, I saw Alan S. Sanders walking up the stairs and when he saw us he came to our table. "Have you heard about Martha?" Mr. Sanders asked.

"Molly just heard," I said. "Do you know what happened?"

"I was called by a lawyer from Fairfax," Mr. Sanders said, and he sat at the table and continued speaking. "The lawyer said the police found her car this morning. She had a wreck. He said the car had very little damage, and he said Martha received a severe blow to the head and that was what killed her."

"She shouldn't die if it wasn't a bad accident," Molly said.

Mr. Sanders said, "She must have hit her head on something that would hurt her. It was a freak accident."

"Poor Martha," Molly said. "She was planning to go back to school, maybe even going to Colorado College with me."

"Molly," Sanders said. "I know this is not the time to discuss this, but you know I wrote Martha's will. She left everything to you and her sister Evelyn."

Molly ignored the comment. She composed herself and began to talk quietly, "I don't want her estate. I just want her back. I don't want to talk about her money."

"I know that," Sanders said. "Like I said, Molly, this is neither the time nor place to discuss it. I just don't want you to worry about business. I will take care of it." He patted her on the shoulder. "If there is anything more I can do, just let me know. Now, I have to get up to the Agency and see what her parents will need."

"Thank you, Mr. Sanders."

Molly packed clothing for the four days of mourning and it was dark when we reached the Thunder home near Grayhorse. Cars were parked in the driveway and outside the yard fence. Cook fires were burning in the backyard and several people were busy around the fires preparing for a late night meal.

Sonny and Roper were drinking coffee near one of the fires. I was anxious to talk to them and see if they had learned more about the wreck, but first, I would go inside the home with Molly to speak with and console the Thunder family.

Cousin Molly would be sad and would cry and try to get her mourning into the four days. Then, as we have been taught since we were children, she would go on with her life. That is hard to do but you have to try, and I would try to help her.

CHAPTER
11

The group of friends and relatives that gathered to bury Martha Thunder stood on the ridge of a low prairie hill overlooking the Thunder home. Evelyn Thunder sat next to Molly and I stood behind them and the prairie was quiet except for a wind that stirred the tall grass outside the fence of the Thunder family cemetery and the chugging of oil wells.

Nom-peh-wah-the of the Thunder Clan stood near the casket and repeated a clan prayer and when Grandfather Sun was directly overhead his prayer ended and the men in their black suits who worked for the undertaker began lowering Martha's casket into the ground and mourners began their prayer songs.

I was prepared for this to be a difficult moment for Molly but she did not cry nor did she react in any way except to sit and stare at Martha's casket as it was lowered into the earth. She placed her arm around Evelyn who was crying.

When the full service was over, Evelyn and Molly walked with Mr. and Mrs. Thunder to their car and Molly drove them down the hill to their home. I stood and watched. The men in black suits arranged the flowers onto the grave site and began shoveling dirt back into the grave. There were cars parked randomly on the slope of the hill and many more cars parked around the grounds of the Thunder home. A stream of people followed the long walkway to the home, the older people wearing their traditional clothing and the young people dressed fashionably and some of the young men dressed in western hats and boots.

For a moment I looked toward the distant hills and began counting. From the hilltop I counted forty-seven oil derricks. It seemed like a strange thing to do, and it was, but I was still concentrating on the derricks when Ted and Mavis walked by me.

"Cousin, you're always thinking," Ted said.

"Just counting oil derricks," I answered.

"Come on, cousin. Let's go eat and you'll feel better."

CHAPTER

12

The home Molly inherited from her parents is several miles from town and the Half Moon family that once lived in the small house and watched the grounds for her parents now live in the main house with Molly. They are nice people and they worry about Molly like a daughter.

For convenience Molly keeps a place at the Carolina Apartments. It has a large living room, a kitchen she does not use, and a bedroom, and it is two blocks from the Bon Bon. I have been concerned about Molly and I was pleased when she asked me to pick her up at the apartment and help her complete her application to return to Colorado Women's College.

We crossed the first bridge over Bird Creek at the west end of town and followed a tree-lined road. "You and Ted will come and see me in Colorado, won't you?" We drove the short distance to the Saint Louis Convent, the Catholic School for Girls.

"Of course, we will. Ted and I will even visit you."

I have always thought the convent would make an interesting painting. It is a five-story native-stone building with barns and other outbuildings in a wooded setting. The main building, that was paid for by a donation from Mother Katherine Drexel, has steep gables and the windows and doors are trimmed in white. All the trees have been coated with a whitewash that covers the base of each tree and gives the grounds a neat appearance.

We parked in the front drive. "I'm a little nervous about coming out here," Molly said.

"Why?"

"This is my first time here since graduation."

Inside we were met by a friendly nun who remembered Molly. "Molly, it is good to see you. We heard about Martha's tragic accident and we want you to know how much we sympathize with you and Evelyn. We have offered many prayers."

"Thank you, Sister. I will relay your message to Evelyn."

"How may I help you?"

"I wish to speak with Sister Mary Nadine."

"Of course, Molly." The nun, whose name Molly did not speak, turned quickly and went to find Sister Mary Nadine.

Sister Mary Nadine turned out to be a woman who clearly has discipline and is physically strong. She led us into an austere sitting room. Sister Mary Nadine expressed sympathy for Evelyn.

They discussed a letter of recommendation for college and Sister Mary Nadine told Molly she would have the letter ready the following Monday, the twenty-second.

We were ready to leave the school when Molly turned and asked Sister Mary Nadine, "Do you think it is possible that I might see my old room?"

"Of course, just follow me." She seemed pleased that Molly would ask. Then she paused. "No, Molly. You lead the way."

"Okay, just follow me," Molly said. "I remember this place so well. That is the practice room where you gave me saxophone lessons, Sister. You were so kind. The piano teacher would strike my hands with a ruler if I hit the wrong piano key.

"Sister Mary Nadine. I want to thank you for the way you taught us to properly set a table and what fork to use." Molly laughed. "I don't mean anything negative, but I believe that may have been the most useful thing I learned while I was here."

"So, we were successful on that mission, Molly."

"I normally sat at that table. I would not eat as much as the sisters wanted me to eat, but I did not want to be heavy like my mother. Around this corner is the back staircase that is narrow and dark. See how dark these stairs are? Reminds me of the first time I walked into the convent. We were told by the people at the Agency and the church that this would be best for me. I knew they would rather have me at home. Momma kept telling me to face it like a little woman. The way the nuns were dressed in your black-and-white habits fascinated me and scared me just a little. No, I was scared a lot."

"You didn't show it, Molly."

"Good. I tried not to. This is the fourth floor and this room was home during those years. My parents would leave me here Monday morning. On Friday I would sit by the window and watch for them. When I saw Dad's car turning into the driveway I would run downstairs and meet them.

"There were some girls from another tribe whose parents lived a long way away. I felt sorry for them a little, but they were sisters to each other and I think that made it easier on them. Still, it would have been hard. Of course, I've never had a sister so I can't really say.

"Martha and Evelyn would tell me that things could be a lot worse but that didn't help. Of course, if I had known Momma and Papa were going to have that freak accident I would have fought and screamed and never let them out of my sight. Their accident was as odd as Cousin Martha's accident."

"I knew that, Molly."

"I thought you might have. Do you remember Bessie Little Hawk, Sister Mary Nadine?"

"I remember her, Molly."

"Well, Bessie was a little older than I was and she said her Papa told her that the tribe was paying the church very well for educating us. Is that true?"

"Yes, Molly, and I have always tried to see that the tribe got its money's worth."

At the bottom floor Molly looked into a small chapel where two girls were kneeling in prayer. "Wonder what they did?" Molly did not receive an answer and we walked on.

Sister Mary Nadine extended her hand to Molly. "You have turned into a nice young lady. I will report that to Mother Superior and she will be pleased."

Molly took a deep breath. "Sister Mary Nadine, I will see you on Monday to pick up the letter."

"I will have the letter ready, Molly, and I am glad that you are going to finish school."

When we were outside Molly did not speak. She turned and shielded her eyes from the bright sunlight and looked at the large building for a moment then got into the car. I drove and when we turned onto the main road Molly smiled and shifted in her seat to face me. "Okay, let's go eat."

CHAPTER

13

I sat on the platform in the front lawn watching the sunset. I had been doing something wrong in mixing the colors of a sunset and thought I might go back to mixing from primary colors. Anyway, the sun was beautiful and I was lost in thought and was a little startled when I noticed a young man standing not more than ten feet from me. His name is Louis and he is Mi-keh-wa-ti-an-kah's grandson.

"Sorry to bother you. I guess I should a said something to let you know I was here."

"You're okay, I was just a little preoccupied."

"Grandpa Mi-keh-wa-ti-an-kah asked me to tell you he wants to talk to you at noon tomorrow, and can you be there?"

"Yes, I can be there. Tell your grandfather I will be there at noon. Should I come to your grandfather's home?"

"Yes. I'll tell him." With that Louis left to deliver the message.

The sun was lower in the western sky and the colors deepened. I wondered what Mi-keh-wa-ti-an-kah had to say, but I would wait until noon the following day.

• ◆ •

The summer kitchen of Mi-keh-wa-ti-an-kah's home has a large cooking stove and two dining tables. The windows were open and the air flowed through the room. His home is a center of activity for his grandchildren and great-grandchildren and many friends and relatives. His wife, Tha-xa-weh, a member of the Buffalo Face Clan, keeps food prepared throughout the day for visitors and family that might drop in.

Mi-keh-wa-ti-an-kah sat down with Louis and me and he prayed. The clan tattoos on his chest had probably been there forty years, yet the tattoos were fairly clear. When we were through eating the old warrior spoke.

"I have asked my grandson Wa-sha-ah-ke-pah to witness what we say. Your Grandfather Xui-tha-ho-tse said you know how to conduct yourself.

"Last winter when we cut cedar you asked the reason for needing a Pipe. Your grandfather is no longer here so I will tell you. We will hold a meeting for a man to become a Non-hon-zhin-ga. It has been seven years since we did this and we may never do it again. I must face the truth as I see it.

"Your grandfather, Xui-tha-ho-tse, and I planned to hold this meeting at his camp on Cedar Creek. That is why he said you should clean the spring that day. It is a good place to gather. If government people know we are meeting for this ritual, they will say it is bad. Some people would want to take pictures of us and some people would try to sell us something.

"The black robe priest would tell Osages we are doing wrong. The preacher with the book would tell Osages we are wrong. It is better no one knows we are holding this ritual.

"We will hold this ritual in the moon when the deer rut. This man who will become a Non-hon-zhin-ga has the seven skins of our brothers that he needs. This man took a long time to gather these things. It is hard to do. Our brothers are not as plentiful as they once were. He had trouble finding all of them. He was respectful to them, he is a good man. The food and gifts he gathered are good. We cannot find people from all the clans that know the rituals. People from other clans will sing the prayers. That is not exactly right but we are going ahead with the ritual.

"In the old days we would use a lodge of a Non-hon-zhin-ga. Now, because we want to hold this ritual in secret we will build a new lodge.

"Wah-ni-un-tah, I ask permission to hold the ritual at Cedar Creek."

I waited a moment and gathered my thoughts.

"I am honored you ask to use the camp on Cedar Creek. I want you to use that camp whenever you need it and I will say nothing about the ritual. I will tell no one of the ritual."

"Wah-ni-un-tah, you have given your permission. That is good. Is there something you want from me?"

"I ask to bring my cousins Me-tsa-he and Wa-tsa-ka-wa to the ritual."

"Bring your cousins. That is good."

I shook Mi-keh-wa-ti-an-kah's hand and I shook the hand of Louis. Mi-keh-wa-ti-an-kah nodded to Louis and Louis gave me a beautifully beaded tobacco pouch.

On the drive home I thought about the ritual I would witness. I also thought about that day in February when we cut the cedar wood and about Grandpa and Mi-keh-wa-ti-an-kah walking through the woods and standing and talking and laughing in the rain and sleet. It was a good memory and I was pleased that the memory would go on beyond that cold wet day in February.

CHAPTER

14

Ted and I attended Haskell Indian Institute in Lawrence, Kansas. The students call it HI. We wanted to be a part of a football tradition several notable players had established. Ted played tackle and I played next to him at end. Since leaving HI we have organized a team made up of Indians, mostly Osages, but any Indian that makes the team can play. The last few seasons we have made at least one trip back east to play some good teams.

At Haskell Ted knew everyone and he would walk the campus wearing his boots and Stetson hat and a group of students would follow him. Ted's group walked from building to building always having a good time. Ted is likable, and extremely intelligent, but even intelligent people must study.

There was a Chippewa girl I thought Ted was getting serious about, but it turned out neither of them was serious.

Once, I saw Ted truly angry. It was following a football game that degenerated into a brawl. Our center, a guy named Ben White Owl, was standing and watching a little pushing and shoving when a guy from the other team came from out of nowhere and hit Ben full in the face with a helmet. Ben sank like a sack of flour and blood started spurting from his nose.

Ted was angry with tears running down his face, and he stood for a moment watching and I think he was unaware that he grabbed the guy and raised him above his head and slammed him to the ground. Then Ted picked him up, punched him full in the face, and that guy's blood went everywhere. It took several minutes for the coaches and referees to separate Ted and the other team. Ted was swinging like a windmill for at least two minutes. I tried to help him, but I didn't make any difference.

Building his home was something Ted liked. He would stand in the yard wearing his Stetson hat and his pant legs tucked in his boots, smoking cigars, and watching the workers. Ted has always been a big guy and during construction he put on a little weight. Not a lot, he just filled out.

After a week of watching Ted stand around, one of the carpenters built him a chair. Later that day I dropped by and did not have a place to sit, so the carpenter built three more chairs and a small table, all painted white. After that Ted spent most of his days sitting and watching his house go up.

Ted is known to entertain well. His parties could be called lavish by some standards. Most of the parties take place in the summerhouse, and on at least one occasion the chicken house. Sometimes, I suppose, things just get out of hand.

Ted gave the architect simple instructions, a white adobe home with red-tiled roof and arched doorways and windows. Later, he told the architect to make all buildings white adobe and red tile. It is beautiful.

For the most part Ted left the builders alone, but he reasoned that Osages were taller than the average person. Therefore, at least the front door of the main house should have a large opening. He asked me to determine the door size so what I proposed was this. I am five feet eleven inches tall and Ted is six feet one inch. Therefore, the average Osage must be six feet. The average American male must be around five feet eight. So, the front door should be four inches higher than average. Ted agreed. Only the Native Church with the Christian cross mounted atop the steep cone shaped roof is not adobe. Ted keeps the church locked.

When I reached Ted's place it was late morning and he stood by the fence on the far side of the lawn with Mavis Davis, the young lady from the train station. Mavis was dressed in English riding clothes and carrying a riding crop that she waved to me as I was getting out of the car.

"Hey, Cousin. Glad you came. You remember Mavis?"

"Of course. Hello, Mavis."

"Hi, John. How do you like my outfit?"

"Very nice. Have you and Ted viewed the fox this morning?"

She laughed and said, "Ted said we just might go riding but he started working on the track. He still wanted me to have some riding clothes, so," she turned in a circle as if to model the outfit, "this morning he took me down to the London Shoppe and bought me this outfit."

"You look nice," I said. "So now are you going riding?"

"Nope," Ted said. He put his arm around Mavis and gave her a sort of rough squeeze. "But it looks good on her, huh?"

Mrs. Bigcreek called to Ted from the porch, telling him Mr. Alan Sanders was on the telephone. Ted was gone for a few minutes and when he returned he put his arm around Mavis's waist and she put her arm at least halfway around Ted.

"What did Mr. Sanders say?" Mavis asked.

"He has the money."

"Do we need to go into town this afternoon to pick it up?"

"Any time. I just have to sign something."

"Ted says I'll like Mr. Sanders."

"I am sure you will. What is the track?" I asked.

"That's what I wanted to see you about. I met a Cheyenne guy. He's going to the Olympics, already made the team."

"The Olympic Games in Paris?"

"Yeap, and I invited him to train here. He can stay up there in that apartment over the garage."

"That's a good idea," I said.

"Yeah, I thought so, and there's a Caddo guy that made decathlon. I invited him too. He'll be here tomorrow, I think."

"What's the Cheyenne's name?" I asked.

"Joe Eagle."

"Eagle. That's a nice name. Bald Eagle or Golden Eagle?"

"He didn't say, Cousin, but they both play football and as fast as they are they should be a lot of help next fall."

"I'm sure they will be if they made the Olympics."

"I need you to mark off a track there on that field so they can train. You know, measure off the track and mark it. You're good at stuff like that."

"I'm sure I can lay out the track. Tom can bring over all that equipment we don't use. Are you going to buy Mavis a spirit leader's outfit?"

Ted smiled. "I'll have to think about that."

Mavis looked up at Ted and gave his waist another squeeze. I think she thought it was a good idea.

CHAPTER

15

Ted and I were out walking the ground early. The plans for the track and field were on a worn-out paper that Joe carried in his hip pocket, but it looked official. Building a track did not seem that difficult.

"Hey, Ted," Joe Eagle called from the fence. "There's that guy named Sanders on the telephone." Ted went into the house to speak with Sanders. "I'll be right back," he said.

Joe Eagle is a friendly sort. He has the long smooth muscles of a Cheyenne and he looks like a distance runner. "I appreciate Ted giving me a place to train. I'm kinda behind on the training schedule I set for myself. I don't worry 'bout it much, though. I know them guys I'm gonna run against and I'll be all right if I can start training pretty soon."

"I bet you'll do all right," Mavis assured him. "With Ted's help you're sure to win a medal. Probably a gold one, that's the big one, ain't it?"

"Yeah, that's the big one," Joe said.

Ted came back from the telephone conversation with Alan Sanders. "Mavis and I have to run into town for a while. Why don't you go with us, Joe?"

Ted left for town and I continued walking the field trying to get a feel for how the track would fit the land. A taxi drove through the gate and across the field and stopped just a few feet from me.

Will Chapman, the Caddo athlete, got out of the taxi with what I assumed were his personal belongings in a purple athletic bag with the words Haskell Indian Institute Athletic Department stenciled on the purple bag in large white letters.

Will smiled and extended his hand. "Hi. I'm Will Chapman. Are you Ted's cousin John?"

"Yes, nice to meet you. My name is John Grayeagle. Ted and Joe Eagle went to town. He said you were coming. Ted said you play football."

"Yeah, I do. Heard about your team."

Will Chapman isn't quite as tall as I am. He is a muscular type with a thin face. I think I see the competitiveness in his eyes. That competitiveness gave me confidence that Will Chapman will give a good account of himself in the Olympics.

Will and I studied the land for about an hour before Tom drove through the gate on the tractor pulling the trailer with the equipment. He was smoking a cigarette that he probably rolled by hand while he was driving the tractor. I have seen him do that.

We worked several hours laying out the track. When we were eating the lunch Mrs. Bigcreek prepared, Will reached into his pocket and produced a worn-out blueprint for building hurdles. The second blueprint was the layout of a shot-put field and the dimensions of a discus and javelin field. Will told us he also needed a bell on a pole at the finish line of the track.

We worked steadily and it was almost dark when we finished marking the track and field. We sat on the bed of the trailer and studied the track and Tom smoked.

Tom told Will about his experiences in Paris during and shortly after the war. After several stories about Paris Tom said Paris had probably changed a lot since he was there.

We were still sitting on the trailer when the headlights of Ted's Stutz Bearcat turned in to the driveway and we could see that Joe Eagle was running in front of the car.

The car came to a stop in the driveway and Joe Eagle walked to the yard and sprawled onto the platform. He looked exhausted.

"How far did he run?" Tom asked.

"From Bartlesville. We came through Okeesa," Ted said.

"He ran all the way," Mavis added. "He shore can run."

Okeesa is an Osage word that means halfway there. Okeesa is about thirteen miles and if that is halfway Joe had just ran twenty-six miles. I was impressed.

CHAPTER
16

The new car was a white Buick convertible. I did not need a new car. The Oldsmobile was less than a year old and was running well. The young salesman got down on one knee and described his young family's needs in detail. The whole situation was silly because I also had the truck and Grandpa's Pierce Arrow. It was more than silly, it was embarrassing.

Anyway, I drove the new Buick to Ted's place for the party, hoping the party would be a diversion from being unable to paint and being concerned about Molly. The party was well underway when I arrived. There were cars parked on both sides of the long driveway and more cars and trucks were parked randomly on the grounds. I parked near the gate and walked to the house.

It was a perfect April evening with the crescent of the moon partway up in the east. I stopped to look at the white adobe buildings and red-tile roofs that were so well lighted. Even the track, stables, and chicken house were lit up creating a festive atmosphere. All four generators were running.

People were in small groups around the grounds and the music of the western fiddles and guitars and yah-hoos and ah-has were coming from the summerhouse.

I went to the main house where Mrs. Bigcreek was cutting a cake. She is even tempered and I have never seen her angry, but Hank says she can be assertive. He used the word *bossy*.

"Hello, John," Mrs. Bigcreek said. Two ladies I do not know were helping her and the two ladies kept working.

"Hello, Mrs. Bigcreek. Did Henry come tonight?"

Mrs. Bigcreek half smiled and kept looking at the cake. "Henry's been looking forward to hearing this Bob Wills play his fiddle. I never heard of Bob Wills till Henry came home the other night and now Bob Wills is all he talks about. Henry says that some day Bob Wills is going to be famous."

I went out the side door onto the patio where tables with food and drinks were lit by candles. Small lightbulbs strung overhead gave it a festive feel. I crossed the lawn to the summerhouse. Most guests were in small groups and were holding a glass or a bottle and were talking. Most of them were smoking. Ted likes to give away cigars and serve whiskey and moonshine and wine.

I was looking for Molly. She had not done much since Martha died, but she planned to come to the party to get away from all of the sadness, as she put it. Evelyn Thunder planned to come with Roper, so Molly came with them. I am certain Evelyn also needed a diversion.

Cloud and two cowboys were talking rodeo. Cloud was telling a story that apparently had something to do with riding a bronc or a bull. His right arm was waving in the air for balance and his left hand gripped an imaginary cinch around an imaginary bucking animal. His hat was pulled down low over his eyes as if the animal was real.

A small group of people gathered around the lawn chairs that were built during construction. A lady in a yellow evening dress held a long cigarette holder and was moving to the music while she related a story. The yellow feathers of her hat pointed downward around her head, and at one point in the story she took a deep drag from her cigarette and then delivered the last line of the story and the group around her laughed.

Ted and Mavis were standing near the door with a gentleman who wore a tweed suit and hat. "Come here, Cousin," Ted said. "I want you to meet a friend a mine. This here is Walter Whitman."

Mavis reached in front of the man and shook my hand. "Hello, John. How have you been?"

"I have been fine, Mavis. How about you?"

"Oh, I've been real good."

"Hello," and we shook hands. "Are you really Walt Whitman?"

He laughed. "Hello, John. I am not The Walt Whitman, but I am Walter Whitman." He was obviously English. The accent was not a fake. "Teddy tells me you've traveled a bit."

"Just a bit. A very little bit."

"Teddy says you have spent some time in London."

"Yes. It is a wonderful city. Lots of history." It seemed I was talking loud.

"Yes, lots of history, splendid. You and I need to talk sometime. Maybe tomorrow or the next day." He smiled and tugged on his hat, pulling the brim down and just a little to the right. "Yes. Let's you and I get together and talk."

"That would be fine."

"From what Teddy tells me, you and I really should talk," Walter repeated. "Not tonight, of course, but soon."

"Yes, Walter, maybe next week."

"Let's talk on Monday. I have taken an office at the bank building just south and across the street from the Triangle Building. The Fidelity Bank, I'm quite sure. Just drop in anytime."

"That is a good location."

"Yes. Had a devil of a time getting in."

"I will come by early in the week."

"Yes. Please do. Why don't you drop in on Monday?"

"Okay. I will drop by on Monday afternoon."

The fiddle player was starting a new song and it must have been a favorite. The crowd applauded and hooted and yelled when they recognized the song.

Mr. Whitman turned and pushed his way past the crowd and into the summerhouse.

"He's pretty cute," Mavis said, "but not as cute as my Teddy."

"Your Teddy is a real cutey," I said and I was still talking loudly.

Ted shook my hand again. "Cousin, I'm glad you came. It wouldn't be a party without you."

"Is that a new belt buckle?" It seemed as good a thing as any to say.

Ted took a drink. "Yep. Pretty good, en it?"

"Looks nice." I was still talking above the music.

"Nice? It looks fantastic under that little tummy," Mavis said.

"Have you seen Molly?" I asked.

Mavis broke in. "Ted's next party is going to have music from Kansas City."

Ted said, "She was dancing a little while ago. Looked like she was having fun."

I asked Mavis, "What kind of music from Kansas City?"

"Charleston. A band coming from Kansas City and Ted is gonna teach me to Charleston. Ain't cha, Ted?"

"They said they'll be here and if I learn to Charleston by then I'll sure as hell teach you."

The ceiling of the summerhouse is vaulted with dark wood rafters that are six feet higher than the walls. The band was playing on a small stage that was about a foot high, and the dance floor was getting crowded and the room filled with smoke.

The bar in the corner was attended by two red-headed gentlemen who wore white shirts and black bow ties. Some people brought their own liquor tucked away in flasks in their coat pockets and in ladies' purses.

The band started another song and the crowd cheered and hooted. Joe Eagle was dancing with the lady in the yellow dress. She held the long cigarette holder and she was talking and Joe was smiling and nodding his head until Evelyn Thunder cut in on their dance. Then Evelyn and Joe danced away, and Evelyn was talking, and Joe was still smiling and nodding his head. When the song ended another young lady approached and put her arm around Joe Eagle and started the new dance. Word had gotten around that Joe and Will were Olympians. Will Chapman did not dance so he talked and mostly listened the rest of the evening.

Ted and Mavis started dancing. Ted is big and he sways when he dances and resembles his clan symbol, the bear, I have always thought. The song was a loud one and everyone seemed to enjoy the music. Molly spotted me. She was wearing one of those dresses with a sparkling belt around the hips. The dress was light blue and her sparkling headband and bag matched the blue dress. Molly danced across the floor through the crowd of dancers.

"Hey, Cuz. How ya doin?" she yelled.

"I'm doing very well," I almost shouted.

"What?" she yelled. "Evelyn is here tonight. Why don't you go dance with her?"

"Okay," I yelled back. It was nice to see her smiling. "I like your dress."

"What?" she yelled.

"Ted said you are dancing well," I shouted. "He said just look for the blue dress to catch sight of where you are," I yelled.

"Hey that's a good idea, a real good idea," she yelled.

Molly laughed and I laughed. We were not laughing at the same thing I am sure, but it was nice to see her having a good time. A cowboy in a black hat and a striped shirt grabbed her by the arm and yelled something and they danced away from me and into the crowd. Maybe later I would ask her what it was I had suggested that was such a good idea.

The room was smoked up and the noise louder than before.

Bob Wills was wearing a white hat and in the middle of the song he held his fiddle above his head and did a little dance and the crowd yelled and hooted. The music was good music and the people responded to it.

I think the measure of whether or not music is good is how well people respond to it. I was thinking about that and realized no one there cared how or what I thought of the music.

A scuffle broke out near the bar. Hank grabbed one of the men and turned him away and toward the dance floor. The other smaller man did not seem to really want to fight. "Sorry 'bout that," the big man said.

"That's okay, Fred." Hank was still holding him. "You boys know to get along or you have to leave the party. You sure won't get invited back if you fight."

Fighting was always a problem at parties like this.

The song was a slow one and the singer, a man named Freddy, was singing about losing the affection of his girlfriend. Ted and Mavis were dancing and Ted had the bear swaying look.

Barbara Williams was drinking lemonade. She was not dancing but was walking toward me to the beat of the music.

"Hello, Barbara."

"Hi, John, wanna fight?"

"Maybe later. How have you been?"

"Been fine. Took that trip back to Kentucky." Barbara has short dark brown hair and is a very attractive young lady.

"How is the old plantation?"

"It's still there. I'm here."

"You still can't talk your dad into letting you work in his office?"

"Nope." She is tall, probably five foot seven and has dark intelligent eyes.

"I like your dress."

"Yes. Fashionable and black."

"Want to go outside?" I asked.

"Sure."

"Why don't we grab a sandwich before the break?"

"Sure. I'm always ready to eat."

We walked to the patio of the main house. There were already people at the buffet and Mrs. Bigcreek had done an excellent job of making the food look good.

"Let's see what Ted's cooked up." Ted always serves what we call mountain oysters at his parties. Barbara took two of them. "Several bulls gave up a lot for this party!" she said, and she filled her plate with other things. Barbara did not seem to be drinking.

The band was cranked up and a lot of music was coming from the summerhouse.

We sat at a small table. Barbara was taking a bite of a mountain oyster and she leaned toward me and looked very stern and asked, "Have you ever played croquet?"

"Yes. On occasion."

"Do you ever sew?"

"No."

"Daddy thinks I should be playing croquet and tennis and sewing and cooking all day long."

"Sounds like an easy life."

"I don't want an easy life, I want an interesting life."

"Try painting."

"I thought of that."

"Come out some time. We can discuss art and painting."

"Why do we have to discuss art? Can't we just paint?"

"People do not just paint, they discuss painting. I thought everyone knew that."

"Will your Aunt Mary be there? I like her but I don't think she likes me."

"Oh, she likes you. She is just afraid you and I will get married and she doesn't want that. She wants my uncle to arrange a marriage for me."

"Do you Osages still do that?"

"For the most part no. However, Aunt Mary is an old-timer and she thinks arranged marriages are the only ones that work."

"She may be right."

From the patio we could hear the band finish the song and the dancers applauded and cheered and the band took a break. The dancers made their way outside and toward the patio.

"It seems your Aunt Mary is pushing more than your uncle."

"That's the way it works. The older women are behind things like that."

"But your uncle will actually handle your arrangements?"

"I didn't say I would do it. In fact, I am sure I will not do it." She smiled as if she had trapped me on that one. "But in the cases where marriages are arranged, the older women are every bit as much a part of the decision as the men who do the talking."

"That is interesting. Maybe I could pick an Osage girl for you to marry and you and I could see each other on the side."

"Just pick an Earth girl. I am a Sky clan, so I must marry a woman from an Earth clan."

"I'm pretty earthy. Does that count?"

"You look earthy to me, but I don't think that is what they had in mind, but I'll ask. I will definitely ask. Why don't we get up and let some of those people sit down?"

While walking toward the summerhouse, we met Ted and Mavis and Bob Wills.

"Good evening, Mr. Wills."

"John, if you don't stop calling me Mr. Wills, I'm a-gonna start calling you Mr. Grayeagle."

"Okay, Bob." We shook hands. "That was a good session."

"Yep, it seems to be a good time," he said looking around at the crowd, "and the boys and I are having a good one."

A young lady wearing a silver-colored dress with layers of shiny fringe grabbed Bob and kissed him full on the mouth. "That's for all that good music." The quick movement knocked Bob's hat off of his head.

"All that good music? Wait til the next session." Bob was smiling. He always has a good time. Mavis picked up his hat and put it back on Bob's head. A little crooked but it was on his head. "Thanks," Bob said.

"I'm hungry," Ted said. "Let's go eat."

They walked to the buffet with Bob's hat still sitting crooked on his head.

Evelyn Thunder and Roper and the English gentleman came by with their arms locked together. Evelyn wore the mink coat she bought to take her mind off her sister's tragic accident. "Come on, Walt, let's fix you something to eat," she said.

The Englishman looked back over his shoulder and smiled and said, "We're fixin to go fix something to eat."

Mavis held Ted's arm. "My Dad is going to run Ted's ranch. Ain't he, Ted?"

"Sure. He can't do any worse than I'm doin'," Ted said. "I'm goin to keep on with the horses."

"And the track and field," I added.

Ted laughed. "Yeh, the track and field."

"Ain't he the cutest thing?" Mavis asked.

Barbara and I walked to the summerhouse. "I don't trust her," Barbara said.

"She is probably harmless, and what can we do?"

Molly was standing outside the summerhouse. Barbara hugged Molly and said, "Molly, I've been away for a month and I just heard about Martha. I am so sorry."

"Thank you," Molly said and she was going to say more, but at that moment what sounded like a high-powered rifle was fired. The shots came from the south side of the main house. A moment later two more shots fired.

Several ladies screamed and people began looking for a place to hide. One of the tables on the patio was knocked over. People came out of the summerhouse and the scene was chaotic. I saw several people hurrying toward their parked cars.

"What the hell is goin on?" Ted asked me.

"I don't know."

Ted started around to the south side of the house and Mavis called to him, "You can't go round there, Ted."

"I gotta find out what's goin on. Somebody might get hurt."

"Yeah, and it just might be you."

"I'll go with you," I heard myself say.

Another shot was fired. People were half crouching behind the patio walls and standing near tables or trees waiting to hide if things got worse.

Then another shot was fired followed instantly by the ring of a bell. Someone yelled, "Yah-hoo-eee. I hit the son of a bitch."

Cloud came around the corner of the house waving his hands to motion that things were okay. "Everything's all right, everybody."

Cloud was shaking his head. "A couple drunk oil field guys was shootin at Ted's bell out there by the track."

We started back to the patio and met Bob Wills. "Sorry about that, Bob," Ted said.

"Oh, that's all right, Ted. We run into a lot of situations in our line of work. I think the thing to do is to get started playing as soon as we can."

"Good idea," Ted said. "Let's get this party cranked up again."

CHAPTER
17

Bob started rounding up the band members. One fiddle player was missing but the other three returned to the summerhouse and started tuning their instruments.

Mrs. Bigcreek came out to the patio and stood looking at the chairs and a few broken dishes scattered on the patio. She uttered a few words in Cherokee then started picking up.

Several people pitched in with cleaning up and in a few minutes the band started playing one of the favorites. Bob Wills may have been young and not well known, but he handled that crowd like a master. The party started up again, and the fiddle player showed up, and the party was quiet compared to the few minutes before the shooting started.

Evelyn and Roper were smoking. Evelyn held her cigarette case out and offered me a cigarette. "Here, this will help."

"I don't smoke, but thanks anyway."

"I don't smoke either," Barbara said, "but I'll take one."

The band played two more songs and people started drifting in from the cars and other hiding places.

"Hiding may be more fun than dancing," Barbara said.

Mavis came across the lawn leading a man by the arm. "John and Barbara, this here's my Uncle Otis. Otis Davis." Mr. Davis smiled and we shook hands.

"It is nice to meet you, sir," I said. Otis Davis is about as tall as me. His dark hairline has receded and he has dark eyebrows and he used strong cologne. Earlier he wore a western cut coat and tie that he removed and he looked more relaxed.

"We've heard a lot about you," I said.

"It's nice to have a niece that brags on you."

"Mavis said you put up oil derricks."

"Well, yes I do, and I also try to get a little piece of the deal." He smiled. "But sometimes you are better off just taking a good wage." She smiled up at her uncle. "I been tellin him about the house ever since he got here," Mavis continued telling us about her uncle. I was about to learn more about what he does for a living when we were interrupted by the sound of a siren. It was two sirens. "It's the police," Barbara said. "I knew they would be here when I saw those cars leave."

It was the police. At least it was the county sheriff. The patrol cars drove to the front gate and the sirens stopped. The sheriff and one deputy got out of the first car. Ted walked to the gate to meet them. The sheriff is a heavyset guy, maybe a little overweight but mostly a strong stocky build, an old cowboy really. "What's goin on here, Ted?"

"Well, Sheriff, one of the guests had a little too much to drink. I don't know where he got the stuff."

"Yes. I would wonder about that myself."

"Anyway, he drank too much and started shooting at a bell hanging on a pole out there in the field."

"A bell, huh?" The sheriff looked serious for a moment. He seemed to study the situation. "I know how it is when folks you probably don't know come on to your place to party." He placed his hands on his hips, "And, by dang, I'll bet a dollar to a donut it's somebody that ain't from around here." For a moment he seemed to be searching for more pieces to our little puzzle, then he asked, "Is that Bob Wills playin in there?"

"That's Bob," Ted said. "He's got himself quite a band."

"Well, I'll be damned." He pushed his hat back a little. "You know I heard him down in Tulsa last fall."

"You're welcome to stay and join the party," Ted said.

"I might stay and make sure things don't get out of hand." He turned to the deputies that came in the second car. "Alfred, you boys go on back to town. Check on that bootlegger out there in Lynn Addition. Make sure he ain't sellin to people headin out to this party."

"Okay, Sheriff."

"Marvin and I will stay here and make sure things are okay. We don't want somebody getting hurt."

Ted said, "Sheriff, you go on over to the patio and get something to eat. You must be hungry this time of night. I have to check on the lemonade in the summerhouse."

The deputies in the second squad car left, and the sheriff and Marvin went to the patio to eat.

Evelyn was dancing with Willie Gore. I had not seen Willie in a while. Willie didn't seem to have the hang of the two-step, but he had a lot of feeling and rhythm. His boots hit the floor hard to the sound of the fiddle music, and his hat was tilted back on his head and he held his elbows out and there was a wide smile under his mustache.

The oil field roughneck that started the shooting was standing by the bar and smiling to all the dancers. He may have gained a little prominence with his bell shooting.

Several people went to the south side of the main house to try shooting at Ted's bell. Occasionally, someone would hit the bell and the small crowd would give out with a cheer. I saw Molly dancing with the sheriff, and I saw a man who I think maintains an office near the Bon Bon. I have suspected he is a lawyer. The gentleman seems to know me, and he always nods a greeting when I see him on the street or at the Bon Bon. He danced with a lady in a long white gown and they moved like trained dancers. They adjusted to any of the music Bob and his boys played and I enjoyed watching them.

After a while the gentleman approached me and said, "Mr. Grayeagle," and he shook my hand. "My name is Edward L. Farrell. This is my wife, Dianne."

"It is nice to meet you."

"Could we step outside for a moment?" Mr. Farrell asked.

"Yes, of course."

Outside, he continued, "I am an attorney at law and I have been doing legal work for Mr. Baskins at the Grand Hotel."

"I have seen you at the Bon Bon, but I did not know you worked with the hotel."

"I am aware that you were gracious enough to loan funds to build and open the hotel, and I thought it would be a good idea for me to at least be acquainted with you."

"Well, it is nice to meet both of you," I said.

"It is a pleasure meeting you and maybe some time, say next week, we could have lunch."

"That would be good," I replied.

"Well. We're going to get back to the dance floor, sir." With that they returned to dancing.

Everyone was aware of the sheriff. All alcohol bottles were out of sight and replaced with soda bottles and the red-haired gentlemen at the bar placed a basket of lemons and oranges and limes on the bar. Occasionally, they would slice one of the oranges and squeeze the juice into a glass. Not that anyone was fooled by the show.

I saw Molly and Will Chapman dancing. Later, Willie Gore was dancing with Mrs. Dianne Farrell, and Mr. Farrell, Esquire, was dancing with the lady in the yellow dress carrying the long cigarette holder. Mr. and Mrs. Farrell know their dancing.

I asked Barbara to go to the south side of the house to watch the shooting. However, she said she would rather dance and at that moment she spotted Walter the Englishman, and he accepted her invitation and they looked happy dancing.

On the south side of the house a small crowd had devised a method for wagering on their bell shooting. The deputy was embarrassed that he could not hit the bell, but he was taking a shot between each shot. He kept shooting and missing and then he would examine the pistol and look puzzled as if the problem was with the weapon.

Tom showed up at the shooting. I had not seen him all evening, but I was not surprised. He always attends our family gatherings and stays in the background. Tom had his .22 caliber single-shot rifle, his squirrel gun. I have seen him shoot squirrels in the head at the top of some pretty tall trees and he never missed the bell, until later in the evening when he had too much to drink.

The draperies were open in Ted's bedroom and I saw Mavis and her Uncle Otis touring the house. He was examining the windows. He unlocked one of the windows and raised it and closed it and he was explaining something about the window to Mavis.

I suppose at a gathering of this kind the level of noise is as good a measure as any to gauge the level of a good time. If that is true, the party was definitely starting to pick up.

I fired three rounds and never came close. Then I walked to the backyard fence to look at the moon and more or less get away from the crowd. A familiar sound came from the hill, it was hounds chasing a coyote. I could hear the yelping and barking as the pack moved along the ridge of the hill. The coyote would win. Of course, he does not always win, but I always pull for him.

I felt a tap on my shoulder and turned to face Barbara. "Ted wants you to come to the house for a minute."

"Good. I had forgotten about that. Come with me."

"Ted invited me. Said to come to the study."

"Let's wait a minute. Do you hear the hounds chasing the coyote?"

"Yes. I always pull for the coyote."

"Good."

During construction of the house Ted and I made a trip to Santa Fe to pick up light fixtures. A lady at Santa Domingo Pueblo made the clay fixtures to the specifications of the architect. The fixtures are pottery with light openings.

A large Navajo rug covers the center of the room. The fireplace at the end of the room to the right is classic as are the two paintings of the mountains near Santa Fe on the wall to the left. Ted and Mavis were waiting. "The others will be here in a minute," Ted said.

Two boxes were gift wrapped and sitting on the library table beside seven wine glasses and a bottle of 1920 Ch. Moutou Rothchild. With a bit of ceremony Ted opened the wine and poured the seven glasses. He had become quite good at opening wine. The narrow windows were pushed open and the music and the sounds of shooting at the bell were clear.

Mavis said, "I think what y'all are doin is just real nice. Real thoughtful, my Momma would say."

In a moment Molly and Evelyn and Roper came into the study. Molly saw the wrapped box and smiled. "Okay, what's up?"

"Cousin Evelyn and Cousin Molly," Ted said. "We know you two been kinda down. Bad things have happened." He picked up one of the packages and handed it to Evelyn. "We wanted to do somethin for you." He handed the other package to Molly. "Just want you to know we've been thinkin 'bout you."

All of us were quiet.

"Cousins," I said. "At one time we had our parents to handle things like this. Now I guess it is just us."

Molly unwrapped the package. It was a statue of a horse head from the neck up made of crystal. Molly held the crystal horse and looked at it for a moment and set it onto the table. "It's beautiful." She hugged Ted and then Mavis. She hugged me and she was crying just a little. She and Barbara hugged and Barbara was crying just a little too.

Evelyn opened the other gift and it held a bronze buffalo.

Ted poured the wine, "Here's to friends and relatives," and we drank the wine.

"Roper," Molly said, "thanks. I know you picked it out."

"I'm very glad you like it."

"You guys know I am a sucker for crystal."

"We're all suckers for something," Roper said. We heard applause and hooting from the summerhouse. I assumed Bob Wills had performed his little dance again, but later I learned it was the sheriff's dancing that received the applause.

The party went on for three more hours and around two o'clock Bob and the boys ate and drove to the Grand Hotel. We found blankets in the study and Barbara slept on a couch and I went outside to the platform on the south lawn. There were still several cars parked outside the fence and people were milling around the grounds. About dawn I awakened to the shot of a gun and I sat up, startled. Out on the track Ted and Roper and Willie Gore were engaged in a fifty-yard dash, although I would probably not call it a dash. Joe Eagle had fired the starting gun. I recognized Ted in the darkness because he runs with his chest out and his fists clinched. Evelyn Thunder was standing at the finish line in her mink coat and Ted gave it his best and it was close, but Evelyn declared Willie the winner. I laid back down and went back to sleep.

CHAPTER
18

I promised the Englishman Walter Whitman I would stop by his office on Monday, and it was Monday. I tried painting during the morning but kept thinking about the appointment. Blaming my inability to paint on the appointment was easy. Finally, I gave up the notion of painting and dressed for lunch.

A long line of trucks were slowly chugging along Main Street pulling oil field equipment from the Santa Fe Station to the western side of the old reservation, and driving was slow.

Men crowded the sidewalks carrying books and rolled up maps. Some of them pushed through the crowd and some were in groups, talking. In ten days the tribe would hold an oil lease sale and the town would be even more crowded.

The Fidelity Bank Building elevator operator was a courteous gentleman who is the descendant of slaves. I learned that once when he and I were the only people in the elevator.

The elevator was crowded and he greeted me cheerfully and took me to the fourth floor after stopping at the second and the third. A fellow dressed in white workman overalls was painting Walter's name on the glass door. Walter Whitman extended his hand to me. "John, I am delighted to see you."

"It is nice to see you, sir."

"Please excuse the disorganization. My furnishings have arrived and I am just moving in. Nothing really to move, I suppose. Just this desk and some chairs."

"Things look fine to me." The room did have a sparse look. The outer reception room and a second office were empty.

"Quite a party ole Teddy threw the other evening, eh?"

"Yes. Ted knows how to have a party."

"Would you like a shot of brandy? That's all I have. Brandy." He was looking out the window that faces Main Street.

"No, I am fine."

"Good. Too early in the day to drink, really."

We discussed the difficulties of travel to the United States and briefly discussed the economy of the old reservation that is now Osage County. After a short time he came to what was on his mind.

"Teddy tells me you spotted funds to build the hotel across the street."

I was a little surprised and it took a moment. Then all I got out was "Well." Followed by a pause.

"I don't mean to pry, you understand," Walter said.

"No, no. You are not prying, you are talking business."

"Yes. That is the manner in which I intended my statement to be taken."

"Well. It was my money that financed the building and opening of the hotel. However, I had nothing to do with the transaction. That was all handled by the Osage Agency, which is, of course, a branch of the United States government."

"Really?"

"Yes, really."

"I understand the government to be involved in your business, I suppose, but I am unaware as to what extent." He paused a moment. "You are telling me that the United States government negotiated a loan to the owners of the hotel to build a hotel with your funds, and they did not need your approval?"

"That is pretty much it. I was very young at the time."

"Are you showing a good profit?"

"I do not share in the profits. I receive a normal interest on the funds, I think. It seems the hotel does well, though. They always have their rooms rented."

"Yes, of course. I am put up there now. It is comfortable. I was a bit surprised to find such lodgings away from the city."

"There are several buildings financed by Osages."

"Would you like a cup of tea?" He asked. "I suppose one can find a cup of tea in Pawhuska?"

"My cousin Molly and her friends drink tea at the Bon Bon."

"The Bon Bon?"

"Yes. It is a nice little place down the street about two blocks. We can walk there from here."

I moved near to the window to look down to see the traffic from above. Two stories below and across the street I could see into the office of Alan S. Sanders. Mavis Davis's Uncle Otis was sitting in Sanders's office and they were talking.

"Interesting view isn't it?" Walter said.

"Very interesting. There is Alan Sanders's office."

"Sanders. I've heard that name several times since I have been in town. How well do you know him?"

"He did some legal work for my parents and for my grandfather. He seems to be well connected at the Agency."

Several people were waiting for the elevator so we walked down the stairs to the street level. We crossed Main Street and walked north on Kihekah Avenue.

"Pawhuska is interpreted as Whitehair, the name of an old chief, I understand, but what does Kihekah mean, John?"

"*Kihekah* is interpreted as chief."

"Interesting."

We stopped by Harry Kirk the tailor and I introduced Walter, who agreed to have his next suit made by Harry. We walked on to the stairs that lead up the hill to the Agency. Reaching the Agency is about a seven-story climb. However, we just climbed the first flight to the Bon Bon outdoor confectionery.

Walter was delighted, as he said, to have a selection of tea and to have it served in a civilized manner. We were sitting at a corner table and Walter was facing the stairs to the Agency and I could see the traffic of the street. Madame Richarde stopped checking the flowers on the tables and took Walter's order for tea and my order for coffee.

"John, do you know there are eighty-seven lawyers in Pawhuska? That means about one of every one hundred people in this little town is a lawyer."

"Are you a lawyer?"

"No. That would mean eighty-eight lawyers in Pawhuska." It was a pleasant day and the strong coffee gave me a lift. "The other night at the party you said you and I should talk."

"Yes. You see, I am an investor of sorts. I have some of my family funds and funds that belong to friends. Not huge amounts, mind you, but we wish to venture into an oil drill."

"I understand that can be exciting as well as profitable."

"I suppose I am in it more for the adventure, and my family and friends are more interested in the profit. After meeting you and Teddy the other evening, I'd rather hoped you might come along on the venture. However, after hearing the status of your personal funds I rather doubt that you are interested."

"Don't count me out, Walter. I am looking at the prospect of handling my own affairs, and while I cannot make promises, I would like to look into it. Like most artists, I know very little about investing."

He raised his cup of tea toward me as a sort of toast. "Very well, but let's not let any business dealings get in the way of having tea and attending Teddy's parties."

I raised my cup in agreement and sipped the coffee.

"There is a matter I would like to discuss with you," I said and Walter nodded his approval. "I have a friend that you met at the party, her name is Barbara Williams. Her father is one of the eighty-seven scoundrels in town. Well, let's say eighty scoundrels. He is one of the remaining attorneys."

"Quite good, old boy." Walter smiled. I was wondering when he would call me "old boy."

I went on, "She is a capable person who wishes to pursue a profession, and being a woman she is unable to do that. I noticed you have taken two office rooms and I thought I would ask who will occupy the other office room."

"I remember Barbara as that rather tall striking lady dressed in black. She and I shared a dance or two."

"Yes, that is Barbara."

"I don't have anyone in mind to occupy the office. Other than being a very charming lady, what skills does she possess?"

"At the moment I do not know that she has a skill that would be useful to your undertaking, but she is a quick learner and can be a persuasive person."

"I will give this some thought, this is America, I suppose."

Walter finished his tea and bread pudding of which he approved. I finished the coffee and walked with him to the corner and pointed out to him the Heritage Bank Building where T.E. Williams's offices are located. Walter told me he had tried to get an office there but could not get in.

I drove home with the thought of working on the painting of the cathedral, but the day was just too good, too beautiful.

Sometimes watercolors are nice to work with and on that day I took the water paint and brushes and walked over the hill and waited in a stand of blackjack trees by a deer trail that leads down to water. I had seen a large buck with three does there. At sunset the buck and his herd appeared and I was surprised to see two fawns. My plan was to catch a glimpse of them then quickly paint the small herd, but it was getting dark and watching them make their way down the trail to the water was enough. I would paint them on another day.

CHAPTER

19

I was in front of Elliot's Hat Shop when I heard a car horn. It was Molly and she motioned for me to get into her car. The traffic was crowded and slow and getting in was easy.

"I did it, John. I ordered the car."

"What car?"

"The blue car to match my dress."

"You ordered a blue car to match your blue dress? Is that the blue ss you wore to the party the other night?"

"Of course, silly. It was your idea."

We laughed about the miscommunication. She was happy to be iting for the car. She said it would take at least two months before car could be delivered.

"Let's go to Wong's, John. They have a new dessert. The recipe is bably a thousand years old, but it's new to us. If we just eat sert we can still eat at Aunt Mary's."

At Wong's Restaurant we sat by the window so Molly could tch the traffic. "Did you take the blue dress over to Mr. Oglethorpe he could get the color right?"

"Yes. He said he could do it. Mr. Oglethorpe said he would mail cloth to the factory. In Detroit, I think."

"Could be that all those black cars people are driving may some y be all sorts of colors."

"I don't know about that but I'll be driving a blue one."

"What are you planning for the first time you wear your dress and drive your car?"

"I've been thinking, but I haven't come up with much. I'll just coordinate rather than match all of the time."

It was good to see her being more like herself. We stopped by her apartment for a coat and drove across the two bridges and out onto the new paved highway going west to Aunt Mary's.

"I like the convertible. Gives me a chance to wear this fur that I thought I bought a little late in the year."

I pushed the accelerator and the car responded. "I haven't seen much of Ted," Molly said.

"Not since he found Mavis."

"Or Mavis found him."

"They found each other. Barbara doesn't trust her."

"Oh really?" Molly said, but she was not serious.

We took some curves a little fast and the car handled them. We left the main highway going north onto a narrow dirt road that led through the Burbank Oil Field to Aunt Mary's home. Workers were putting up oil derricks as fast as they could get timbers and pipe. The derricks were two hundred twenty yards apart running north and south and east and west and every hole they drilled produced a good well.

"Look at that sunset," Molly said. "Stop for a minute."

I brought the car to a stop and we got out and leaned against the fender to watch the sun set.

"What do you think about those derricks? Don't they kind of spoil the sunset?" Molly asked.

"I've thought about that. The first time I saw them I thought they were ugly. Now they really don't bother me."

Molly laughed. "You're no artist."

I laughed too. "I can not explain why I don't mind the derricks. The things are not natural and out of place, but they do not bother me like they did when I first saw them."

"Well," Molly said. "I still think they're ugly."

So, Cousin Molly and I stood leaning against the car watching
e sunset. "You know," she said. "Those things really don't bother
e that much either."

The sun dropped lower, turning the sky and clouds pink, then the
ouds turned burning orange, and then deep red, and the copper-
lored grasses changed to bronze, and the whole prairie glowed.

"God, that is beautiful," Molly said. The sun dropped beyond the
rizon and the grassy horizon became the dark color of the wooden
rricks silhouetted against the dark sky.

"The sun sets every day," she said.

We drove down the short hill to the clear shallow water at the
ossing and there was barely enough light to see the stream and the
aterfall where we swam and fished when we were children and
enagers. There is a flat area by the pool where Aunt Mary's fam-
camped, and they lived there.

It was dark when we walked to the backyard. The scent of meat
d hominy cooking was good. The fire had been brought to full
me and allowed to die, and when the flames had died the meat
rips were placed about a foot above the embers. Aunt Mary was
nding over the cook pit, concentrating on turning the strips of
eat.

The worshipers had gone into the roundhouse at sundown. There
ere several people sitting on the two platforms and in chairs. The
rkness allowed us to see only the forms of people sitting in the
rd. The meeting was starting and the low even beat of the drum
ways creates an atmosphere that relaxes me and builds me up.

"Where have you been?" Aunt Mary asked.

"We were watching the sunset," Molly said.

She laughed and said, "Go over there and eat."

"Who is running the meeting?" Molly asked.

"Wa-tsa-moin," Aunt Mary said. "They just now went in."

Wa-tsa-moin is sometimes interpreted as "Warrior" and some-
nes he is called Warrior. Wa-tsa-moin is a member of the Bear Clan
d his war honors from the past are numerous.

"I saw Ted's car. Is he in the meeting?" Molly asked.

"He brought a Caddo named Will with him, a runner." Aunt Mary was stoking the fire under the coffeepot. "Ted thought I might want to meet the Caddo runner. Same tribe as Mi-om-pah-weh-li, Moon Head." She paused, unable to remember his European name. "John Wilson, that's his name, the Caddo." She laughed. "I can't remember anything anymore."

"My uncle was a runner. He was a messenger," Aunt Mary said. "That's why Ted thought I might want to meet this runner. My uncle could run for miles and miles." She finished turning the meat and stirred the hominy.

The summer kitchen has two long tables for eating, but we sat on the platform outside and ate. I enjoy eating near a fire when the air is cool. The steam-fried meat gravy and the hominy and fry bread were good.

As children, Molly and Ted and I came here with our parents in July when the corn was ripe. For four days we would help Aunt Mary and Marjorie and Bob dry corn. Molly and I talked about the corn-drying days.

We were here on this ground and watched when the workers came to build the roundhouse. Wah-kon-tah-gi, the old people called it, the house of God. They were just regular carpenters but Aunt Mary gave them a lecture about the significance of the building and they treated the work with respect. It was important to my mother and several times she said she appreciated the workers for treating the job with reverence. On the day they finished building, the last thing they did was to place the cross on the top of the church.

Aunt Mary is an East Mooner and the door of her church faces east. The question goes back to when Grandfather Peyote was brought to the Osages. Some thought the altar should face east and some west. So, there was a compromise of ancient teachings and new teachings.

I have visited Aunt Mary's backyard all my life and for the first time I thought of painting it. Since Grandpa died I have thought about losing Aunt Mary and some day that will happen.

When the church was completed Aunt Mary traveled to western
klahoma to the home of the Caddo prophet, John Wilson. She
ked him to come to her place to build an altar. John Wilson came
id made the altar of cement so it would be permanent.

The Osages said all John Wilson thought about was the moon and
sages call him Mi-om-pah-weh-li, or Moon Head. He must have
one his work well because there were three other meetings on the
d reservation that night.

The low even beat of the drum continued. Willie Gore sat on the
latform, he was driving for Gla-moin, of the Bear clan. I kept
inking about Willie dancing at Ted's last party. Willie is Chero-
ie and a nice person. Willie and Hank Bigcreek are related, I
ink.

The moon overhead was near full. We wrapped up in blankets
id sat on the platform watching the fire burn and talked more
out our childhood. After midnight Ted and Will Chapman
oke protocol and came out of the meeting and joined us for a
hile.

Will said he knew John Wilson and thought they were related
rough his father's family. He was surprised to know John Wilson
as so prominent in Osage country.

When Ted and Will returned to the meeting Molly and I rolled
o in blankets and slept on the platform. I sleep well to the beat of
drum. A little before dawn Aunt Mary woke us. She had her hand
ı Molly's shoulder and was shaking her a little. "Sister, get up
om there." Aunt Mary spoke slowly with a hint of scolding. "Why
idn't you go inside the house and sleep on a bed? You're going to
itch cold."

Molly was half awake and did not move. "I'm all right, Aunt
ary. Really I am."

At sunrise the worshipers came out of the meeting, and I thought
several days earlier when we saw E-ne-op-pe and Hum-pa-hu giv-
g their morning prayer to Wah-kon-tah. I know Aunt Mary some-
nes still has her prayer at dawn. On this morning she was cooking
ır those who were praying to Wah-kon-tah as well as to Jesus.

Those who had prayed and sung all night and the cooks and visitors ate and talked and later would sleep for a few hours and would then return to their homes.

Molly and I left after breakfast. Ted was wrapped in a red striped blanket and would sleep on the platform for several hours.

CHAPTER
20

I cranked the telephone and asked the operator to ring Walter Whitman in the Fidelity National Bank Building. She gave me the number and I wrote it down. The operator rang Walter's telephone and when he answered I told him I would drop by to visit him. The telephone is convenient, but I am not in the habit of using it. I probably should use it because I understand laying the line was expensive.

When I reached his office Walter was busy with a matter of several rolls of maps and a man whom I took to be a geologist. All geologists carry rolled-up maps and wear hiking boots. The door of the office was open and Walter motioned for me to come in and to wait.

I looked down onto the busy street. A long black car was stopped in front of Mr. Bander's Mercantile Store on the corner. The driver held the car door and Mr. Bander waited for He-se-moie to get out of the car. Grandpa told me He-se-moie is a member of the Buffalo Clan and his wife Nom-tah-shkah is a Water Clan. He-se-moie is a dedicated Road Man of the Native Church and both dress in traditional clothing. The storekeeper helped the elderly couple out of their car and they slowly made their way into his store. At one point in his life He-se-moie tried wearing white man's clothing, but he was self-conscious and went back to Osage clothing.

Nom-tah-shkah has always been good to me. Even when I was a boy and did not know who she was, she would stop and talk with me. Once she gave me a round gorget made from the shell of a fresh-water mussel. Grandpa said that was her clan and the pearl like gor-get represented the brightness of the Sun. I still have it stored away somewhere.

Osages purchase a lot of blankets and broadcloth from the Mer-cantile Store. I suppose trade cloth is a more commonly used term for the thick wool cloth from France many Indian people use. It is a strong and durable cloth and rather expensive and has become a tradition for many Indians. The old couple were probably preparing for a gathering of some sort. Could be the I-lon-shka dance the Hominy people were planning for the summer. I heard they were trying to return to normal living after her sister was killed in a car wreck. I hope they can, she is a good person.

I watched until the couple were inside the store then I turned my attention to Alan Sanders through his window in the Triangle Build-ing. Mr. Sanders was meeting with Mr. Bartholomew who handles guardianships for the Agency. The two men shook hands and Mr. Bartholomew left.

After a few minutes the geologist left Walter's office. "Was that a geologist?" I asked.

"Yes. Do you know him?"

"No. I just wondered." It was just a little test I set for myself. There is a lot I should learn about white people.

"It is a nice day, Walter, and I asked Barbara to meet me at the Bon Bon in about thirty minutes. Why don't you come along? It can-not hurt. I did not tell her you might come along, so it will not be awkward if you do not come."

Walter put his hand to his chin and was thoughtful. "You're quite right, old boy. I do need a break and it will not hurt to have tea with Barbara, will it?"

I suspect that Walter needed a break from his office like I need a break from my painting.

At the Mercantile Store the older man He-se-moie was sitting in a chair. I shook his hand and introduced Walter to him. He-se-moie shook Walter's hand.

He-se-moie asked, *"Where did you find this white man?"*

All I answered was, "England."

He-se-moie was cordial and showed a trace of a smile. There was enough information in my answer that I did not need to translate for Walter. Walter told He-se-moie it was nice meeting him.

His wife was making the purchases and she came over and said hello and asked if I was moving on with my life after Grandpa's death. I told her I was doing well and that I thought often about her loss and that I wished her well.

When we walked back onto the street Walter asked, "Does he speak English?"

"He speaks very little English." I did not explain to Walter that He-se-moie is like many older Indians who allow business or government people to think they can neither speak nor understand English. There is no telling what some of them will say when they think Osages cannot understand them.

We crossed the street and Walter stopped briefly to look in the window of Watson's Western Store at a pair of boots and a Stetson western hat.

"How would I look in that hat and those boots and a vest, John?"

"You would look silly, Walter."

"I tend to agree with you, old boy." And we walked on toward the Bon Bon.

It was a cordial meeting and I believe Walter has a feeling of trust in Barbara. He is, however, concerned that she is a woman. Walter had not met T.E. Williams and clearly he does not want to start off in a new town by breaching some unwritten local code, such as hiring the daughter of a local lawyer who is trying to keep the daughter at home. I had to assume it was something I did not understand. I was impressed with the professionalism with which Barbara handled herself. Not surprised, just impressed.

Too much strong coffee had me a little on edge. I noticed in Europe that French people drink coffee like Osages, in a deep, wide cup without handles. The Richardes serve coffee in either a small, regular coffee cup with a handle, or in a deep cup without a handle, like Osages. I drink it like Osages, but either way I was on edge that morning.

Monsieur and Madame Richarde once considered the notion that Osages prefer a heavier dessert than the French people prefer. Ted had suggested serving fry bread, but after considering it for a day or two the Richardes concluded they were not ready for fry bread. They did, however, add two or three heavier pastries.

When Walter and I parted ways I kept thinking about He-se-moie and Nom-tah-shkah, the older couple who were shopping. They had been friends of my parents and of Grandpa and they had always been good to me. I decided that next week I would drive to Hominy and visit them. That would be good.

CHAPTER

21

Barbara enjoyed driving the convertible. She wore a white dress trimmed in dark green and her hair was tied with a dark green scarf so the wind was not a problem. We stopped briefly while cowboys moved a herd of cattle across the highway. She watched the cattle bawling and pushing and the cowboys yelling and waving their ropes. "Men get to do everything."

"Some men," I said. "A lot of men are stuck in jobs they do not like. Anyway, I read that somewhere."

"At least they have jobs. They get up every morning and go do something while women are stuck at home. Surely you cannot argue with that."

"No, I won't argue with that." The cattle soon crossed the highway and we drove on to Ted's place.

"There is something else I think I have figured out, John."

"What is that?"

"I know why Will and Joe's running is so interesting."

"Why?"

"Because they are world-class athletes. I hadn't thought of that. They are going to go up against the best in the world. I don't blame Ted for helping them. I would if I could."

"That is true, they are world-class athletes. Of course, Ted would help them if they were training for the county fair as long as they can play football."

"He probably would, but I would not find what they do as fascinating." She was serious. "Just think of it. They are going to Paris and run against guys from Germany and France and South America and the Netherlands and just all over. How many countries will be there?"

"I don't know. You know Will is going for a personal record today?"

"That does make it exciting, doesn't it?"

"It does for me," I answered.

We parked on the circle drive in front of the main house next to Aunt Mary's car. Will Chapman was stretching and warming up for a run at the high hurdles. The hurdles were in place and Molly was helping Hank measure the interval between hurdles and she waved and called to us.

"What are you guys doing?"

"We are pretending we are in the stadium in Paris," Barbara called back and she struck a pose with her hands on her hips like one of those models in a magazine.

"Good," Molly answered. "I'll pretend I am one of the official timers."

The high hurdles are a one hundred ten meter distance and there are ten hurdles. The way Hank had it laid out the race starts on the far curve of the track to our left and straightens out and passes in front of us and finishes on the straight away to our right. The finish line is near the Native Church.

Aunt Mary was sitting on the first row of the three rows of bleachers watching what was going on.

"Hi, Aunt Mary," I said.

"Hello," Barbara said.

"Ha-weh," Aunt Mary responded. "Thought I'd come out here and watch that man run. My mother's brother, my uncle, he was a runner. He was a messenger."

"I remember Dad telling about him."

"He would carry messages. And even if he could ride a horse, he would rather run," she said slowly. "He would run for long ways, over hills and 'cross creeks. He knew where he was going. He knew where all them camps were. My father always told us that we depended on the runners.

"I remember my uncle going into the bark house where the old men would be meeting. They would give him a message and he would stay in there 'til he had it memorized, then he would come out of the bark house, and he would start runnin toward that other village. Sometimes they would send several runners at once, so they could send the same message to the people in all the villages.

"And my uncle, he would carry a little pipe to show that he was a messenger. Sometimes he would carry it in his hand and sometimes he would have it tied to a strap he had tied round him."

Aunt Mary was deep in thought and I wanted her to tell us more, but she noticed Will was ready to begin his run and she stopped talking. I knew she was still thinking about those far-distant days.

Ted was standing at the starting line and loading the pistol, and Molly and Hank stood near the finish line holding stopwatches.

When everything was ready, Will walked to the starting line and took off and folded the warm ups and laid them on the grass and continued stretching. He kicked the starting blocks, checking them. Will looked serious, and when he was sure the starting blocks were firmly into the track surface, he stretched a little more. Then he began getting his spikes settled into the blocks.

Will was relaxed and looking down the track to the finish line. The day was quiet with only the sounds of a few birds and the chugging of an oil well in the distance. Will took the starting position and Ted held the pistol into the air and called. "To your mark. Get set." Ted paused a moment then fired the pistol that held real bullets that gave a report far louder than the pop of blanks used in competition.

Will did not care that the sound of the gun was different, he was out of the starting blocks instantly and took the first hurdle on the curve.

"He is so graceful," I heard Barbara say.

Will took the second hurdle as quickly, then the third as easily and as gracefully as the first and then Will was on the straight away and you could see the power in his legs and he was still taking the hurdles perfectly and breathing perfectly and it was an exciting time. Molly yelled, "Come on, Will. You can do it, Will."

Will cleared the final hurdle and kept the pace without flaw, crossing the finish line, completing what looked to be a perfect run, and it was a lot of excitement for the small group of friends who had become fans.

Aunt Mary held her hands tightly in front of her chin much like a prayer pose and when Will crossed the finish line she was clapping her hands quickly and she was excited.

Will gradually slowed to a walk near the church and he was breathing heavily. He turned to walk back toward the finish line with his hands on his hips, still breathing heavily, and Molly ran to him with a towel and a bottle of water, and she threw the towel on his neck, and he took the water.

Hank was smiling broadly and holding the stopwatch in the air. "A new record," Hank called to Will.

Ted was walking on the track with his hat pushed back on his head and he motioned to me as if he was throwing a football. Ted said, "And when he's running against somebody he'll do even better."

"He don't need to run against nobody and he don't need to beat nobody," Aunt Mary said. "He runs cause he likes to run. That's why he's good at it."

"Aunt Mary," I said. "Before the run started you were telling us about your uncle who was a runner."

"My uncle. His name was Ke-no-to. He was Buffalo Clan. My mother, she was Buffalo Clan.

"And when I was a little girl and there would be weddings they would always have foot races at weddings. It was exciting and I would run in the races. I never lost a race at one of them weddings all the time I was growing up. Now days I even walk slow, but in those days I could run. I didn't run to beat the other runners. I ran 'cause I liked to run."

CHAPTER

22

We sat at a corner table of the Bon Bon, sipping tea and coffee. I was starting to be comfortable with Barbara, like before. Molly climbed the stairs and waved to us when she reached the top step. "Hey, what are you guys up to?"

"Nothing. Just killing time," Barbara said.

"John, Aunt Mary came to see me." Molly sat down at the table. "She wants to have a little dinner at my place and she wants you and Ted there. Said I should visit you and ask you to come."

"Are you going to visit me?"

"Yes. You know she will ask if I went to your home and invited you in person."

"Yes, she will. I'll be home later if you want to stop by."

"Good. That will cover me."

"I don't suppose you know what she wants to talk about?"

"Nope. Just have to wait til noon, day after tomorrow. Why don't you get there just a little early? I told Aunt Mary I would cook."

"Are you going to cook?"

"Sure. Well, Mrs. New Moon is cooking." Molly smiled. "Hey, I can cook, you know," and Molly leaned over and hit me on the shoulder.

"Yes, I know. You cook real good," I said.

"Roper was looking for you," Molly said. "Said he has some new roping calves and he wants to do some roping next Sunday at his place."

"What time?"

"Around two o'clock is what I think he said. Well, you'll see him before then."

I looked at Barbara. "Want to go?"

"Sure, I'd love to go."

"We'll be there," I told Molly.

"Got to run," Molly said.

"Where you going?"

"Got to see what Mrs. New Moon needs for the dinner."

Madame Richarde asked, "Do you want anything, Molly?"

"Nope. I have to run. Thank you though."

We watched Molly walk down the stairs to her car. Madame Richarde returned with a new dessert. "Here try this. On the top of the house."

"Thank you," I said. "It looks good."

"John, did you hear Mavis say that her dad would be here in a few days to take over Ted's cattle operation?"

"Yes, I heard that. I think if the guy knows what he is doing, Ted will let him do it. If the man doesn't know anything about ranching, I am sure Ted will not let him do it."

"I hope you're right. Some of these people around here are greedy. Well, maybe it is not even greedy. They just see so much money floating around and they want some of it. At least that is what Daddy says."

Barbara looked thoughtful and went on, "I am not just talking about Mavis wanting money and what it will buy for her. Sure, she probably falls into that category, but more than that, she and Ted seem so different from each other."

"I've wondered what your dad thinks about what goes on around here."

"Daddy is honest and I am most proud of him for that." She smiled a little, "and he does all right as far as making money is concerned. But, he is a little confused about things that happen." She paused. "After dinner Daddy likes to sit and talk. He thinks we are conversing, but it is really just him talking and Mother and me listening."

"What does he think about you and me seeing each other?"

"He thinks you are intelligent and artistic. He is particularly impressed that you consider yourself an artist." Again she smiled a little. "Sure you want to hear this?"

"Sure, I'm sure. Stand up and take it like a little man. That is what my mother always said. She was raised by her grandparents and her parents and that was their advice to her. Of course with her it was a little woman. If you have it coming, stand up and take it."

"Good advice. Smart people," Barbara said.

"So, what else does your dad say?"

"He thinks you handle yourself well. He also thinks there are so many Osages that die under strange circumstances that there is danger in just being an Osage." She was serious and had a troubled expression. "He thinks you are aware of that danger and that you may have in mind a way of protecting me. Is he right about that?"

"I would say he is right. Of course, Grandpa and his generation could protect themselves and their families. How well I am able to protect someone is uncertain. He really did not teach me that, and I have never been faced with a challenge quite like that.

"In Grandpa's time they knew who and what the enemy was. That was a long time ago. These days? I am sure we have enemies and I know there are people and things I should not trust, but I am not certain who or what those things are."

"You can trust me."

"I know that."

Barbara sipped more tea and I more coffee. We talked more than we had ever talked. Barbara said she was serious about wanting to work and to accomplish something, to create or build or turn out paperwork. She said she envied the waitresses at the restaurants. I told her that I wanted to be in the military during the war when I was fifteen years old and that I could picture myself in a uniform. My daydreams placed me near to combat but always shielded me from getting hurt.

Barbara told me that during her teen years she fantasized about being a nurse in the war in Europe. I told her about my daydreams of being with Grandpa and fighting the Pawnees in hand-to-hand warfare.

Several people left the Bon Bon and others took their places at the tables. Mrs. Rosa Hoots was one of the people who came to the Bon Bon and I asked about Black Gold. She said he was definitely in the Derby and they would be taking him to Kentucky in a few days.

It was a good day for us.

CHAPTER
23

About five o'clock in the morning I awoke to enormous cracks of thunder accompanied by bolts of lightning that lighted up my room like midday. Then the thunder rolled across the prairie away from me for what seemed a long time. I heard the rain hitting the roof and the upper part of the windows and the wind picked up. I got up to close the lower part of the windows enough to keep most of the rain out. I have learned that I sleep much better when the weather is violent and on that morning I felt secure in my warm bed with the cold rainstorm just a few feet away. I tend to think there is a bit of caveman in each of us. Probably more in me than most people.

I was on the verge of sleep and still enjoying the rain when Tom knocked on the door.

"John, it's rainin an I'm goin fishin over at the falls on Sand Creek. Wanna come with me?"

"I can't, Tom. I have some things I promised to do."

"Think I'll go on over."

"Tom. I will bring my fishing stuff with me and when I am through I will meet you there. I should be there by three and I'll bring something to eat."

"Good. I'll be there."

I would rather go fishing with Tom than have a meeting with Alan Sanders. I also would enjoy sleeping a little longer.

Later, when I got out of bed it was what could be called a steady, gentle rain. Doris had breakfast ready and I looked over my sketches from the previous evening. I think I could see something in them. At least the one sketch of the Rocky Mountains was not flat.

Tom had waterproofed a canvas bag. I don't know what he rubbed into the canvas to make it waterproof, but it does the job. Although it does smell kind of funny. I put a can of Prince Albert tobacco and cigarette papers into the bag and brought it along to put with Tom's lunch.

I found a parking place in front of the jewelry store by the Triangle Building. By cutting through the Triangle Building I had to walk less than a block to the Grand Hotel coffee shop where Barbara and her father were waiting for me.

Mr. T.E. Williams is always a gentleman and I enjoyed meeting him and his daughter for lunch. We discussed the rain and contrasted it to dry weather, then we ordered lunch. Mr. Williams said, "Barbara tells me that you may be interested in doing some investing on your own."

"Yes, sir. I have given the idea some thought." Our conversation was interrupted by Mr. W. W. Baskins. He was a heavyset man with dark hair, most of which was missing. His mustache was dark and full and his nose was rather pointed. He always wore a dark suit.

"Hello there, Barbara and T.E." He extended his hand to T.E. and patted Barbara on the shoulder. "John, it is always a pleasure to have you in the hotel."

"Thank you, sir. It is a pleasure to be here."

"Our attorney, Ed Farrell said he had quite a time out at Ted's last week."

Baskins motioned the waitress to come to the table. "Maxine, would you put Mr. Grayeagle's ticket on my tab?" He swung his arm in a circular motion indicating the table with Barbara and T.E.

"Yes, Mr. Baskins."

"Thank you, Maxine."

"Thank you, Bill," T.E. Williams said. "Business must be pretty good."

Mr. Baskins looked serious and a little sad. "I wish that were true. But it is difficult making a profit in the hotel business these days."

"I'm surprised," T.E. said. "It seems that you do a good business here."

"Yes, I am aware it may seem that way. However, the operating costs associated with a quality operation like we have are enormous."

"I am sorry to hear that," T.E. said.

"Yes. So am I," Barbara added.

"We are not in any serious trouble, mind you. Still servicing our loan to John, here. But we would like to show a better profit." His expression lightened and he said, "But don't let me ruin your lunch with my problems."

"Oh, you are not ruining our lunch," Barbara said.

Baskins added, "I do hope I have not intruded too much into your conversations. Truly, enjoy your lunch." Baskins left the coffee shop and went into the main lobby of the hotel.

"That is quite a surprise," T.E. said.

Barbara said, "The hotel is sure enough taking in a great deal of money. The coffee shop does well, and the drugstore," and she looked toward the drugstore that opened into the coffee shop, "heaven knows, it does well. The stores out front, they pay their rent to the hotel and the meeting rooms and banquet rooms are always busy."

"I know it is my money we are talking about, but I am at a disadvantage here," I said. "I've always wanted to be an artist, so I studied art not business. I just do not know much about business. I know I should. Everyone should, I suppose."

Barbara went on, and I think she was getting a little wound up, "There is that speakeasy in the basement and the speakeasy on the second floor. All of that plus the guest rooms. The guest rooms are always full."

"I think the hotel is doing all right," I finally said.

"I just do not see how it could be losing money," Barbara said, and I know she was angry and somehow I appreciated her anger.

T.E. did not express an opinion.

"Did you notice, Mr. Baskins said he is still servicing the loan. Does that mean that he is only paying interest and not paying on the principal?" Barbara asked.

"That is how it sounded to me," T.E. said. "John, do they pay only interest?"

"I don't know, the Agency people handle those matters." I felt a little stupid. "I suppose I could find out." Barbara looked at me and I could see frustration in her expression.

I think Barbara had arranged the lunch hoping that a spark of something would ignite an interest in some form of business. We discussed ranching and retail stores and I suppose other businesses, but when we finished I knew things had not gone as Barbara planned.

It was still raining so I hurried across Main Street to the canopy of the department store. The water was near the top of the curb when I crossed Kihekah Avenue to the Triangle Building.

The secretary said Mr. Sanders was expecting me and asked me to go into his corner office. He was facing the window and his feet were propped up onto the windowsill. He was not wearing a coat.

"Hello John, how are you doing?"

"I am doing fine, sir." Alan Sanders was still facing the window. I looked beyond Sanders to the fourth floor of the bank building and saw Walter Whitman standing looking out at the rain. Walter looked down at us and he did not acknowledge us.

"John. I sit up here and watch the people down on the street. Even on a day like today when it is raining pretty hard out there, they are busy. Working. Trying to make an honest dollar. It makes my job of helping people a lot easier." He turned in his chair and faced me and continued, "I was up at the courthouse the other day. Heard Ted had himself quite a party a week or so ago."

"It probably was not as wild as some of the stories make it sound."

"Probably not. Never is. People like to exaggerate stories like that."

"Ted likes to see people have a good time."

"I hear Ted has a girlfriend. Isn't from around here but that she's a real nice girl. You know her, don't you?"

"Yes. She is a friendly girl named Mavis Davis."

Sanders laughed a little, "Mavis Davis. That's a cute name."

I asked, "Do you remember that day we saw you getting off the train at the Santa Fe Station?" Sanders looked thoughtful. I continued, "Ted and Molly and Roper and I were eating and you came in the restaurant and visited with us for a few minutes."

"Yes. Of course, I remember that."

"Well, Mavis was on that same car you were on. She got off just after you."

"Well, what do you know about that? Same train I was on."

"Her uncle is Otis Davis."

"Otis Davis, don't think I know him. Is he from around here?"

"I know he works in the oil field. I don't know how long he has been here." I was puzzled but I tried not to show it. "He works setting up derricks or helping to set them up."

"It's good she has some family in town. Do you think Ted is serious about her?"

"They seem to get along well. How serious he is only Ted knows. And only she knows, I assume."

"Well, let's hope he finds a good woman before too long. A good woman will help Ted keep his life in order. Not that his life is not in order, but there are pitfalls out there and so far Ted has avoided them, but you never know."

"No. I suppose one does not know."

"Anyway. I don't know this girl named Mavis, nor her family. I was just thinking that if she's as nice a person as everyone seems to think she is, she might be just what Ted needs."

Alan S. Sanders held a case file with both hands. He tilted his head back so that he could look through his glasses that had slipped down on his nose. "John, I have your grandfather's last will and testament ready to file for probate."

"Do you foresee any problems?"

"No. None whatsoever. There are, however, a couple of things I would like to discuss with you."

"What are those things?"

He laid the document on his desk and leaned back in his chair. "John. Your grandfather left a sizable estate, and he left it all to you."

I did not respond. It seemed everyone knew that.

"Now, John, you are a college-educated young man. It would be silly for you to start off with a guardian. On the other hand, if you run into difficulties, well," he was searching for words, "well then, I'm always here to help. Do I make myself clear?"

"Yes. That is clear and I appreciate it."

"However, there is one thing that I believe you need to do." Again, he looked thoughtful. "You need to make a last will and testament of your own."

"I will give it some thought."

"I know I'm right, John, and as your attorney I feel obligated to tell you. It is the only prudent thing for you."

Alan Sanders picked up the other file from his desktop and held it up for emphasis. "I have taken the liberty of starting work on a last will and testament for you." He laid the file back down on his desk and he smiled.

"Now, John, I've known you since you were a boy." He was interrupted by a loud clap of thunder and the thunder made me think of Tom out at Sand Creek. Alan Sanders took a breath and sighed and went on. "I want to look after your best interest for a very good reason. That reason is that I see a lot of myself in you, John." There was another clap of thunder and it seemed to roll away from where I sat for a few seconds and he waited. "John, when I was your age I had a lot of plans for my future. I wanted to be a judge. I wanted to make a lot of money and be a gentleman judge. I more or less got wrapped up in my law practice and time just got away from me. We never had children. My wife has friends around town, other ladies whose lives revolve around local clubs and church." He seemed to ponder those things for a moment.

"John. You have an estate. A substantial estate."

"That is true. I just never thought of making a will."

"Most people don't. We wait and we put it off and then, one day, heaven forbid, we're gone and our loved ones are left to fight for whatever we may have left behind."

"I suppose that is what Voltaire was referring to when he said something to the effect that the young do not foresee dying, therefore, they do not plan for that inevitable conclusion." I doubt that Voltaire ever said such a thing, but it seemed to be a chance to move the conversation along. Certainly Sanders did not know whether or not about Voltaire.

He took my comment to mean that we were in full agreement and he slapped his knee and stood up behind his desk. "You hit the nail on the head, John. Voltaire said exactly what I mean."

I thought I may as well play out this high road. "It is an age-old problem."

"Tell you what let's do, John. I will finish writing your will and let you know when it is done." A powerful clap of thunder vibrated the room and I thought of Tom on Sand Creek. "And, when the will is done you can come in and sign it."

Outside, I stood under the small canvas canopy of the Triangle Building for a moment and watched the rain falling. Mr. Sanders had studied the complex systems of the law and Mr. Baskins must have studied business and I assume understood how the hotel business works. I had studied art and knew nothing of business or the law. My raincoat would protect the upper part of me and the boots may keep my feet dry, but part of me would probably get soaked. I was right.

CHAPTER

24

The cook at the Club Café took just a few minutes to prepare a couple of roast beef sandwiches and a bottle of Coca Cola. Tom would have an opener on his knife.

Driving north and east to the falls on Sand Creek I thought about Baskins and Sanders. I knew they knew business and they knew the law, still, they seemed like ordinary people to me.

There was also the question of Mavis and her Uncle Otis. I saw him and Sanders talking in Sanders's office. Mr. Sanders was lying about not knowing Otis Davis. Maybe it had something to do with attorney and client privilege, but that was pretty weak.

After leaving the highway I followed a small lane through the woods to a clearing where I parked next to Tom's car. It was still raining and I could hear the roar of the falls below the hill.

The small trail that led down the hill was slippery and I had to concentrate to keep from falling. I was thinking I must paint the falls. I have tried painting a rainy setting and it is tricky.

The trail down the hill ended by the first waterfall where the rapids begin. From there the rapids fall and crash and roar one hundred fifty yards to the left. I did not see Tom so I followed the trail downstream to the left. The water was as high as I have ever seen it and there were places where the trail was covered by water and the roar of the water was loud and wonderful. I know I inherited my love of the power of nature from Dad.

Dad and Tom and I first came here when I was a boy. Since then I returned many times with my father and mother. Tom and Ted have been my fishing partners since my parents' accident. Standing by the rushing water I had the urge to tell my dad that I was there at the falls and that nature was roaring out of control. It is a strange feeling that I have occasionally about my parents. I find I want to tell them things and they are not there to hear me.

I took my time following the rapids downstream to the place where the path of the water turns to the left. It was there I was greeted by Wolf, wagging his tail and jumping around in front of me. Wolf and I followed the trail another fifty yards and reached the pool where I knew we would find Tom. His fishing gear was on the ground and dry because of the umbrella effect of a huge elm tree.

Tom liked to catch fish with his hands. Dad and Tom called it noodling. Tom always said when the creek is up and the water is flowing fast you catch the big ones.

He was in the water next to the far bank of the stream. Only his green plaid cap and the upper part of his face were visible. He was moving along the edge of a large flat rock that was the far creek bank. He had his hand under the rock feeling for fish. When the water is this turbulent the fish take refuge under the rocks. When he locates a fish he feels around to find the mouth and places his hand into the mouth of the fish. He waits for the fish to bite down on his hand and he pulls the fish from the water. I have never tried noodling and I don't think I ever will.

Over the sound of the rapids Tom heard Wolf barking and he looked up and saw me. Tom dog-paddled out to the middle of the stream and let the current carry him downstream about forty yards while he swam to the near bank. He was then able to wade to shore and Wolf was on the bank to greet him.

Tom patted Wolf and he pulled the bill of his cap down low over his eyes, then he looked at me. "I caught four big ones." He held out his hand to show me how long the fish were. "I got em on a line over there." He pointed upstream.

I handed Tom the canvas bag and we walked to the trees and stood under the elm where no rain fell. Tom was soaked and I was a little concerned about him because it was cool and I was thinking of Grandpa. He opened the bag and looked in. "Thanks for the sandwich."

"Hope it's dry."

"It's plenty dry. And thanks for the tobacco."

Tom stood eating, holding the sandwich with his right hand and looking downstream. Then he pointed downstream with his left hand. "Look down there."

I looked downstream and saw nothing other than the rushing, whirling water and the trees and boulders lining the stream. "I don't see anything."

"Act like you see something."

"Okay," I pretended to look downstream. "What's going on?"

"There's a man watching us. He got here right after you and Wolf. I think he was followin you. He didn't see me cause I was in the water."

"Do you recognize him?"

"No. When I get through eatin I'm gonna roll a smoke and smoke it."

"Okay."

"Then I'm gonna go over there and pull that string of fish out of the creek. If he's a game warden he'll haul me in right then and there." Tom pointed downstream again for effect. "If he starts after me I'm gonna jump into the creek with the fish and let the fish go and swim on downstream with the current. I don't weigh much and I'll float fast enough with the stream that he'll never catch me. You're okay cause you ain't fishin."

"Good plan, Tom, but if there is a fine we can pay it."

Tom ignored my comment and finished his sandwich. He did not want the second sandwich. Neither did I, so Tom gave the sandwich to Wolf, and Wolf finished it quickly. Tom rolled his tobacco, lit it, and he took several drags from the cigarette and dropped it and stepped on it.

"You stay here for a minute," he said smiling. He walked to the edge of the water and pulled the first line of fish from the water. It was an impressive string of fish. Together the two catfish must have weighed over forty pounds. Then he pulled the second line from the water and it was the same, and he carried the fish toward me staying in a position to see the man and to run if needed.

Tom laid the fish by me and went back to get the other line. He carried the second line and handed it to me. "If you'll carry this I'll get the other line."

"Is he still there?"

"Yeah. He's there."

There was no one else fishing the falls, and we carried the fish and Tom's fishing gear. Following the stream, Tom stopped and removed three fish free of the stringer and returned them to the water. "We don't need all of them fish," he said.

It was getting dark.

"Tom, did you get a good look at him?"

"I'll know him when I see him."

We climbed the small steep hill to the cars in the clearing and we loaded the fish and gear into Tom's car.

Tom said, "I'll go first. Maybe this guy will follow us. Just past the fork in the trail there is a place where I'll turn into the trees. I can get a look at him when he drives by and I'll see what he's drivin.'"

Tom's plan made sense. Maybe we did need to know something about this man in the trees. On the drive home I did not see any lights in my rearview mirror.

It was dark when I got home and the rain was starting to let up. Tom showed up about twenty minutes later. He said the man was just a few minutes behind me. He was driving a black 1920 Chevrolet coupe. Tom pointed out that a lot of people in the Osage drive black Chevrolets, but it was still good to know.

Doris had cooked a meal to go with catfish. Tom cleaned the fish and gave it to her and it took just a few minutes to cook. The coffee we drank during that brief wait warmed and relaxed me.

The day had been long and wet and a little cold and I was tired and I was pleased to be dry and warm and sitting in front of the fireplace. After a while Doris went to her room. Tom was sitting in an oversized chair and smoking a cigarette along with his coffee. Like always he needed a shave.

"Tom. How did you see that guy in the trees today?"

He set the coffee down on the table beside him. "I'm sure he was followin you. I was almost underwater and he just didn't see me."

"That's what I was thinking. So it looked like the guy was following me."

"Yep. That's what it looked like to me."

"What did the guy look like?"

"He was about as tall as you. He was about your age, I'd say. He was white. Couldn't tell what his hair looked like 'cause he had a hat on. Wasn't a cowboy hat, just a brown hat with the brim turned down all the way around. Johnny, your dad and mother, they always took care of me. I was like a stray dog when they took me in."

"Tom, you were loyal and they appreciated it and they liked you." I realized Tom and I had never had a conversation like this one.

"Yep, they did. I always knew that." Tom rolled another cigarette. "There is something I never told nobody before. Being small like I am was good when I was a jockey, but beyond that I've had to do more than other people to pull my weight."

"Seems to me you always pulled more than your weight. It doesn't matter, you're a part of the family."

"That's why you can count on me, Johnny."

CHAPTER

25

During the early morning the clouds and rains that cleaned things so well moved on through the old reservation and the sun was bright, and we drove the convertible. The air was good. I was concerned about the roads because of the rain, but it seems every year the roads are better. Now the road is graveled all the way to Molly's place. Molly asked me to be there by eleven and we would eat at noon.

I was thinking about Barbara. I admire her for pushing to establish herself in a business career, and I wish I could help, but I know very little about business. I could act as an investor, but I don't think she would accept that.

Molly's house is seven or eight miles from our place. She drives past my place on her way to town. I drove past the two-room schoolhouse where Molly attended grade school before she went to the convent. She received a good education at the small school. They teach the basics.

From the school it is a short distance to the rock gate of Molly's private drive that follows the hill down into a valley. A tree-lined creek runs through the valley and Molly's herd of whiteface Herefords were grazing on the floor of the valley and on the far hillside.

Molly's home is a two-story white frame residence and has a small residence next to it and there is a large red barn where we played as children.

Randall and Daisy New Moon are Delaware Indians and once lived in the small residence, but since Molly's parents' accident, the New Moons and their two children live upstairs in the main house.

The New Moons maintain a good size garden including about an acre of red corn near the house. They still plant squash with the corn like in the old days. The red corn they planted had broken through the soil and formed little green shoots in the middle of the mounds. Across the creek the New Moons raise an acre of blue corn. Randall New Moon looks after Molly's horses and her growing cattle herd. Roper says Randall knows what he is doing with cattle.

I parked in front of the house outside the fence and Molly came out onto the porch and she was smiling and waved and she walked down the eight or nine steps to the sidewalk. The heat of the sun had already burned much of the moisture from the air.

"Hey, Cuz," she called. "I heard you and Tom tried to drown yourselves yesterday."

I climbed out of the car. "Tom thought he was an otter."

We met at the front gate and Molly had me turn and look at the cattle. "You know," she said, and she tilted her head just a little. "I like raising cattle." Tilting her head is an expression she has had since she was a child. "Hey, I helped cook this morning and Aunt Mary said I did good."

"Good. I'm looking forward to dinner."

At noon Wah-she-u-tse stood at the head of the table in Molly's dining room and prayed. He is older and he wears Osage clothing, like Grandpa and like Aunt Mary. His facial features are clearly defined and his mouth tends to turn down at the edges and he has a sharp nose. Wah-she-u-tse is a tall man with broad shoulders. He is still, even in his old age, a strong-looking person.

Wah-she-u-tse is from the town of Hominy. He won many war honors as a young man. There are numerous stories about him within the tribe. He is from one of the Hun-Kah clans. The Hun-kah are the Earth People. Some people have interpreted the name of his clan to mean the Isolated Earth People. It is a prominent clan and it is an earth clan, a Hun-kah clan. Wah-she-u-tse has completed the steps necessary to become a Non-hon-zhin-ga. Aunt Mary has known him for a long time.

Wah-she-u-tse is a brother to Ke-wah-he-she who is a follower of Moon Head and is a Road Man. They are a well-respected family in the tribe. Wah-she-u-tse's grandson Daniel Junior drove their car that day.

Aunt Mary and Wah-she-u-tse and his wife talked while we ate. I know Molly well. She is the closest thing I will ever have to a sister, and I know she was pleased with the dinner.

Aunt Mary told them about the time my father, George Grayeagle, purchased his first car. He drove it out to his home and when he came to the gate he started pulling back on the steering wheel and saying "Whoa, whoa, whoa." He said it louder every time. Of course, the car did not whoa and Dad drove through the gate. Wah-she-u-tse laughed and said he did the same thing.

Aunt Mary complimented Molly on her dinner and later when we were in the living room Aunt Mary addressed Wah-she-u-tse.

"Wah-she-u-tse, thank you for coming. I am concerned for my children. These are the grandchildren of my brother."

Aunt Mary continued. *"Children. I would have asked you to come to my home and I would have prepared a good dinner for you and I would have spoke to you. But, I wanted Me-tsa-he to prepare the food here. Here in her home."* Aunt Mary always used our clan names on occasions such as this.

"Children. At one time a lot of things happened here in this home. We would come here and eat and visit. Sometimes we would spend the night or spend two or three days here visiting. It is good for us to be here eating and talking. I want you to know that. That is not the only reason I asked you to come here. I asked Wah-she-u-tse to be here and to talk for me."

Wah-she-u-tse remained seated. For a moment he seemed to be thinking about what he would say and when he was ready he called us each by our clan names and then he began to tell us what he had to say. He spoke to us in the Osage language. Generally, what he said was this.

"Your Aunt Gra-tah-shin-ka asked me to tell you what troubles her. Your aunt is not the only one troubled by things that have happened. These things trouble most of our people. There are people who want to harm us. It could be they want to harm us so they can have our money or our land. It could be they want to harm us for oil. It could be they want to harm us because they do not like Osages.

"In the old days we would fight these people. I fought them. Back then I would find them. If they were not cowards and stood and fought, I would kill them. If they were cowards and ran away, I would chase them and catch them and kill them. These people today, I cannot see.

"The Pawnees would stand and fight. The Comanches would stand and fight. These people I cannot see.

"They tell us that our children are dying from accidents. We know this is not true.

"I am an old man. If I could find these people I would fight them. Maybe I am too old and I would be unable to kill them. Still, I would fight them. Maybe now they would kill me. Still, I would fight them. There are many other Osages who would fight them. Together we would kill them. We have changed a lot, but we still know how to fight. We still know how to die if necessary.

"The Council of the tribe, the Council we marked the paper for. The Council that takes care of our oil. That Council has paid the government much money to find these people who are doing these things. I think the government knows these people better than we do. They will find them. Finding them will take time.

"Your Aunt gra-tah-shih-ka asked me to tell you that until the government can find these people we want you to be careful. Be careful who you do business with. Who you hire to cook your food. We know other Indians better than we know the white people. Hire the other Indians to work if you can find other Indians.

"Do not drink the white man's whiskey. Whiskey lets them say we poisoned ourselves, or that we drank too much and we crashed our car.

"You children are fortunate to have an aunt like Sister here. An aunt that cares enough about you to call you together like this.

"If I can be of help come and see me and tell me what it is that I can do and I will do it. It is good that we stand together on this matter and I will stand with you.

"That is what I have to say."

We sat for a few moments, thinking. He was right. There were just too many Osages who had died without adequate explanations. I spoke. *"My sister and my brother and myself. We thank you for your words,"* I said. *"We know many Osages have died. Some have been murdered with guns and with dynamite. It seems that in the past those Osages that were killed were not related to us. Now, it seems that those that are dying are relatives of my sister Me-tsa-he.*

"Thank you for coming to tell us your thoughts and for speaking for our Aunt Gra-tah-shin-ka about what troubles her. We will follow your words and we will be careful."

Ted spoke. *"Wah-she-u-tse, I thank you. I want you and my aunt to know we will follow your words. We will be careful. Since we were children we have heard stories about you. We have heard that you are a warrior. A great warrior. A man that whenever called upon, you would stand up and fight for our people. It makes us feel good to hear words from you. Again, thank you for your words."*

Molly spoke. *"Grandfather, I thank you for coming. There are mean people in the world. Mean people here on our land. We will be careful. We will look after each other. I do not know how we will look after each other, but we will find a way to do that. I thank you and Grandmother for coming. I thank Cousin, there, for driving you here."*

Aunt Mary waited for a few moments and then she spoke. She thanked Wah-she-u-tse and his wife for coming to talk for her. She gave him a blanket and some tobacco. She gave his wife a blanket. She had not planned on the grandson who came as a driver, and she did not have a gift for him, so she gave Daniel Junior money.

When they were gone, Aunt Mary told us that she had some other things she wanted to say.

The possibility of someone wanting to harm us had seemed too far away and too unlikely. Now it does not seem so remote and we may be in danger.

I told them about the man who was standing in the trees when I went to see Tom on Sand Creek on the rapids. Aunt Mary seemed interested in that incident and she asked me to let her know when I learn his name.

Aunt Mary told us her corn crop from last year was a disappointment and she did not trust the seeds from that crop. She wanted me to go to Mon-tse-no-pi'n who lives in Indian Camp and get corn seed from him. He had the old seeds that we had used for years. She did not know how many years but it was a long time.

Later the conversation drifted to the good times we had shared at the Thunder home, and we exchanged stories about when as children we played in the barn and along the creek bank. Ted told a story about a game of tag when we were in the loft of the barn and I was It and I found Molly. She took a good run at the door of the loft and jumped, sailing to the ground and really crashed, but she jumped up and kept running.

Retelling the old stories helped us to relax and gave me some confidence that we would handle whatever we were facing.

CHAPTER
26

Barbara and I sat at the corner table of the Bon Bon that is closest to the hillside. We were drinking coffee with just a small bit of brandy. The brush and shrubbery that covered the hillside were just on the other side of the two-foot concrete wall of the terrace. The plants had leafed out, and the insects were making their evening noises, and we could hear the sounds of traffic from the street below, and we were not talking much.

I knew Madame Richarde had pastries in the ovens when I first started up the steps from the street. If they bake during the evening it is only a few pastries.

I had spent some time considering Aunt Mary's thoughts and she was right. I did not feel any personal danger but I was unsettled by the things we had discussed. I knew Tom was concerned about the man in the brown hat who had followed me to the falls. Tom was planning to go into town and walk the streets to locate that man.

"John, what is Molly up to?"

"She will be here in a few minutes. I spoke with her, but she didn't tell me what she has been doing."

"John, I hope you don't mind, but I asked Daddy if he could find out something about the financial condition of the hotel."

"I think that is a good idea."

"You don't mind that I did not ask you first?"

"No one has ever asked before working on my business." I had only taken a few sips of the coffee and had not yet tasted the éclair. The ambiance of the evening was relaxing and I felt good. "I like your dress. I like the spring colors."

"Thanks, John." She sipped the tea. "Would you rather not discuss this?"

"No, I don't mind. I just like your dress. You look good in it."

"You really don't mind that I didn't ask you first?"

"I really don't mind, your dad may learn something. Seriously, everyone who discusses my business pretty well does it without my knowledge, and certainly without my consent. I think your dress accents your personality, and that is good."

"Hey," Molly said. "I hope I'm not interrupting anything."

"Nothing important, Cuz, we were just discussing my business and Pawhuska's latest fashions."

"That isn't fair," Barbara said. Then she turned to Molly. "John told me about your family meeting. I think it is good to have family meetings like that."

"Yes, it is," Molly answered. "We used to have meetings like that a lot. My Dad said Aunt Mary would get us together just so she could cook."

The conversation went to other things just as unimportant. Arthur Bonnicastle, an Osage man, descended the stairs to the Bon Bon with a group of friends who were from out of town. At least I did not recognize them. Arthur Bonnicastle has quite a history and Roper once read that the *New York Times* referred to him as a soldier of fortune. I found myself relaxing and fantasizing just a little about who the people with Arthur Bonnicastle might be. Maybe other soldiers of fortune or mercenaries that followed him over the Great Wall of China during the Boxer Rebellion.

Monsieur Richarde came out onto the terrace and played his accordion and I left off speculating on Arthur Bonnicastle and what daring things he may or may not have done.

It seemed odd to be sitting in Pawhuska drinking rather exotic coffees and teas and eating French pastries while Monsieur Richarde played European folk songs on his accordion. It was a pleasant experience but I have to say unusual.

Roper came by. Madame Richarde asked what he would drink and he said, "American coffee."

"There is no American coffee, Roper," she answered.

"Well. Just regular coffee then."

"There is South American coffee," I said.

"That is close enough. What is it, three thousand miles?"

"What's wrong with you?" Molly asked.

"Oh, nothing. I just feel rotten."

"Really," Molly said. "We may just have a family meeting for you. Right here at the Bon Bon."

Walter Whitman had climbed the stairs and came to our table.

"Good evening, Walter," I said.

"Good evening, old boy. I heard the music and just bloody well had to come up and take a cup of tea."

"Pull up an éclair," Roper said, "and a chair."

"Yes, I will pull up a chair." He sat down at the table. "Sorry, if I sound a little out of sorts. I've bloody well had a trying day."

We talked about many things such as philosophy, and we talked economics, and music. We even discussed the wisdom of all of us driving out to Ted's to see if we could stir up a party. Walter deemed that to be a splendid notion. I agreed it was a splendid notion and it probably was, but we did not do it.

It turns out Walter had been in the war. He told us something of it after adding a little whiskey to his tea. Monsieur Richarde produced a bottle of rum to drink with a mixture of fruit juices he also produced. The mixture and the rum tasted good. Much later in the evening after other customers were gone, Monsieur Richarde joined our little party.

Before Madame Richarde retired for the night she sang two songs while her husband played the accordion. Madame Richarde has mannerisms and expressions that reflect painful experiences. Experiences from the war, I understand. She has a nice husky voice that makes her sound unlike an entertainer, which of course, she is not.

Her singing was moving and I thought I could hear the pain from her experiences.

I began to think about my work. My so-called art. At one point after so much brandy, I thought of throwing the subject of my alleged art out onto the table for discussion. Fortunately, I had not had that much to drink. In the lateness of the evening while Roper told a story about a rodeo and Walter told a story about England, I silently compared my art with a romantic relationship that may be ending. If I would have brought it up for discussion there at the Bon Bon my relationship with art may have been discussed by my friends and each of them would have commented on a subject that is still much too close to the center of me. The discussion would then have been forgotten among the other stories. It was a melancholy brought on by the drinking, but I was truly becoming dissatisfied with my so-called art. Still, there was enough of an involvement that I was not ready to bring it up for open discussion.

The streets of Pawhuska remained busy. On Kihekah Avenue below we could hear car sounds and the motors of the trucks of the oil field workers and the loud voices of people, some who work at night and some who do other things at night like the cowboys with their ladies that we heard. From Main Street we could hear the sounds of the big trucks pulling oil field equipment out to the field in the middle of the night, and we heard the chugging of the engines pulling the railcars bringing their loads of oil field equipment and drill pipe and casing to be unloaded, and we could hear trains leaving the rail yard hauling crude oil to market.

CHAPTER

27

I do not like sleeping late, but I was tired and felt rotten. I suppose I could be honest and credit my condition to the brandy. Mavis's father would come into town today. I think around four o'clock. He would arrive at the Midland Valley Depot or the Santa Fe Depot. It did not matter because I did not plan to be there.

Sometime during the day I would drop by the Agency and speak with Mr. Hugel about Grandpa's estate. I would tell him that I want to go ahead with probating Grandpa's will. I would ask if he has learned anything about me handling my own affairs. Mr. Hugel would turn the matter over to the bearded and stern Mr. Bartholomew who would immediately tell Mr. Sanders.

I thought about the last will and testament that Alan Sanders was working on for my signature. I thought I would wait on that. Delay it a while. *Procrastinate* is probably a better word.

Doris was playing a Jelly Roll Morton ragtime record on the Victrola in the living room, and she was smiling when I came into the kitchen. "Have a hard night?" she asked.

"Had an interesting night."

"I guess interesting can be hard." She poured me coffee. "Ted came by. I didn't see any need to wake you up. Said he wanted you to drop by his place around half past one. It had something to do with those runners he has over there. Are you hungry?"

"I am starved."

"Molly called. She said she would meet you at Ted's." The record ended and Doris went into the living room to turn the record over. "John, I want to discuss something with you," Doris said. "Do you remember that cooking school I attended in New York? I guess they called it a culinary school."

"Sure. I think it was worth it, don't you?"

"Yes, I do. Anyway, I've been reading about a refresher course they're offering, and I think I would like to go."

"Sounds good to me. Just make up a budget and I'll get the funds from the Agency. When is it?"

"Some time in July. I'll get right on it. Thanks."

After lunch I drove the convertible to town. Breakfast had helped, but my head was still hurting when I picked up Barbara.

"Barbara, I have observed that life is much better when lived in a sober state."

"Was that your life that you were observing?"

"I'm afraid so."

"So your head is hurting? Is that what you are saying?"

"Really hurting. Think I am going to stop drinking."

On the drive to Ted's place the warm afternoon air cleared my head. Will and Ted were near the track, and Will was warming up and stretching, getting ready for a run.

"Cousin. Glad you came," Ted said.

"Cousin, I wouldn't miss whatever it is you have in mind."

Ted laughed. "I have a couple of favors to ask of you. First, I need a little *mon-se-ska* to help pay for these guys training."

"Sure. I can do that. What is the other favor?"

"I need you to drive Will to Tulsa to meet a man to pick up his formal invitation to the Olympics. Will's been moving around and the invitation just hasn't caught up to him yet. He's gonna meet him at Union Station in Tulsa."

"I can do that too. Is that it?"

"Yep. That's about it."

"Well, Ted," Molly said. "Go on. Tell him the rest of it?" She was smiling.

"What rest of it, Ted?"

"You need to be there by 2:55. His train is leaving then. I thought you were gonna be here earlier than this."

"I'm ready to go," Will said. "I can go like this."

"We better hurry," I told him. "Molly, want to come along?"

"Sure."

The Nelagony road has a lot of curves and I was driving faster than I should have. Not that it matters but the word *Nelagony* comes from an Osage word meaning "good water." There was a place near Nelagony that I found and was thinking about painting. I had never had an interest in landscape painting, but my opinion on that subject was starting to change. There is a lot in nature that I have missed.

The road was dirt but well maintained, and we did not kick up much dust because of the recent rain. Barbara must have been looking ahead because she yelled to me that she thought a train was stopped on the tracks. She was right, it was blocking the road, and we stopped, and the train did not look like it was going to move anytime soon. I felt bad for Will because there was no way we could reach Union Station on time.

Molly asked Will, "What city is the man you are meeting going to?"

"I don't know."

"I promise you, Will, we will get that letter for you," Molly said. "Thanks."

"John said the Olympics are important and you are going to be in the Olympics."

Barbara said, "You know, I think I know how to unhook those boxcars."

"I don't know where you might have learned something like that, but it's worth a try," I told her.

Barbara and Will jumped out of the car and ran the few feet to the train and Molly followed them. I could see Barbara pointing and talking. Will jumped up on the hitching mechanism that connected the two boxcars. Barbara was still pointing and talking. Suddenly Will jumped off the train and very slowly the part of the train to the right of us began moving away from the rest of the train.

Will and Molly started pushing on the train to make it move faster. I doubt that they made it move any faster, but they were giving it all that they had.

Several cars down the track to the left I saw a brakeman had climbed down from a boxcar and was running toward us. I honked at them and pointed to the man. They ran back to the car and got in. To the right two more men had climbed from the train and were also running toward us. They were getting close and they looked angry. I moved the car close but the train was hardly rolling. Finally, there was enough space and we drove through the small opening between the two railcars. The railroad men missed us by at least fifteen feet. Will and Molly were laughing, and Barbara was leaning back in the seat out of breath and laughing. I don't know why I drove so fast, because unless I drove on the tracks the train could not chase us.

We drove into the main entrance to the Union Depot at 2:44 and Will and the girls ran into the station. There was a lot of traffic at the station, and I drove the driveway circle until they returned. When they came out of the station, they were smiling and Molly grabbed the letter from Will's hand and waved it to show me.

"I know this great place," Molly said. "Anybody hungry?"

"I'm starved," Barbara said.

"It's in a hotel and it's kinda fancy, but the food is really good."

"Sounds good to me," Barbara said. "But if we are going to be a while I need to call my mother. She will worry."

We found the hotel and waited in the lobby while Barbara called her mother. When she came back she said, "John. My Daddy will be out of town til Saturday, but he wants to meet with you on Saturday. He left the message with Mother."

The restaurant was on the second floor of the Hotel Tulsa and the maître d' remembered Molly. It was awkward, as the maître d' said, because Will was wearing inappropriate attire. Will offered to walk the streets while we ate, but we all agreed that was not possible.

"This is silly," Molly told the maître d'. "We will be right back."

We went down the street to Sir Edward's Men's Store. Molly asked to see the manager who was a tall gentleman with a mustache who appeared and asked, "May I help you?"

"Yes. My name is Molly Thunder, and this here is Will Chapman."

"It is nice to meet you, Miss Thunder," and he nodded slightly, "and it is nice to meet you, Mr. Chapman."

"Mr. Chapman has qualified for the Olympics in Paris, France, this summer and the restaurant up the street will not let him in because he is not dressed properly."

"Congratulations, Mr. Chapman. That is quite an honor. We certainly have clothing that would be suitable for any restaurant and for the Olympics in Paris, Miss Thunder."

"I did not bring any money with me, so I would like to charge a suit and whatever is necessary for Mr. Chapman."

"Are you an Osage, Miss Thunder?"

"Yes I am."

"Does the Osage Agency handle your affairs or do you have one of those guardians?"

"I have a guardian. His name is Mr. Alan S. Sanders and he has an office in the Triangle Building in Pawhuska."

"A. S. Sanders. Yes, I think we may be able to help you, Miss Thunder. If you and your friends care to wait here for a moment?"

"We will wait. Thank you, sir."

The manager of Sir Edward's Men's Store returned with a smile and Will was fitted for a suit and accessories and luggage. I am certain Will was embarrassed by the affair.

"You will need this in Paris this summer, Will."

"I'll pay you back, Molly."

"That is not necessary, Will. Just win a medal, any color."

We returned to the restaurant and the maître d' maintained his expression and seated us. Molly was right, the food was very good.

When the waiter suggested we have a drink, I felt a little pain in my head and I was pleased that no one ordered a drink. The steak I had was just about perfect. When we left, the maître d' was pleasant and assured Molly the next time there would be no problems.

CHAPTER
28

We returned to Pawhuska through Hominy to avoid the rail crossing at Nelagony. Not that anyone would be waiting for us, we just wanted to avoid it. On the first part of the drive home we talked and we laughed about the train and the waiter at the restaurant. On the last part of the drive the tiredness hit us and no one spoke much. We did not put the top up on the car and it was a little too cool. Will loaned Molly his workout sweater that has the word Haskell Institute on the front and she curled up in the corner of the backseat. Barbara wrapped in a blanket I keep in the trunk of the car. Will and I pretended the cold did not bother us. At least I did.

The sun had set when we drove through the gate at Ted's place. Joe Eagle had finished his run and was walking the track to cool out. The lights of the house were on, and through the row of dining room windows we saw Ted talking to Mavis and, I supposed, her father. I parked next to Ted's Stutz Bearcat and Cloud's black Model T. Tom had cut off of the trunk and the frame around it, to make a bed so Cloud could haul things, just as Tom had done his own car.

"Maybe Mrs. Bigcreek will make some coffee," Molly said.

Barbara said, "I'm sure she will."

The coffee warmed and generated some energy for me. Ted and Mavis introduced us to Mr. Donald Davis. His boots were the boots of a working cowboy and that was a surprise. I had not expected

Mavis's father to know anything about cattle. After the introductions, Mr. Davis told us to call him Lucky.

His hairline had moved back more than his brother's and his features were more weathered by the sun. There was no physical part of him that was not lean and tough. Lucky does not smile as much as his brother Otis smiles, but Lucky's smile is real.

Mrs. Bigcreek's training table accommodated all of us except Will who left to finish his workout and said he would eat later. So we sat and ate and talked.

Lucky Davis told how he would approach expanding a ranching operation. He went into some detail and Ted seemed relieved that he knew at least something about ranching. Later, Lucky slung his coat over his shoulder and carried his well-worn suitcase and Mavis led him to the bedroom where he would sleep the first night.

Molly was still wearing Will's sweater, and she and Barbara were looking at photographs Ted left on a table. I heard Ted ask, "What do you think, Cloud?"

"Sounds like he knows what he's talking about." I like to hear Cloud's heavy Sioux accent. "But he might be like me, Ted. He might know how to work on a ranch. I know how to work on a ranch, but I don't know how to run a ranch. There's a difference."

"Yeah. I thought about that," Ted said.

Molly told Will she would have his sweater cleaned and returned to him. Will said it was all right the way it was. Molly insisted, and after a while, Will agreed. I think she may have liked the sweatshirt look.

The day had been a good day and I was tired. When I drove into my driveway the house looked well lit. With the several cars parked there it looked as if something was going on, but there was nothing happening there. Doris was listening to some jazz musicians on the Victrola and Tom was sharpening his axe and Wolf was sitting at Tom's feet, but there was nothing happening there.

CHAPTER

29

During the week the town of Pawhuska is busy with the business of oil and the shops are open, and the Osages and local residents are buying. On Saturday the deal makers are still dealing in the hotel rooms, but the business of oil is slowed and most offices are closed.

It is on Saturdays when the families who live and work on the ranches come to town to relax and shop. Most of the families do their chores in the morning and are in town early enough to find a prime parking space for the day. That more or less becomes their Saturday headquarters.

I parked on the hill in front of the Agency and walked to the courthouse, where I walked down the stairs to Kihekah Avenue. The stairs lead past three small landings with benches. There are globe lights at each landing and the landings are nice places to sit and read or relax and talk.

I reached the street and was crossing Kihekah Avenue to the Heritage National Bank when I saw Sonny leaving the bank and walking toward me. He was wearing a black western hat dark glasses, and boots, and he was opening a pack of cigarettes and looking serious. Sonny always looks serious. I waited for him on the sidewalk.

"*Ha-weh*, Sonny, how are you?"

"Doin good, John. How do you like my glasses?"

"I think they look good on you."

"Got em in San Antonio. Been down there a while." Sonny lit his cigarette. "How do you like your Grandpa's Pierce Arrow?"

"It's a nice car. Thinking about getting one?"

"Yeah. Just thinkin 'bout it."

"It rides real nice, comfortable. I would recommend it."

"Ever been to New York?"

"Just passing through. That was when I went to Europe. Are you thinking about going to New York?"

"Been thinkin about it. My mom and dad want me to go back down to San Antonio with them, but I think I'll go to New York. People always talkin 'bout New York and I never been there. Think I ought to go."

"You would enjoy it."

"Good to see you, John. Tell my cousin I said hello."

"Good to see you, Sonny. I'll tell Molly you said hi."

The entrance to the bank has a newsstand and tobacco shop that sells newspapers from several cities. Some of the papers are a few days old but you can keep up with the rest of the world. The owner is from Syria, I think. He smiled and said good morning.

Mr. Thurman is the gentleman who operates the elevator. He once told me he is a descendant of slaves. His brother, Cleve Thurman, is a tall, slender man with a mustache and a friendly smile. He is an outdoorsman who walks the hills and streams nearly everyday to hunt rabbits, and squirrels, and quail when in season. He traps raccoons and sells the hides. Grandpa and Dad gave Cleve permission to hunt and fish our property at any time and I assume other landowners have done the same.

"Good morning, John."

"Good morning, sir. How is Cleve getting along?"

He smiled. "Oh, old Cleveland is doing just fine." When we reached the fourth floor the elevator gave two or three soft bounces and was still. Mr. Thurman opened the door, "Watch your step, John."

"Thank you, sir."

Barbara was waiting by the receptionist desk and led me into her father's office. She was acting businesslike.

"John, I did some checking and what I learned is not good." He moved on quickly. "The hotel filed for bankruptcy."

Barbara said, "When we were having lunch and talking to Baskins he had already filed for bankruptcy."

"John, I am not familiar with bankruptcy law. I will have to do a little digging to see what this means, and what, if anything, we can do about it."

"How long will that take? You know, to do a little digging?"

"I am not sure. We should have time to make some type of response, but in this one Baskins does not seem to be playing by the rules."

"Daddy, what about the Indian Service? You know, the federal government? The Agency?"

"Yes, that's right, John. The Agency will be involved. In fact, I would think the Agency would represent you."

"I am sure they will. I just don't know how well they will represent me." I felt restless, so I stood and walked to the window and looked down onto the busy street. "Sir, would you go ahead and look into what I can or cannot do?"

"I think that is a wise move, John."

"I will pay your normal fee. I just need to know what I am doing when I talk to Mr. Bartholomew at the Agency on Monday."

T.E. said, "Yes. Go ahead and meet with Bartholomew at the Agency on Monday but don't let him know you know about the bankruptcy. I should know something about the law by Tuesday."

Barbara and I went out into the hall and Mr. Thurman took us down to the marble-lined newsstand. From the newsstand Barbara went into the bank.

"I'm going to buy you lunch," she said. "But first I have to get some money."

"Sounds good to me. It also sounds like I am broke?"

"You may be, you poor Osage."

Inside the bank there was a set of weighing scales. Barbara went to a cashier's window and the lady at the window knew Barbara and they spoke for a moment. I weighed myself. One hundred seventy-eight.

When Barbara came back I asked her, "Want to weigh yourself?"

"No thanks. Where do you want to eat?"

"Let's just walk for a few minutes." We went outside and walked in the direction of the Bon Bon.

"What is Molly doing this weekend?" Barbara asked.

"I don't think she has anything planned, so I would bet that Molly will be at the Constantine Theater this afternoon watching whatever motion picture is playing. Then tomorrow morning she will be in church, and tomorrow afternoon she will be at Roper's place for Roper's roping."

Barbara smiled. "I like Molly. She is fun to be around."

"She is having a little trouble with her cousin Martha's death. I probably should spend more time with her."

"I have a question, John. Are you just a little curious about what is going on over at the hotel?"

"Yes. I am very curious."

"Curious enough to go over there for lunch?"

"Not really. Not now. I'll go over there sometime, maybe."

"Maybe?"

"Both Grandpa and Dad told me that if somebody does not want you around them, then don't go around them. It is simple, you will be better off. It doesn't matter that you are doing what they want you to do, they do not matter. It is better for you."

"Is that an old Osage teaching?"

"That is how I was taught. There are Osages who would take a more direct approach to a man like Baskins and settle the matter right then and there, man to man. I could certainly whip Mr. Baskins but he would still own the hotel."

"What about the fact that he has a lot of your money?"

"Settling up finances is a separate matter from personal contact with those kind of people."

"I guess I don't understand."

"I am not sure it makes sense, that is just how I was taught." We had stopped and were standing and talking on the sidewalk.

"I have to admit it is logical because if you don't go around someone who doesn't really care for you then you are better off. Still, that is a lot of money." She paused. "I guess it is logical. I'm just confused by your response. Or your non-response."

We were in front of the Post Office Sandwich Shop. "Well, here we are," I said, "one of Pawhuska's finest eateries."

The Post Office Sandwich Shop is a small single-story brick building that looks to have been constructed more or less as an afterthought. It did not take too many bricks to build it. It is between the large brick J. C. Penney Department Store and the Townsend Clothing Store.

We went in and stood along the wall waiting for two of the twelve seats at the counter. A man who came in after us stood leaning against the wall beside me. "Ya gotta match?" he asked. The man was about as old and about as tall as I am. He was a white man, clean shaven, and he was wearing a hat. A brown hat with the brim turned down all around the hat.

It occurred to me that I should remember this man's face precisely, so I took a good look at him. The top button of his wrinkled shirt was buttoned and he wore work boots. I looked close enough that I will know him if I see him again. Then I said, "No. I don't smoke, sorry."

It also occurred to me that there are a large number of men in the Osage who fit Tom's description of the man on Sand Creek. The man in the brown hat placed the cigarette back into the package and leaned back against the wall, waiting for a seat.

Tom came into the sandwich shop. He tipped his hat to Barbara and said, "Hi, Johnny."

"Hi, Tom. Are you going to try the plate lunch?"

"Yea. Thought I'd try the plate lunch." Tom and I ate there often and he always ordered the plate lunch. Tom leaned against the wall next to the man in the brown hat. Tom had his knife out and was whittling on a small stick. He whittles a lot.

Two people got up from their seats, and Barbara and I sat down, and I ordered the pork sandwich and so did Barbara. The sandwich was good. They just slice pork from a roast and grill it, then put it on a grilled bun with mustard and dill pickles. Simple as it is good.

A seat became available and the man in the brown hat sat down. Later Tom got a seat next to Barbara. When we were through eating, we got up and gave our seats to two people leaning against the wall.

"I'll see you, Tom."

"Bye, Tom," Barbara said.

Tom halfway turned his head in our direction and without fully looking at us waved his hand slightly and kept eating.

Barbara paid for the lunch, and when we went out onto the street she said, "Did you think that was an odd man in there?"

"Yes, I did. Real odd."

"Want to go with me to shop for a pair of shoes and a spring dress?"

"No, but thanks for lunch. I'm going to Indian Camp to ask about corn seed for Aunt Mary."

I always enjoy speaking with the old people and had been looking forward to seeing Mon-tse-no-pi'n. It was a beautiful afternoon, when I went to ask Mon-tse-no-pi'n for the corn seed.

CHAPTER

30

Indian Camp is a community on the northeastern edge of the town. In the 1800s it was a campsite for Osages and tribal dances were held in the center of the village. Soldier Creek crosses the northeast corner of the village and a variety of trees line the creek. The land is owned by the tribe and several Osages have built homes there.

In the early days the government cut maybe five or six roads through the village that resemble square blocks, and when the rain falls or the snow melts, the roads are hard to travel.

I turned off the main road into Indian Camp and thought of Grandpa. During the last few years of Grandpa's life the I'n-lon-shka dance was the closest thing Grandpa had to the old days. He enjoyed those dances and he and Mon-tse-no-pi'n were good friends.

Mon-tse-no-pi'n's home is a five-room house painted a dull yellow color. Behind the house is a barn for his horses, and he grows about an acre of corn. Mon-tse-no-pi'n owns a large home in the country where a Ponca family named High Eagle lives and watches over the place. Once Barbara asked me why Mon-tse-no-pi'n did not live at his farm home. I told her it could be that Indian Camp is not too different from a village of earlier times. I think that is it. My dad always called it the Village.

Hu-ah-toin answered the door and told me to come in. Since I was a child, I have thought she looks like Aunt Mary. She asked me to sit on the couch, which was covered with a striped Pendleton blanket, and asked if I wanted something to eat or to drink. I told her water. She left and returned soon with a glass of water.

"*That is good,*" I said.

"*I have hominy cooked with elk meat. You come to the table and eat.*"

I had not eaten elk meat in a while, and the hominy was good, and I ate more than I normally eat. When I finished, I went back to the living room and sat with Mon-tse-no-pi'n. The furnishings were simple and the room had the scent of natural herbs. After a few moments he spoke. "*I have wondered how you have been since your grandfather died.*"

"*I miss Grandfather almost as much as I miss Mother and Father, but I am going on with my life as Grandfather told me.*"

"*Your parents and your grandparents were good people and no matter how long you live you will think of them every day for the rest of your life. That is the way life is and that is good.*" He paused a moment. "*You and I are the same clan.*"

"*Yes. I thought of that while I was driving here.*"

"*The first time I saw your grandfather, we were in a group of boys who received instructions from the old men about the clans and the old ways. Later, we were in the northern part of our land traveling to visit another group of Osages.*

My grandfather was a Non-hon-zhin-ga. We were traveling to take part in a ceremony that would bring another man into the circle of Non-hon-zhin-ga. The night before we reached that village we camped beside a stream. During the night a rainstorm caught the camp off guard. I remember the thunder and rain and hearing the people tying down the tents and covering firewood. The next morning, your grandfather and I walked the hills and forest together looking for horses that got away. We found two horses and the grown people praised us for our work." The old man smiled at the memory. "*We thought we were important.*"

I waited until I was certain Mon-tse-no-pi'n was through speaking, then I spoke. "*My Aunt, Gra-tah-shin-ka, she needs red corn seed and she wants me to ask you if you have extra seed she can plant. She thinks her seed from last year is not good.*"

"I know that corn that she grows. I always save more than I need. You will take corn seed to your aunt. It is red seed and I believe it is good."

His wife, Hu-ah-toin, left the room and returned with a white cloth sack that held corn seeds and she handed the cloth sack to me. *"That is good,"* I said and I handed her the buckskin bag that held tobacco. *"My aunt sent you this tobacco."*

"That is good," Mon-tse-no-pi'n said. *"You must come back and visit me. We should talk. Bad things have happened. It is good we talk and tell each other what we know. The old people always told each other about things that went on."*

When I left Indian Camp, I drove through town toward Aunt Mary's. I wanted to deliver the seed because it is important to her, and I think she may be planting two weeks later than she wants to. Planting corn is a simple act but Aunt Mary brings a sense of ceremony to planting. She plants the old way, in small separate hills, and I have heard her singing corn-planting songs during the planting. It is one of those things few people do.

It was mid-morning and I rode Choctaw to the top of the hill and looked down on Roper's home with its large barn and stock pens and storage buildings.

As a child he practiced roping chairs or dogs or fence posts and his mother started calling him Roper. He wanted me to paint a picture of his place and I think the top of the hill would be a good view.

Roper's mother was preparing a serving table under an oak tree. She is one-fourth-degree Osage blood and her husband is a white man, who spends his time being an old cowboy. They live on her Osage allotment land about three miles west of Roper's place. Very friendly people, like Roper. Late in the afternoon I would ride to the east side to catch the view with the sun setting.

There is no seating for the small crowd of friends and relatives, not that they expected any. They either sit on the top rail of the corral or they back their trucks up to the corral and sit in a chair in the back of the truck.

Roper and Cloud were down in the pens marking the calves with a number. Each of us would draw a number of a calf from the hat.

I asked Roper, "Is Cloud roping?"

"Cloud and Sonny both."

"Pretty stiff competition," I said.

"Yep. Should be good," Roper said. "I haven't heard from Evelyn. She dropped by about eight last night and said she would be here."

"Did you ask Molly?"

"Yep. Molly hasn't heard from her either."

From the judges' stand you get a good view of the grounds. Lucky Davis was in the saddle of one of Ted's horses and was swinging a rope, trying to get the feel of the horse and the rope. There were three ropers Roper had invited that I knew only slightly.

Sonny was saddling his horse. Sonny has always been a good roper, and he took his time checking the saddle to make certain it fit. He was wearing his dark glasses from San Antonio. I believe most people do not take Sonny seriously because they do not know him. I know him and I have always liked him. When he is working with horses he is serious. I like that.

When Sonny was sure of the saddle he put his left boot in the stirrup and swung his leg up and over the saddle and his horse moved slightly and Sonny stilled him. He began swinging his rope to get the feel of it.

"Roper, how many ropers do you have?" I asked.

"Let's see. There's you and me, that's two. We got Cloud and Sonny, that's four, and Lucky, that's five. Lee West is gonna time, so he won't be roping. I guess we'll each rope eight all together."

Each of us put twenty dollars into a hat Barbara held. Roper had already put in one hundred dollars, so the winner got the two hundred sixty dollar pot.

Roper said, "Hey, Ted. I bet twenty bucks Cloud finishes higher than Lucky."

Ted laughed a little, but I think the offer irritated him. "Make it a hundred and you got a bet."

"Okay, one hundred bucks."

I did not feel ready to rope, but I thought I would get into it after a couple of rounds. That's the way it goes.

Cloud was the first contestant. He rode Tonkawa and was in the starting chute. He said he was ready and the gate swung open and the steer bolted. A split second later Tonkawa and Cloud came out of the chute. Within three seconds Cloud had a loop on the horns of the steer and within sixteen and four-tenths of a second the steer was down and had been tied. The white flag that Lee West held came down and Molly's thumb hit the stopwatch. None of us could beat his time and Cloud won the first go-round. Really it wasn't a very good time.

Lucky Davis turned out to be a pretty good roper. His time of seventeen seconds was good enough for third in the go-round. Roper had a time of eighteen and two-tenths of a second. He wasn't satisfied with it. I don't blame him, he is a much better roper than that.

Sonny had problems and finished with twenty-two seconds, but I felt sure he would have done better in later rounds.

It was one of those times when you feel so very bad for someone and yet there is nothing you can do to make things better. That is what I thought when I saw Aunt Mary's Buick moving slowly over the crest of the hill toward the roping arena. At first I thought maybe Aunt Mary was coming to watch the roping, but then I knew she would not do that, and that she would be bringing bad news and somehow I knew the bad news would be for Molly, and for Ted.

Aunt Mary parked near the pickup trucks and cars. She did not get out of the car, rather she waited for someone to come to her car.

I dismounted Choctaw and walked toward Aunt Mary's car and I heard Molly say, "John, would you see what Aunt Mary wants?" Her voice sounded as uneasy as I felt.

"Sure."

The roping stopped and the arena was still and everyone waited. When I reached her car Aunt Mary said, "Grandson, I have bad news."

"What is it?"

"It is about Molly's cousin, Evelyn. 'Bout noon, they found her over between Fairfax and Hominy. She was dead. She was in her car and the car was alright, but she had died. Grandson, you go tell her and bring her here."

I motioned to Molly and walked toward her and watched while she descended the steps of the judges' stand. Ted and Roper met Molly at the bottom of the stairs and walked with her, and Barbara caught up with them and did not speak but walked beside her.

"What is it?" Molly asked.

"It's your Cousin Evelyn." She knew something was wrong and there was no way to make it easy for her. "Aunt Mary said she had been missing all night and they found her this afternoon. Evelyn's car wasn't damaged, but she was dead."

"What?"

"She's dead, Molly. Aunt Mary doesn't know much about it except that she is dead."

"What do you mean she is dead?" Roper asked.

"That is all we know, Roper."

"People don't just die," Roper said. "There has to be a reason. Who told your Aunt Mary?"

"I'm not sure," I said. "Let's go to the house and call somebody and see what we can learn."

We sat in Roper's living room. I called the funeral home in Fairfax and asked the man who answered the telephone if Evelyn Thunder had died, and if so, was he handling the funeral.

The man on the other end of the line sounded uncertain and finally he said, "Yes. Evelyn Thunder is here, and we will be handling the services. She was brought in a little after noon today."

"How did she die?"

"I'm not sure. I believe it was some form of suicide." He paused again. "Yes, it was a suicide. A gunshot wound, I believe. Yes, a suicide by gunshot."

"Do you know what time she died?" I asked.

"No. I know very little about it. All I know is that she was brought in a little after noon today."

"Thank you." And I hung up the telephone.

"What happened?" Molly asked. "Did he know anything?"

"He claims Evelyn shot herself."

"That could not be true," Roper said.

The cowboys and their friends and families loaded their ponies and stood in small groups talking. Roper told Cloud to tell the guests to come up to the house and eat before they left, and to take some food with them, and he asked Cloud to return the entry fees to the ropers.

Aunt Mary sat in her car with the window down. She said, "I think we should talk. You children, you come to John's house this evening. Come there when you get back from Grayhorse. Roper, you come too."

CHAPTER

32

Several hours had passed since we heard about Evelyn. Barbara and I waited in Grandpa's rock house that was lit by two kerosene lamps, waiting for the others to show up for the family meeting.

"I've never been here before, it's kind of cozy. I like the thick rock walls."

"Grandpa preferred staying here. Always slept here. The architect designed a large bedroom for him in the main house, but he only slept there one night."

"What's in those trunks?"

"His clothing and blankets and tobacco bags, and fans. I'm not sure of everything, I haven't felt like going through them."

She pointed to a picture on the wall. "Is that the man who went with you and your Grandpa to cut cedar wood for that pipe?"

"Mi-keh-wa-ti-an-kah?"

"Yes, him. I have trouble pronouncing his name."

"Yes, that is him. That picture was taken in the Garden of the Gods near Colorado Springs. That other man is Mon-tse-no-pi'n, the old man who lives in Indian Camp. The next picture is my Dad and Grandpa and other dancers. That one there is a picture of my grandmother Hui-e-non-zhi and her sister. They were Willow People. That baby Grandma is holding is my Dad."

Barbara smiled. "Is that your high school picture?"

"Yes. Grandpa was proud of that."

"What's in the little cedar box under the bed?"

"You are full of questions. That box has Grandpa's medicine bundle in it. He left me instructions about burying the bundle but I am not ready to do that. Before too long, I will bury the bundle and the cedar box. The little chest beside it is full of silver dollars. Grandpa did not like paper money and I just haven't felt like doing anything with it."

Barbara smiled and her view moved on. "Is that the war club you told me about?"

"Yes. He used it very well, I understand. He once killed seven enemies in one day. After the funeral I brought the club back here and hung it over the fireplace."

"I cannot imagine warfare like that. Shooting a gun is one thing, but a war club is something different, anyway I think it is." Barbara looked at a pencil drawing on the back of a piece of wallpaper. "That is very interesting."

"It is a drawing Grandpa made of the Mourning Dance. Those figures all have a part in the dance, and the one on the far right is Grandpa."

"That is a fascinating drawing. He drew very well."

"My dad could also draw. I hope it runs in the family."

"John, did you hear a car door slam?"

"Yes, we better go inside."

Tom was sitting on the platform in the back yard with Wolf at his side. "Thought I'd have a smoke," Tom said. The glow of his cigarette brightened with his draw on the tobacco. "I think Ted and that girl just drove up."

In the living room Tom and I arranged two sofas and some chairs into a circle. We sat in that circle and talked, using a lot of words to express our sorrow and feelings of helplessness. It seemed to me that we used more words than the old people would have used.

"Could I say something?" Roper asked. "My family has not been touched by all those unexplained deaths. When it happens to other families, I just go to the funeral and then go on with whatever I'm doing."

"We all did that," Molly said. "It's been too easy to take a trip or have a party. But now I am going to face whatever is going on. Whatever that is."

Aunt Mary was thoughtful and like always she spoke slowly. "You children. Don't make yourselves feel bad. You could not know bout people that are mean in the world. You need to figure out how are you going to look after yourselves and look after each other. That is what you need to spend your time doing."

Aunt Mary was right and I could think of very little to say. The others talked for over an hour, and I think it was good that they talked.

When we finished talking, Doris served one of her new desserts, a French form of apple pie. I decided I would explain to Doris everything that was happening. If there was a danger, she deserved to know about it.

Roper had been tense all evening, and when he asked me to step into the sunroom to look at my art, I am certain everyone knew he wanted to talk in private. "What do you think of Mavis?"

"I am not sure," I said. "Ted likes her a lot. She came along and wrapped Ted up pretty quickly. I guess I don't know what to think. Going with my feelings is as good as anything and I have a good feeling about Mavis and Ted."

Roper asked, "What does Molly think of Mavis?"

"You know Molly. She trusts everyone."

"That's true. But, John, if I find that Mavis had anything to do with this, I will beat the hell out of her and her family."

"I would help you on that one, if we ever learn that is what happened. It is possible that she is involved, but we don't know. We can't say anything to Ted. We cannot even let Ted know that we are thinking about it."

Molly came into the room, "What are you two talking about?"

"Roper just wanted to know what I thought of Mavis?"

"What do you think?" Molly asked.

"I do not know what to think. What about you?"

"I like her. I have the feeling that she really does like Ted."

Back in the living room I quietly asked Barbara what she thought of Mavis. "Mavis is just Mavis," Barbara answered. I reacted as if I knew what that meant, but looking back on it I have no idea what that meant.

Things were quiet. Aunt Mary did not stand when she spoke. *"I want to tell you children something. When I was a young girl, we had a time like this. We were still living on the northern part of our lands up in Kansas. There was some mean people that killed two Osages. White men. I remember my father saying Osages signed paper with the government, and that the Osages needed to look to the government for protection. The government people said, if we protect ourselves, we would cause bigger problems. Maybe a war. So we looked to the government for help, but the government did not look for the men.*

"Four families went on a buffalo hunt. For a full day they traveled west to the buffalo plains. The second day, they turned south and made a big circle back toward home, and at the end of the second day they met up with two scouts who had slipped away early. The scouts had found two of the men who had killed one Osage. They planned a war party and killed both white men, then went to hunt buffalo. When they came back, they did not have many hides, and not much meat, but no more Osages were killed. Not many Osages know that story."

We have a tradition of staying with a person who has died until the time of burial and Molly was fulfilling that tradition for Evelyn. I went to the Thunder home near Grayhorse to see the Thunder family and to see how Molly was holding up.

The moon was near full, and the air was clear and sharp, and Willie Gore was tending the fire for the two Ponca ladies who were cooking. I remembered Willie and Evelyn dancing at Ted's last party. I like Willie, he is one of those people who can be counted on during a difficult time like this.

Light from the small Peyote fire showed through the window of the Roundhouse. Roper and Molly and I sat on a platform in the yard. Molly wrapped in a blanket. The constant even beat of the drum and the aroma of campfire coffee told me I was where I should be, and where I wanted to be.

The thought of attending another funeral was, strangely, a challenge for me. No matter how many of us they murdered, we would always respond with a full tribal funeral, and we would go on living our lives, and some day we would somehow find the murderers. That was a pretty weak response, even for me, and I know it was more personal for Molly and Ted and Roper. However, that was the way I felt on the day we buried Evelyn.

Wa-lu-tsa-ka-she is an older and respected man from the Panther Clan. He presided at Evelyn's funeral. The Panther People are warriors and they are an interesting clan. Their traditional members do not visit people who are ill. They say they only make them worse. Wa-lu-tsa-ka-she completed all of the steps to becoming a knowledgeable man, a Non-hon-zhin-ga, a Little Old Man, as it has been interpreted. He also has a reputation as a warrior and as an orator whose counsel is sought for many reasons.

It was noon and Evelyn, the girl who loved life so much, began her journey with Grandfather Sun. The four days of mourning were complete.

Molly and Ted had taken care of their obligation to their cousin. The obligation was a formal ritual in which we all believe and a very personal farewell that went well beyond the requirements of a ritual.

Roper took Evelyn's death hard and that evening I went to check on him. Molly had many people to comfort her and Roper looked alone. I checked his house and the hotel speakeasy and the Bon Bon. I found him sitting in the Catholic church.

He seemed to be studying his Stetson hat. Neither of us spoke and I sat down beside him. He remained deep in thought and every so often he would shift his sitting position and clear his throat, or cross or uncross his arms or his legs, and once I thought he was going to cry. During that time he lit a candle and prayed once. After about an hour he asked, "Are you ready to go?"

Outside, Roper said, "Thanks for coming by, John. It's nice to have friends."

I put on a good front for the burial service and for the dinner that followed. I know we had agreed not to be alone, but after the funeral I wanted to be alone.

The o-lo-shka food from the funeral dinner was in the Buick. I put a .38-caliber pistol under the front seat. I drove north of town and parked the car on the cliff overlooking Grandpa's old camp. I did not expect anyone to follow me but if someone was following me, I would have an advantage by knowing the land and the stream.

There is a rock that juts out into the water, where my Dad and I had often fished. Sitting without movement, I could see the surface and underwater activities the fish, turtles, snakes, and bugs carry on all day.

It had been several hours since I had eaten, and I took the fry bread and a piece of beef that had cooked slowly over the coals. I ate the beef and bread. The beef is a little tough but has enormous flavor. You have to chew it, but it seems the more you chew the more flavor you get out of the meat. I sat for a while relaxing and eating. The funeral had started me thinking about my Mom and Dad and I wanted to be alone to do that, and Grandpa's old campsite was the best place to be alone.

My mother was thirty-one when she died in that car wreck. The same accident cost my Dad his life. I still have the newspaper that quoted the sheriff as saying it was faulty brakes. I remember Tom asking why a new car would have faulty brakes. That is a question I have never forgotten, not as a child, nor as an adult.

Mom was a pretty woman with understanding eyes, and she was emotionally strong. Sometimes Molly reminds me of her. The other day when Molly told me that I am too diplomatic, and that I understate everything, she reminded me of my mother.

It troubled my mother that the people at her church and the people at the Agency thought it better for me to attend the boarding school on the hill next to the Agency. Because her generation was not familiar with European concepts of schooling, she went along with the church and government's recommendation. During that year she was there to pick me up every Friday afternoon and the weekends were good. Then she decided one year was enough. She told me there were too many things that the boarding school would not teach me, things one learns from family. After that I attended Indian Camp School, a public school with an Indian name.

Her name was Pa-hiu-the-zhe and people called her Jenny. She was Deer Clan, and as a young girl Mom had listened to the old people and concentrated to remember many of their teachings, and when she was tucking me into bed, she would repeat the teachings exactly as she had heard them. She once told me she was a good interpreter. "I understand the Osage language and I think I translate it very well," she told me.

Once when I was six years old, we were in a crowd of people on the tracks of the Midland Valley Railroad Station, on the south side of the town. A famous person was at the station and I do not remember that person's name, but many people came to catch a glimpse of that famous person. I was not tall enough to see what was happening but I could hear the famous man talking.

In the crowd behind me I heard a funny voice say, "Damned Injuns. How in hell did they end up with all the land 'round here?"

I had been taught not to turn and look at people because that was rude. I had time to see who it was, because the man with the funny voice kept talking. I finally took off my hat and held it for a moment, then dropped it, and that gave me an opportunity to look at the man with the funny voice.

The man was dressed in a black suit that was a little small for the man, and the man himself looked funny. He was skinny, and he had stooped shoulders, and he chewed tobacco, and some of the tobacco had ran down onto his beard. He must have thought me rude, because he caught me looking at him.

Finally, the big man he was with told him to "Shut the hell up."

He did shut up, but not before he said some rude things. The skinny ugly little man kept looking at me, and I kept looking back at him, and then I heard my mother say, "Don't pay any attention to him, John. He is ignorant, and you are above his ignorance."

"Think you're better 'n me?"

"I know you are better than him," she said to me and we walked away.

I thought the man would surely want to fight my mother and me, but he did not move. He just kept grinning at me, and his friend took him by his arm and said, "You sorry little son of a bitch, you're gonna get the hell kicked outa you," and he pulled the skinny little man away. I do not know where he took him, but I could not see or hear him, and that was fine with me.

Later, when the famous person was gone, and the crowd was smaller my mother said, "There is nothing anyone can say about Indians or about being an Indian that will make you feel ashamed of being Indian or make you want to be something other than an Indian." She had told me that before, but on that day at the rail station, I understood more of what she was saying.

Then my mother said to me, "I am proud of you, John. You stood up like a little man to that ugly *E'n-shta-keh*." I knew my mother was serious because she broke one of her rules by using the Osage word for white man.

Because of those oil wells, I have a better education than most people, and I have traveled more than most people. Somehow, I have always been certain that Grandpa was better educated than I am. Considering his standing in the clans and the rituals he had completed, I consider him to have credentials just as I have a college degree. His certificate was in the people that were always called to witness ceremony.

I think I am a pretty good judge of people, and it still bothers me that the little man, who was obviously insignificant even in his own world, would think he could talk like that in front of my mother. My mother knew who she was long before Osages had oil wells, and she and Dad and Grandpa taught me how to deal with people like that little man. Grandpa would have laughed about him, and then put him out of mind.

I know how right my mother was when she said there was nothing anyone could say that would make me ashamed of being Indian, or that would make me want to be something other than Indian. I was not embarrassed for him, but probably could be embarrassed for his family, whoever his family might have been.

I chewed another piece of beef and the fry bread was good and I sat on the rock feeling safe. The little man bothered me because he was insignificant. That was it. Because he would not have bothered Grandpa, I wondered if my generation was losing an important part of being Osage. Cloud once said his Sioux people gave up a lot just to survive, and it troubled me that I might be in that position.

It occurred to me that I had not thought of that little man for years, and when Evelyn died I thought of him. Maybe someone as insignificant as that little man became significant by killing Evelyn, and he knew he could get away with it.

The sun was starting to set, and I heard the motor of a car parking near the edge of the boulders. It was not a Model A, but I made sure of the gun beside me.

I heard Barbara calling to me. She and her father were standing near the edge of the boulders, and I told them to wait, and I would come to them.

"I'm sorry to bother you, John, but I was afraid for you and I thought you might be here, so I came on out."

"That's all right, glad you came. How are you, sir?"

"I'm fine, John. Barbara asked that I come with her. I hope you don't mind."

"Not at all. Like I said, I'm glad you're here."

"Are you really alright?" and her voice sounded concern.

"Of course, I am alright." I was happy to see her. It also pleased me that someone would care enough to drive out to Cedar Creek to check on me. I remember thinking at that moment that I felt close to Barbara. Very close, and it was an unusual sensation for me.

"Daddy, you go on back and I will ride with John. Is that okay with you, John?"

"Sure, I wish you would." I was relieved it was not the man in the brown hat, and I knew it.

34

Tom had breakfast about the time the sun came up. Two hours later he joined me while I had breakfast on the sunporch. He rolled a cigarette and told me about a colt that was for sale. Tom will always be a jockey at heart, and every so often he will get horse-racing fever. I told him that if he still liked the colt after the second look, we would buy it. He smiled and told me he had looked at it four times already.

"That guy that followed you up to Sand Creek is named Kenneth Carson," Tom said. "He may be a little crazy."

"Why do you think he is crazy?"

"He just looks like it, acts like it. He stays at a boardin house south a downtown, over near Bird Creek. He still don't know I saw him at the falls that day. I talked to him. He thinks I'm dumb. I know I'm dumb, but I ain't as dumb as him."

"Why does he think you're dumb?"

"Cause I acted dumb when I talked to him." Tom studied his cigarette for a moment then lit it. "I bet he was the one up on the hill watchin the house."

"I've been thinking that too. Be careful around him, Tom."

At the Agency Mr. Hugel smiled broadly and with a firm grip he shook my hand. "Come in, John. It's good to see you."

"Thank you, sir."

"John. We've been giving your request a great deal of thought. You understand this is a very complex question." He clasped his hands together and he stopped smiling and he looked serious. "Frankly, John, I don't see much wrong with it and by next Tuesday we should make a recommendation to the central office."

"Where is the central office?"

"That is in Washington, D.C." He pointed to the picture of President Calvin Coolidge. "That there is my boss, John, and I have to be pretty darned sure of myself when I make a decision like the one you are asking me to make. And you, you should think long and hard before handling your own affairs."

"I plan to buy some books and read and learn about business. I can enroll in classes at the college in Tulsa."

Mr. Hugel smiled and shook his head. "John, John, John." He stood and walked around the desk and placed his hand on my shoulder. "While the Indian Service is handling your accounts you have the benefit of expert financial managers. John, there are people back east who pay considerable sums of money for the services that you receive without it costing you a dime."

"I know that and I appreciate it." I waited a moment. "But you think you will know more by Tuesday?"

"Yes. Drop by on Wednesday. We should know for sure."

I wanted to inquire about the hotel but decided to take Mr. Williams's advice and wait.

I left the car parked at the Agency and walked the stairs down to the Bon Bon where Barbara and Molly were waiting. "Hey, Cuz," Molly said, "did you ever notice how a cup of tea, an éclair, and some sunshine can change your view of the world?"

"Yes. I have. I think Mr. Hugel at the Agency may have had a double dose of tea and éclairs this morning."

Molly smiled but did not comment.

"Did you ask about the hotel?" Barbara asked.

"No. I stuck with the plan and played dumb. Convincing him I am dumb was not difficult."

"Molly, are you going to see Sanders?" I asked.

"No, he would tell me that I will inherit all of Evelyn's estate. He would act real sorry about her dying so he can show how nice he is. Then he would tell me how valuable the estate is and what he plans to do for me."

"You're right. I don't think I will see him either."

"I'm going shopping," Molly said. "You guys might want to drop by this evening. Mrs. New Moon said she was fixing something special."

On the edge of town I pressed down on the accelerator and felt a surge of power from the engine. Barbara turned in the car seat to face me and smiled. "Where are we going in such a hurry?"

"I guess I just got a little anxious. I've been thinking about business, and it occurred to me that I have assets but I do not really know what I have. It has always just been home, but who knows, I might start thinking of property in terms of assets."

When we reached home, Doris said Mr. Sanders had called and did not leave a message.

"Think I will look at the long house."

"Why do you call it the long house?"

"Because it is long. That is what my mother called it. It does not have anything to do with the Long House religion that some tribes practice."

I had not been inside the long house since Grandpa's funeral.

"You do not lock the door?" Barbara asked.

"No. Tom is normally around."

When I walked into the room I thought about Whitedeer standing and praying during Grandpa's funeral dinner. Some light was coming through the windows and I left the door open to let more light in, but the room was still dark. Several tables placed end to end made three long tables with seating for large dinners.

"How many people can sit down and eat here?"

"I think Mom said about one hundred twenty."

We walked through the door and into the kitchen. "I've never seen so many dishes. Maybe you could open a restaurant. How many dishes are there?"

"Doris says there are a little over four hundred place settings, she called them, with plates and silverware and glasses and cups and serving bowls."

"And they are beautiful. When would you use them?"

"We used them for Grandpa's funeral."

"I forgot about that. I wasn't here."

"When Mom and Dad were alive, we used this place a lot. Of course, we did not always have one hundred twenty people eating. Doris comes out here occasionally and keeps things clean."

"Look at those pots and pans. They are huge."

We walked back into the dining room and Barbara turned to me. "John, you really should leave this place as it is. It is interesting. It's beautiful."

Something blocked the light from the outside door, and we turned toward the light. Mr. Alan Sanders was standing in the doorway, "I hope, I'm not interrupting anything."

"Mr. Sanders, come in. No, you are not interrupting. Mr. Sanders, this is Barbara Williams."

"Hello, Barbara. I hoped Molly might be with you, John. I feel so bad about Evelyn, and I know Molly must feel terrible."

I believed Barbara to be staring at Mr. Sanders, and I am certain it was because he was certainly acting just like Molly said he would act.

"This is a difficult time for her," I said. "And I apologize for not letting you know that I would not stop by your office today."

"That is okay, John. However, we need to talk. I drove to Grayhorse to see Mr. and Mrs. Thunder. I know they are grieving and I did not go over there to talk business. I just wanted to pay my respects."

Neither of us spoke for a moment, then Alan Sanders said, "John, why don't I communicate with Molly through you?"

"That would depend on Molly, and probably the staff at the Agency."

"I will speak with Hugel at the Agency. I am certain that we can work through this without disturbing Molly in her grief."

Barbara was still looking at Sanders, and I could see she resented him.

"Let me discuss this with Molly," I said, "and when things are right, I will contact you."

"Good, very good. We can get Evelyn's business settled quickly." I did not answer him, and the silence was a little awkward. "John, I have done a great deal of work on your will. I think I have come up with a good solid plan for you, Molly, and Ted."

"I am afraid I cannot speak for Molly and Ted."

"The way I see it, John, you and Molly and Ted are first cousins and your estates are intermingled. Not entirely, you have your own original allotments, but much of what you have inherited has been divided with Molly and Ted.

"John, I suggest very strongly that you, Molly, and Ted leave your estates to each other. In that way you will be taking care of each other." Mr. Sanders looked at his watch and placed it back into the pocket of his vest. Looking at his watch seemed to be a nervous gesture. "I have written each of you a will. All there is to do now is to sign them."

"I wish to include some items that Ted and Molly may not want in their wills."

"Like what, John?"

"Like Tom Woodson. He has lived with our family for a long time, and I do not know what he would do if I were not here. I assume he could live with Ted or Molly, but we have never discussed it."

"Is he a relative? Is he even Indian?"

"No. He is a friend. He is a white man that drove for Grandpa and worked for Dad. I think you have probably seen him. He is a jockey and he is a small man."

"Oh yes. I remember him and you may include a small bequest like that. I don't mind that." He smiled and it seemed the smile was almost genuine. "I have scheduled you and Molly to sign your wills on Monday." He paused and was going to continue on, but I spoke.

"Molly will need more time to review what you have written."

"There really is not much to read. What about a week from Friday, then?"

I nodded my agreement.

"John, I suggest you leave Woodman cash, not headright interest. It isn't right for us to take care of half of Osage country." He smiled again.

"I will be prudent with those items," I said. "I will drop a list by your office by Monday."

Mr. Sanders extended his hand and I shook it and he tipped the brim of his hat to Barbara and said, "It was nice meeting you, Miss," and he paused. "I am sorry, I am not good with names. It was nice meeting you."

"Miss Williams," I said.

"Yes, Miss Williams." Mr. Sanders walked to the door and turned and stood looking at the tables. "This is a nice room." He looked up at the light fixtures and reached to the wall and turned the lights on. "A man could use this room for a lot of things." Then Mr. Sanders left the long house.

"My God, what an ass," Barbara said. "What an unbearable, arrogant ass."

I did not answer and Barbara went on. "John, he was rude to you."

"Yes. I suppose he was."

Later we sat on the white wooden lawn chairs and I did a pencil sketch of Barbara. It was not a bad sketch, but her anger and resentment toward Mr. Sanders showed through in the sketch, and anger and resentment are seldom in her personality.

Mr. Sanders has always been aggressive and he works to make his smile appear sincere, but on that day I picked up traces of anger toward me in his voice and in his mannerisms. Also, Barbara was right about the arrogance in his behavior.

Barbara had promised her parents she would eat with them and she went home to keep that promise. I went back to the long house and sat for a while and tried to sort things out, and I came up with nothing. It was late and I was tired when I lay down on the bed, and just before I fell asleep, for the first time in my life I had a mental picture of Grandpa as a warrior, faced with danger and silently speaking to another Osage in the sign language of his hands.

CHAPTER

35

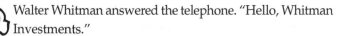 Walter Whitman answered the telephone. "Hello, Whitman Investments."

"Walter. This is John Grayeagle."

"John, old boy. It is good to hear from you. How are you getting on?"

"I am getting on well, Walter." I thought for a moment and decided that I had no choice. I would simply place my trust in Walter. "I have a rather unusual request." I did not want to sound too dramatic. "Walter, I must ask your complete confidence."

"Yes, John. You have my complete confidence."

"This is not a social situation, it is a very serious business situation."

"I understand, John. Are you saying you want to arrange a meeting in a place that is less than public?"

"That is exactly what I am saying."

"In my profession, John, I often conduct business in complete privacy. For that reason I have kept an eye out for such places since I came to Pawhuska." Walter cleared his throat. "You know, of course, the location of the hill just north and east of town, where the oil wells are on the ridge of the hill near the Osage cemetery, and then the hill reaches higher to a peak?"

"Yes. I know where that is."

"I think that would be perfect. You go up there and take your easel and brushes just a little before sundown and set up for painting," he said. "I will show up with my camera and we can both catch the sun setting. That should look innocent enough. Two artists catching the beauty of the setting sun. You know, John, people seldom take artists seriously."

Walter went on, "We can see for miles around and we should be able to talk without being overheard."

This was not what I had in mind, but it made sense, so I agreed to meet just before sunset.

Walter was right about his reason for meeting on the hilltop. No one would hold a secret meeting on top of a treeless hill.

I reached the first level of the hill where the cemetery is located and could see Walter on the higher ground near the peak of the hill. The wind was strong on the hilltop and the grass had not been heavily pastured and was tall for spring and was blowing in waves.

I set up my easel on the ridge of the hill near the cemetery and sketched the outline of the valley to the south and west of the hill where the town is located. The hill beyond the valley to the west was a solid green of trees, mostly blackjacks.

I thought about the conversation we would have. Walter came down the hill carrying his camera. He waved once while he walked toward me. Walter was putting on a convincing show for anyone who might be observing us.

He called to me, "How are you, John?"

"I am fine, Walter. Thanks for coming."

Walter came near enough so that I could hear him, "I just hope I can be of assistance, John. You sounded quite concerned on the telephone. What, pray tell, is happening?"

"You are aware that two of Molly's cousins have died recently?"

"Yes. I am aware of that. Terrible thing, really."

"Yes it is. Before we begin, Walter, I want you to know that I question whether or not those deaths were accidental."

"From what I hear, old boy, I rather seriously doubt that either of the deaths was accidental. Not that I know anything specific, you understand, but in general, a lot of Osages die from causes that are other than natural."

"It seems that way to me."

"I am not an Osage, of course, so the locals assume I am one of them, heaven forbid." He was setting up his camera on a tripod. "Not that they are all bad. I am given to understand there are some good chaps among them. Still, there are some bloody mean people among them too." He made an adjustment to his camera to make it level.

"What I want to ask of you, Walter, is that you keep an eye out for me on a particular individual."

"Who might that be?"

"Mr. Alan S. Sanders," I said. The sun was starting to set. There were enough clouds in the sky that the sunset would be beautiful.

"Alan Sanders."

"Yes. He is attorney for Ted and for Molly and he wants to be my attorney."

"Is he one of those guardians?"

"He is guardian for Ted and Molly."

"As I understand that guardian business, that means he has substantial, if not total, control over their business."

"That is true. I really do not believe he killed Molly's cousins. However, there are some things about the situation that do not add up. Your office affords a good observation point to see who comes and goes in Sanders's office."

"I see. I remember that day you viewed him from my office window. Of course, John, I will be pleased to help. However, I would ask that this little reconnaissance operation be kept between you and me." He had both hands on the camera and seemed to be studying it. "I am certain you understand my reasons."

"That is in everyone's best interest." I felt good about our conversation.

"How do you propose we communicate?" Walter asked.

"Maybe you could leave a note for me at the middle landing of the stairs that lead from Kihekah Avenue up to the courthouse. There are three landings. Tom has fixed a place to leave notes. You must sit on the bench on the north side of the landing. Sit on the extreme left side of the bench and with your left hand reach behind and under the bench. Tom has attached a shelf that will hold a paper rolled up about an inch thick."

"That is splendid. When I have something to report I will place a red vase in the window of my office." Walter was angling his camera to take a picture of the town. "This is real intrigue. I think I am going to enjoy this little operation."

"I also need to know about people from the Agency. I don't really know who else I am looking out for."

"Don't worry about it, old boy, I'll keep a close eye out for any suspicious-looking characters." He smiled. "The not-so-suspicious-looking are probably the scoundrels."

"Walter, I want to thank you for your help. We need help in whatever it is we are up against."

"I am quite pleased to be of assistance. You know, there isn't much that I have done that I believe in since the war ended. I have a feeling this is worthwhile."

After the discussion I began sketching, and for a few minutes I sketched well, and Walter took more pictures.

"John. I have been nosing around a bit and I am intrigued by what I hear about Osage ritual. My question is, do those old Osages really memorize those prayers word for word and phrase for phrase?"

"Yes they do, Walter. It is an amazing accomplishment. Of course, every society must have a record, and they did not have typewriters."

"That is true. Sometime I would like to talk to you about it."

"Certainly. Not that I know that much about it. All I know is what my Grandpa and my parents told me."

I waited a few minutes and watched the colors turn as the sun dropped behind the horizon. It was beautiful, and to think there will be another one tomorrow. I folded my easel and put the sketching pencils away. Walter waited until I was partway down the hill before he followed me, carrying his photography equipment.

CHAPTER
36

Tom said Grandpa's Pierce Arrow should be driven to keep it in good running order. He said he heard that somewhere. So, I drove Grandpa's Pierce Arrow. The car is so luxurious I am embarrassed driving it without Grandpa sitting in the backseat.

Barbara laughed when she got into the car. She stroked the dashboard and the seat covers and rubbed the golden door handles. "I am going to ride in style today."

"I don't know what to do with this thing."

"I think driving it is one thing you can do with it. It is your car, isn't it?"

"I suppose it will be mine when Grandpa's estate is settled. So, if I don't get shot before then, I suppose you could say it is my car."

"Don't talk like that, John."

Walter and I agreed to secrecy and I could not change that, but it made me uncomfortable to keep that information from Barbara. Not telling Ted and Molly was going to make me even more uncomfortable, I knew that for sure.

The receptionist told us to go on in to Mr. Williams office, he was waiting for us and like always T.E. got right to the point.

"John, my initial reading of your legal position was accurate. My sources are treating this subject with extreme secrecy." He took a deep breath and looked at Barbara, and I detected something of a father who has let his daughter down. "John, I am afraid you have been swindled out of a great deal of money. The paperwork is in order, but that is not unusual in a swindle.

"You remember I told you earlier that both W. W. Baskins, personally, and the Grand Hotel as a corporation filed for bankruptcy? Well, I thought we would have a little time to get ready for it, but the hearing was held at the same time they filed. It was a quiet affair in Oklahoma City. The Agency staff have signed off on the settlement, and you will receive ten cents for every dollar you invested in the hotel."

"Is that legal?" Barbara asked.

"Normally, I would say no. However, that may not matter because the federal government has agreed to the terms of the settlement."

"So, was Baskins telling the truth when he said the hotel was not doing well financially?" I asked.

"Not at all. He was lying. The word around Oklahoma City is that it was a swindle. Baskins arranged the sale of the hotel to a third party. So far, I do not know who that third party is. I suspect Baskins is a part of the third party. The way the scheme works is Baskins is technically out, and you are paid ten percent of what is owed you. The court forgives the ninety percent. That is the way it works."

Barbara was angry. "Daddy. They can't do that. They simply cannot do it."

"Barbara, they have done it," T.E. said.

"Then, as you see it, there is nothing I can do?"

"That appears to be the situation, John. I think it would be wise for you and Barbara and me to keep our meeting a secret. Who knows, we might learn something."

We took the elevator down and walked out onto the street. The clouds were drifting away, and the sun was starting to break through.

Barbara said, "Let's walk by the hotel. That will be a start on this new non-strategy." We walked toward the hotel. "In fact, let's go to the hotel for lunch."

"In a day or two, like we agreed."

When we reached the corner to cross Main Street to the hotel, there was a red vase on the table by the window of Walter's office.

"Why don't you want to have lunch at the hotel? I know they stole from you, but lunch is part of our strategy."

"Grandpa said not to go around people who do not want you around them. You will be better off and what they think or want does not matter."

"I just want to see the look on Mr. Baskins's face when you walk into the hotel restaurant."

"I don't care about the look on Mr. Baskins's face."

"If it was me they cheated, they would pay." Barbara paused and thought. "No. I would kick the crap out of them, or hire someone to kick the crap out of them. Then they would pay. You could bet on that."

"Well. Hopefully, I will recover the money or the hotel. Although, at this time I don't see how I am going to do either of those things."

"You know, John, sometimes you can be darned frustrating."

"Yes, I know. Let's go eat. Eating is good for frustration."

CHAPTER

37

The note from Walter was written in code, more or less. The code, I suppose, was for the benefit of someone other than myself who might find the message.

tuesday morning
to the goat
greetings
ass visited by od who is uncle of md
ass paid money to od
i hope this helps.
will continue observation.
the osprey

So, Alan S. Sanders had paid Otis Davis some money. Apparently Walter was enjoying the operation, as he called it.

I rang up Molly and Roper on the telephone and asked them to meet at Molly's apartment.

It is a nice hillside apartment and there were birds chirping in the trees just outside the open windows. I told them, "I have learned that Mavis's Uncle Otis and Mr. Sanders have a business relationship. I don't know what they are doing, but there is something going on between them."

"Where did you hear that?" Roper asked.

"I cannot tell you because I gave my word. But I believe it is true."

"It don't sound good," Roper said. "But what's really wrong with it?"

"When I asked Alan Sanders about Otis Davis, Sanders said he did not know him. And do you remember that day at the restaurant in the train station? Sanders and Mavis got off the same train."

"I have been thinking about that," Roper said. "Mavis seemed to know Ted right from the start. Do you remember that?"

Molly said, "You know I do not like to think about it, but Mr. Sanders was the one who wrote Martha's and Evelyn's wills. And now Ted and I will end up with everything they had and their parents are being left out. And now Mr. Sanders is working on a new will for me."

"What about Sonny?" Roper asked.

"I'm sure Sonny's will is the same as Evelyn's and Martha's. Everything is divided between them and Molly," I answered. "Sanders wrote it."

Roper was thoughtful and spoke slowly. "Then, all of the headrights of the Thunder family and the Grayeagle family and the other side of Ted's family would be concentrated in you three people. And, to state it bluntly, the last one alive would inherit everything."

Molly said, "I talked to Sonny. He believes both Martha and Evelyn died in accidents. He read the police and Doctor Wells's reports in the newspaper, and he believed every bit of it. He said he was going to talk to the sheriff. Of course, the sheriff won't tell him anything, just how tragic the wrecks were and how hard he was going to work to keep Osages from drinking poison whiskey."

None of us spoke for a moment. Then Molly said, "If all of this is true, then Ted is safe for a while. Isn't that right?"

"Well, yes. If you look at it that way I guess there is something good about it," Roper said. "But on the other hand, if someone would kill for a lot of money, they would probably kill Ted for what money and land that he has now."

I said, "Well, Molly and Roper, I think we better do like Aunt Mary said. We need to stay in a crowd, particularly at night. Oh, I almost forgot. Sanders has scheduled a day for us to sign the new wills he is preparing."

"What about Ted?" Molly asked. "If we talk to him he will probably tell Mavis. So, we can't tell him."

"Like you said, he will be safe for a while. That should give us time to do something," Roper said.

We had not really done anything, but for some reason I felt better.

We sat on the ground near the finish line of the track. Hank Bigcreek and Molly approached us and Hank called out, "Ted, do we set up the hurdles now?"

"Sure, go ahead."

Will Chapman was stretching and warming up for a run at high hurdles. Hank and Molly started setting up the hurdles.

Molly stopped working on the hurdles and walked to the finish line and began ringing the lap bell. She rang it six or seven times.

"Hey, everybody," Molly yelled. "I have an announcement."

She took us by surprise. "Okay," I said. "Let's hear your announcement."

"Wait a minute. You guys gather around, because I want everybody to hear this."

While we were gathering around her, Molly climbed up and stood on the bench with her hands on her hips. "My announcement is this. I refuse to allow anything to interfere with the way I live my life. If I cannot live my life the way I want, then I'd rather not live it at all."

Our little group of friends and cousins applauded Molly.

She slightly shook her head negatively. "I am not going to be reckless and I'm not going to be careless. But this business of being afraid is not for me. If somebody wants to shoot me, then they are just going to have to shoot me, but I am going to go on enjoying myself and live my life the way I want to."

"That's damned good to hear," Ted said. "I feel the same way."

Our little group gave Molly another round of applause. "Now we'll set up the hurdles," Molly said and with that she jumped down from the bench.

Molly's announcement seemed to cheer up our little group of friends and cousins. Somehow, it seemed as if a burden had been lifted.

Ted started ringing the bell and stepped up onto the bench. "Now I have something to say. I want to invite you guys to a party I am having at the Grand Hotel on Tuesday night. It's in that Red Room on the second floor."

"The speakeasy," Molly said.

"That's it. The speakeasy. Eight o'clock," Ted said.

"Barbara and I will be there. What's the party for?"

"Just show up. I'll tell you when you get there," Ted said. "Molly, can you make it?"

"Okay, Cuz. Like I said I don't want to be reckless. I just want to keep on living. It feels good. You know, being afraid isn't good."

On the drive into town Molly asked me to stop by the church. "Why don't you come with me?" she said.

"I will do that?"

"I won't be long. I want to pray just a moment. Maybe see if Father Olfengaille is there and speak with him a moment."

I sat waiting near the back of the church, and Molly walked down the middle aisle and knelt and then sat. She then lit a candle and prayed. I don't know how long she prayed. Probably for ten minutes.

When we left Molly said, "I suppose I should come when Father is scheduled to be hearing confessions."

"That would improve your chances of catching him."

"Just being in the church is good for me. I feel safe there."

"Does it remind you of your mother?"

"Yes, it does."

"That's what it does for me," I said.

"You know, Cousin. We were lucky to have the parents we had, even if we didn't have them that long. Not everyone is that lucky."

CHAPTER
39

The evening before the Osage Tribe's oil lease sale, Molly and I sat at the Bon Bon and T.E. Williams introduced us to one of his partners named Clay. I cannot remember his last name. He had a mustache and was from Chicago. His other partner would arrive from Tulsa at nine o'clock on the following morning on what has been called the Million Dollar Special. It is a train that runs on the morning of Osage lease sales.

Clay and his partner would go up against some of the big players in the oil business, trying to get a lease from the tribe. Clay wanted to meet an Osage so Barbara brought Molly and me to meet with him. I had no idea why they would want to speak with us about their business. Barbara also asked me to go with her to the train depot on the following morning.

The man named Clay sipped his coffee and said, "The streets are certainly crowded."

"Yes," Molly answered. "Lease sales are exciting. We sometimes make as much money from the lease sales as we do from the sale of oil."

Mr. Clay went on. "So let me get this straight. The tribe owns all of the oil under the million and a half acre reserve?"

"That is true," I said.

"And the oil companies and speculators must purchase the rights to drill for that oil from the Osage Tribe. Is that true?"

"That is true also."

"Then," the man went on, "I have been told it is a pretty good deal for the oil companies, because any other place there would be several landowners to deal with. Here in the Osage, a company can have an approved lease within a day or two. Whereas in Pennsylvania it may take two or three months."

"That is true."

"So, if we are the successful bidders on a tract tomorrow, we could legally be ready to commence drilling on the day after tomorrow, which is Friday?"

"That is true. You would probably have an approved lease by tomorrow. However, the sale will probably last for two days."

Clay said, "I heard there are six hundred sixty-six leases to be auctioned. That would be over one hundred thousand acres. The fellow at the Agency is predicting over twelve million dollars will be paid into the tribe by tomorrow night."

"Hopefully, that is also true," I said.

"So, then, every time a barrel of oil is produced in the Osage, you receive at least a small part of it. Is that true?"

"Yes. A very small part of each barrel, but that is true."

Walter Whitman walked up the stairs to the Bon Bon. He saw our group and tipped his hat to us. I waved and Molly motioned him to come sit with us, but he put up the palms of both hands to us and shook his head negatively and pointed to a newspaper he held under his arm. Walter sat on the lower landing of the Bon Bon. He ordered tea and read the newspaper. I appreciated his playing his part so well.

There was a constant stream of people walking through the Bon Bon terrace, going up and down the stairs to the agency. The people at the table next to us appeared to be putting a last-minute deal together. I was not trying to listen, but they were talking loud and became very excited when one of the men pointed out that one Osage lease had produced over two million barrels of oil in ten months. The man then grabbed a piece of paper and scribbled some figures and announced that they could each net over a million dollars apiece each year.

We finished the conversation with T.E. Williams and his partner, and they walked down the stairs to Kihekah Avenue and turned toward their hotel. After speaking with the investors I understood their reason for wanting to meet an Osage. Their reason was they knew nothing about the Osage system and I believe they knew very little about how one might drill for oil, in the Osage or anywhere else.

Barbara and I walked with Molly to the Carolina Apartments and walking back toward the Bon Bon, Barbara said, "I spoke with Daddy just before I left home this morning." We kept walking. "He said the man who purchased the hotel from the bankruptcy court was Baskins's brother. His name is Leroy Baskins."

"I see."

"Daddy still thinks it is fraud and he would like to try to do something about it but he doesn't know what. Anyway, he wants to meet and talk about it tomorrow morning."

I drove Barbara home and assured her I would be safe driving home. When I reached home, all of the lights were on.

Tom was sitting on the platform in the front yard and he was smoking a cigarette. Cloud was sitting with Tom. Tom said, "Johnny, I asked Cloud to stick around for a while."

"Good to see you, Cloud."

"If you need me, John, I want to help out."

I explained to Tom and to Cloud the whole picture. I also told them that I felt safe physically, because I thought Baskins would be content to steal the hotel.

"You may be right," Tom said. "Just the same, we ought to be ready."

"Tom's right," Cloud said.

CHAPTER

40

There was quite a crowd on the passenger dock of the Santa Fe Railroad Station. We were waiting for Mr. Williams's second partner to arrive on the Million Dollar Special from Tulsa. Just before nine o'clock we could hear the engine chugging and rail sounds of the train and then the whistle. The train carries the biggest names in the oil industry, and a ripple of excitement ran through the crowd, and some of the people gathered near the edge of the dock to look down the track.

It was exciting when the financiers, and geologists, and engineers, and promoters rushed from the train onto the loading dock. We were introduced to a tall, slender man, Mr. Fred Turner, and we quickly got into the car and drove to the Grand Hotel where Mr. Turner left his luggage. The hotel was busy with tables set up in the lobby to register anyone who might attend the sale. It was a central list so that people in the business might find each other. I let them off at the Agency and parked the car. Barbara and I walked down the stairs to the Bon Bon.

It would be a busy day and the aroma coming from the bread ovens covered the whole terrace and the stairs that made up the Bon Bon. Several people were waiting to be seated, and Madame Richarde led us to a table and explained to those people who were waiting, that we had a reservation. Of course we did not have a reservation, but Madame Richarde takes care of her regulars. That is a trait of the French that I like.

Madame Richarde returned to our table, "I like your dark glasses, Barbara."

"Thank you, Madame Richarde. How do you like my new eye glasses, John?"

"Your glasses look fine," I said. "I know you're wearing them to shade your eyes from the brilliant sunlight, but I think they make you look rather sophisticated."

Barbara laughed. "I have a new flapper dress to wear to Ted's party tonight at the hotel. Have you figured out what Ted wants to talk about tonight?"

"I am afraid to think about it."

"I know what you mean. I have the same suspicion," and she began humming the wedding march.

"That's what I'm afraid of."

"I told Daddy that you would meet him in Elliot's Hat Shop about five minutes from now."

"Okay. Why am I meeting your Dad in five minutes?"

"Daddy thinks it is better if you are not seen talking in public, and Mr. Elliot and Daddy are close friends. Daddy said we can trust him. Just act like you are looking at a hat."

I told Barbara I would meet her at the Agency campus in a few minutes and I walked down the stairs and turned right on Kihekah Avenue and walked to Elliot's Hat Shop. Inside the hat shop Mr. Williams was smoking a cigarette and waiting for me. He came to the point.

"John, Barbara probably told you it was Baskins's brother who purchased the hotel property from Baskins."

"Yes, she did."

"My sources tell me there is nothing that can be done. However, John, I want to work on it. I want you to know that the law simply should not work this way." T.E. inhaled the smoke from his cigarette deeply and held it for a moment, then blew the smoke out into the air and pressed the cigarette into an ashtray.

"I suppose we should continue to keep quiet about it," I said.

"Yes, we should." He paused and thought for a moment, then decided to go on with what he wanted to say. "John, I want you to know that I am taking a risk by helping an Osage on Osage matters."

"I know that, and I have been careful to keep Barbara from appearing to be involved in my business. However, if Barbara and I have a social relationship some people may interpret that to be a business relationship and I have no control over that."

"That is true, and it bothers me. I want you to know that I admire you for trying to protect Barbara. I do not think there is a real danger to Barbara."

Mr. Williams and I shook hands, and I left the shop first.

I climbed the stairs to the Bon Bon and felt that someone was watching me. I stopped and asked Monsieur Richarde if Roper had been by. He said that Roper had not been by. I walked back down the stairs and near the bottom I met Kenneth Carson. I did not acknowledge him and he did not acknowledge me. Tom was right, Kenneth Carson is not real smart. An amateur like me caught him trailing me.

The Agency campus was busy. Cars were parked on both sides of Grandview Avenue and on the drive behind the Agency buildings and on the lawn.

Perhaps four hundred people were between the main Agency building and the dormitory of the Osage Boarding School. They were, for the most part, wearing suits and hats. Some were sitting on the ground and in chairs, and many of them stood. They were all holding papers or briefcases, and some had boxes of papers and rolled-up maps in the boxes.

Maybe fifty Osages sat in chairs under trees in the outer areas of the group of people. It is the business of the tribe, and many Osage people are understandably interested. Every time I see the older Osage people in a group, I think about painting a picture of them. Walter took several pictures.

Officials of the Agency were working at and around four tables under an elm tree. The auctioneer was a tall man who stood at one of the tables and called numbers and meaningless words at a rapid, even tempo. He had removed his coat and showed his red suspenders and he held a microphone in his hand.

The man in red suspenders was creating excitement by melodically repeating dollar figures. "Four hundred thousand. Who'll give me four hundred thousand dollars?" He looked over the crowd and pointed to a man near the front who apparently had bid that much. "I've got four hundred thousand. Now, who'll give me four hundred fifty thousand? Four hundred fifty thousand dollars. Who'll give me four hundred fifty thousand dollars? I've got four hundred fifty thousand dollars. Who'll give me five hundred thousand dollars?" A young man who I understand is from Tulsa bid the five hundred thousand. The auctioneer took a deep breath and continued. Sometimes it seemed that he was almost singing with the use of a single note.

"I've got half a million dollars. Who'll give me six hundred thousand? Who'll give me six hundred thousand dollars?" and he pointed to the man near the front again. "I've got six hundred thousand dollars. Who'll give me seven hundred thousand dollars?"

The bidders narrowed to three men and continued going up, until the man near the front bid one million two hundred fifty thousand dollars. Finally, the auctioneer banged his gavel down onto the table and called, "Sold to the man in the striped shirt for one million two hundred fifty thousand dollars." The crowd applauded and the younger man gave the winner a casual military-type salute. The auctioneer said to the man near the front. "Mister, that's why we call this here old tree, the Million Dollar Elm."

"Let's do another one," the auctioneer said. "A million dollars, boys, and you can drill one hundred sixty acres of Osage land. When you hit oil, and I am sure you will, just give the Osage Tribe its share and you keep the rest. Buy yourself a new car and buy Mama a new pair of shoes."

The crowd laughed and the auctioneer prepared to sell the next lease and I saw Mr. T.E. Williams join his investor friends across the crowd from Barbara and me.

Mr. Frank Phillips of Phillips Petroleum Company was bidding on a property. Everyone seemed to know when Mr. Phillips did his own bidding he was going to be the high bidder, and he was the high bidder at one million four hundred thousand dollars. Barbara saw Molly on the other side of the group of men. Molly was talking to Mr. Buffalo Standing and Barbara waved but Molly did not see her, so Barbara walked over and stood by her.

Molly always enjoys tribal gatherings. She introduced Barbara to Mr. Buffalo Standing who is a member of the elected tribal council. Mr. Buffalo Standing is over six foot five inches tall and wears a white man's suit with a vest, and a silk scarf. His hair was parted in the middle into two braids. He is a nice gentleman who seldom speaks during council meetings. He voted in favor of paying the federal government to look for the murderers of Osages. Of course, they all voted for that.

A reporter for an eastern newspaper asked if I thought the influx of oil money had changed the lifestyle of Osages. It seemed like a silly question and our interview was interrupted by the excitement caused by bidding on one of the prime leases. Everyone was familiar with Mr. J. Paul Getty. Everyone knew that sometimes he bids against himself on leases he is interested in. He has another man bid against him on leases he wants in order to thin out the bidders. However he does it he seems to end up with good leases that cost a lot. I suspect Mr. Phillips and Mr. Skelly and Mr. Marland and the others engage in similar strategies.

When the excitement settled down, I told the reporter that oil money had changed most Osages. It certainly had changed the way we live, I told him. The reporter asked Molly and Mr. Buffalo Standing the same question. I drifted away to watch the auction. A photographer took a picture of Molly and Mr. Buffalo Standing with the Million Dollar Elm in the background.

T.E. Williams's clients, or partners, were the successful bidder on two leases. They paid a little over one hundred thousand dollars for each of the leases and were pleased with the outcome of the bidding.

Kenneth Carson stood on the edge of the crowd, leaning against a blackjack tree, not involved in the bidding. He was observing the crowd. I am sure he was observing us.

I suspected Tom was nearby and I tried to not be noticed looking for him. Since I was a child my parents told me to never stand and look around at a crowd. My father said it was unbecoming.

Near the end of the day, several high-priced tracts of land were auctioned and brought the total to over fourteen million dollars. Midland Oil paid nearly two million for one tract, and Phillips paid one million seven hundred thousand for the next highest. Most of the leases sold for under seventy-five thousand dollars.

The Osages who observed the auction carried their chairs and blankets and returned to their cars. The Agency workers were tired, and they gathered their papers and boxes and hurried to the stone Agency building while other Agency workers began picking up the papers left strewn on the Agency grounds. The bidders lingered for a while discussing their drilling plans, then some of them slowly moved down the hill to the hotel rooms and restaurants. Some waited to hear official word confirming their bids and their right to drill for oil.

"We are going to be in the Red Room at the Grand Hotel about eight," Barbara told her father.

"We'll probably eat and go back to the office," T.E. said.

The partner, Fred Turner, was calculating on a piece of paper. "Do you know the money from the sale today would buy twenty-three Model T Fords for each member of the Osage Tribe?"

"Don't tell John that," Barbara said. "He is a sucker for cars. He already has three cars and a truck."

It was late when the Osage Tribal Council gathered in a small room on the top floor of the Agency building. The council went into session and approved the results of the auction. They also voted to enter lease agreements with all of the top bidders. The Agency staff drove the $14,193,800 to the bank on Kihekah Avenue and to the bank on Main Street where the bankers were waiting for the deposits.

I was tired and wanted to get away, so I drove home, alone. My plan was to sit on the platform on the lawn and study the sun as it set, but I could not think about painting. I felt uneasy about dealing with people in secret, and I thought about that. I was not good at dealing with people in secret.

I thought of my mother's stories about when she was a child, and how she would sit and listen when the people gathered. They sat in a circle, and she told me how each of them spoke when it was their turn to speak, and they said what they thought, or they did not speak at all.

CHAPTER

41

I was disappointed with Mr. Baskins, and I thought about it when we entered the lobby of the hotel. I kept thinking somehow the matter could be corrected and I could foreclose on the hotel. I see now that I just did not understand how things work.

We took the elevator to the second floor with Molly more or less leading the way. She knocked on the door and the small wooden window slid open and a man looked us over.

Molly said, "We're with the Bearsky party. You know Ted Bearsky. A big Indian guy."

"Oh, yeah," I heard a man's voice say.

Then another voice said, "I know Ted."

The sliding window closed and the door opened into the cloakroom. A small sign above the door read "Cloak Room." Will said, "Dang, I didn't even wear my cloak." There were a lot of hats on the shelves. No western hats. The westerners wear their hats. The businessmen check their hats, and the geologists and engineers check their hats and wear helmets.

The room was smoky and alive. A piano player played Scott Joplin stuff. Party music, Molly called it. The room was crowded. A young woman with a coarse voice said, "Ted's over there. Follow me, honey."

"Thanks," Molly said and turned to us and said, "Follow us, honey." We followed the wall of the crowded room for a few steps past another room where a man appeared to be guarding the door. I had been to the Red Room before but had never gone into the guarded room that is used for gambling. We wove our way through the crowded Red Room to reach Ted and Mavis.

It was at least some of the same crowd from the auction earlier in the day. The investors would wait until tomorrow to pick up the signed lease agreements at the Agency. There was some celebrating going on and probably some letting off steam. The salesman who sold me the Oldsmobile was in the crowd.

Ted had four tables placed end to end. He and Mavis and Mavis's father, Lucky Davis, were at the table with Hank Bigcreek. We joined them.

"Sit there, honey," Molly said to me, pointing to a chair.

"Sure."

Alan S. Sanders entered the room shortly after we came in. He followed our little group to the tables. "Good evening, Ted." They shook hands. I had never seen Alan Sanders out on the town.

"Good evening, Mr. Sanders," Ted said. "I think you probably know everybody here." Ted indicated our party by the sweep of his hand that held the cigar. I could tell Ted was feeling good. Not tipsy, just genuinely feeling good and enjoying himself. Mavis also looked happy.

A barmaid was waiting to take our orders. Sanders nodded to all of us and approached Molly. "Molly," Sanders said, "there is plenty of time to talk business during working hours." He held up his palms toward Molly, to suggest he knew he was acting inappropriately. "I just wanted to let you know how sorry I am for you and your family."

Molly said, "Thank you, Mr. Sanders." Then she turned to the barmaid and said, "I'll have a lemonade."

"Do you want anything in the lemonade?"

"Just lemons," Molly smiled.

We all ordered. Will ordered lemonade. As Ted said later, Joe Eagle said he was going to break training real good. I wished I was in training for something.

Within a half hour Roper joined us, then Otis Davis joined us. Ted did another one of those mass introductions for everyone at the table. I watched carefully and Sanders appeared to be meeting all of the Davis family for the first time. After the introductions Sanders explained that he must leave and he left.

The group numbered about twenty people when everyone got there. Walter Whitman was included in the group. In his introduction of Walter, Ted told us Walter was a newcomer to town and we should welcome newcomers.

I think Ted was about to tell us why he invited us to the hotel when an oil investor who had been one of the successful bidders and who had drunk more than his share of whiskey came to the table and purchased a round of drinks for the table. He wanted us to know how much he appreciated the Osage Tribe. He told us, "I think of Osages as my partners in a business." He sounded emotional. "And Osages have always treated me right and I want to treat the Osages right."

"Thank you," Ted said. "We want you to know that we think of you people as partners too. Now will you shut the hell up?" Everyone in the room that heard the remark laughed, including the man who bought the round of drinks.

Ted put his arm around the man, "I apologize, sir. I was just joking. You must forgive me. And after you have forgiven me, would you stay here and listen to what I have to say?"

"I would count it a privilege, sir." He raised his glass a little in the direction of Ted.

"Put your damned glass down," Ted said to the stranger. Again people in the room laughed. It seemed Ted had the attention of the entire room.

Ted was still standing with glass in hand. Mavis stood next to him and he put his hand around her waist. "I wanted to invite my friends here tonight to tell you all that Mavis and I are gonna get married."

The entire room applauded. I suppose I was a little disappointed because I do not know Mavis, but I felt good that Ted was happy. Barbara got into the spirit of the evening and joined the spontaneous toast for Ted and Mavis. Molly hugged Ted. Then she gave Mavis a hug.

"When's the big day?" Molly asked.

"A week from Saturday, April 24, at my place," Ted said. "Our place," Ted corrected himself.

The rest of the evening in the Red Room turned into a party for Mavis and Ted. The piano player was joined by three other musicians and they played some good ragtime music.

There were numerous toasts to Mavis and Ted and several toasts to the families of both of them. The inebriated investor proposed a toast to all Osages. Roper proposed a toast to all of the investors and drillers and rough necks and the nonsense went on and on. I wasn't really drinking on those toasts.

Molly spent a lot of time on the dance floor and called people Honey the rest of the evening. We drank a toast to the men in the factories who make the pipe and to the miners who mine the ore to make the pipe. One geologist toasted the geologists who find the ore to make the pipe.

Once, I saw Mr. W. W. Baskins enter the room for a moment. He saw our table and I caught his eye and waved. I am not a good smile person but I tried. He waved back and smiled and left the room. There was a man with him that I assumed to be his brother. Barbara caught the little exchange and said, "Not bad, John."

"Thank you."

"You may make a decent hypocrite yet."

CHAPTER

42

At Mavis and Ted's announcement party I drank practically nothing and the next morning my head felt fine. I was on the sunporch alone and enjoying the morning air and the coffee. Our plan was that Molly would stop by and I would go with her to look for a gift for Mavis and Ted.

A long black car that I did not recognize turned into the driveway. An Indian was driving so I knew it was not a salesman. As the car came closer I could tell that Wah-she-u-tse's grandson was driving. The car stopped at the end of the front sidewalk and Hu-la-tse, who we also call Daniel Junior, got out and opened the door for his grandfather Wah-she-u-tse. It was then I remembered that his grandmother's name is Wah-so-po-me, of the Night Clan.

Some people have interpreted Wah-she-u-tse's clan to be called the Isolated Earth People, and he is one of their most prominent leaders. He won many war honors during the past century. I remembered that day when he came to Molly's place to speak to us on behalf of Aunt Mary and I could not remember his wife's name. I did remember people called her Rose, but I could not call her Rose.

They were deliberate in their walk up the sidewalk and I met them at the bottom of the front steps to the house and invited them in. I offered them something to drink and they accepted water and Doris brought them water. I had told them I was moving on with my life and that our family was doing well, I inquired about their family's welfare and he told me they were doing well.

Then he spoke. *"Wah-ni-un-tah, on that day when I came to your sister's home to speak for your aunt."*

I nodded my head to indicate that I remembered that day.

"On that day our grandson drove for us to your sister's home. That grandson, his name is Hu-la-tse and he has a son that is near one year old. Next month on the twenty-first day of the month we will give this little one, E-lon-tha, we will give him his name. At that time we would like you to come and eat with us and witness the naming."

"I am honored, Wah-she-u-tse and Wah-so-po-me that you have come to my home and asked me to come for the naming of your great-grandson. I will be there."

"We will serve breakfast on that day and the naming will be at our home when the sun comes up."

"I will be there."

"Are you and your cousins being careful in the way that you do things?"

"Yes. We are following the advice you and Aunt Gra-tah-shin-ka gave us on that day we were at Me-tsa-he's home."

"That is good. Your aunt is a good woman. We have known her a long time and she has good ways."

A few minutes after Wah-she-u-tse left, Molly drove through the gate and parked her car. She waved while getting out of the car and came to the sun porch.

"Ha-weh, Cuz. Ready to go shopping for the bride and groom?"

"Sure." I tried to think of something smart aleck to suggest we buy for them, but I could not come up with anything clever, so I said, "Give me a few minutes."

Molly went into the studio and looked at the sketches. "Not bad, Cuz. Really. Kinda makes me want to go to Colorado."

I did not respond, but her comment made me feel better, even if it does take practically nothing to put Molly into a mood to take a trip.

●◆●

The rain from a week ago was still keeping the dust down and the drive into town was good. Molly asked what Daniel Junior wanted. I explained it to her about the child naming. She told me that she was already invited and was planning to ask me to go with her.

Molly said, "Speaking of invitations, Ted is driving out today to invite Aunt Mary to the wedding. I hope he doesn't forget."

Molly and I needed to spend a day together so we could talk. We discussed the wills Alan Sanders was preparing for our signatures. Molly had thought it over and could see nothing wrong with signing the will. She said Alan Sanders had looked after her interest in the past and signing the will was probably the right thing to do.

We looked at several gifts. Molly decided on wineglasses that had red glass cups with silver stems and red glass bases. I knew when Ted and Mavis made their announcement that she would end up buying them several gifts before the wedding day actually arrived.

At about mid-afternoon I saw the red vase in Walter's window. I suggested we walk up the stairs to the Courthouse and take a little break on one of the benches. Molly is always ready to do something a little different and convincing her to climb the stairs to the courthouse was not difficult.

Molly sat across the landing from me. I felt a little silly, but I managed to retrieve the note without Molly noticing and I would read the note later.

We went back down to the street and we just walked in the direction of the Bon Bon. "I have been going by the church to pray at least once a day," Molly said.

"That is good. I know I should do that."

"Only if you really want to. I am thinking that in a day or two I will go visit Sister Mary Nadine at the Convent".

Sonny was at the Bon Bon with an Osage Sky Clan girl from Hominy and a girl whose father owns a clothing store in Hominy. The store owner's daughter is tall and blond and has pretty eyes. We sat down at the table with them.

They were talking and I took the note from my pocket and read it.

april 16
to the goat
observed unidentified male following m.t.
is our little puzzle being solved?
would like a spot of tea and coffee
the osprey

Sonny said he was still thinking about going to New York, and I told him it was a good place to visit. The women continued talking about New York and about the difficulties and the good things about a trip there.

My thoughts strayed to a comment Wah-she-u-tse had made. He said it seems we hold more funerals than when he was young and was a warrior and had fought the enemies of the Osages.

Sonny drew me back into the conversation by asking how long it took a train to get to New York. I told him I thought it took three days. They discussed what one might do to make the train ride enjoyable. Sonny said he was ready to leave and stood up and told us goodbye and the two young ladies left with him.

"It is always nice to see Sonny," Molly said.

"Yes it is. He always seems to be working on something fun."

"I hope he enjoys New York."

"I am sure he will, and New York will probably enjoy Sonny."

43

The thought of someone following Molly disturbed me. I knew Molly's stalker would turn out to be Kenneth Carson, still I wanted to see the picture that Walter took. Walter was coming to the house for dinner around six and I would wait until then to see the picture.

We were gathering at our place to eat and to ask Mavis and Ted if there was something we could do for their wedding. Our eating habits have been more interesting since Doris decided to attend the refresher course in New York. That evening she was going to try another new recipe.

Tom volunteered to build a fire outdoors. He wanted Doris to cook some beef over the fire, but Doris is not much on cooking outside. When she first came to work for us we teased her about being raised on indoor cooking. That was the first time she spoke up for herself. She said Indians were like cavemen cooking over an open fire.

My mother thought that was clever. Now, after seven years, Doris says pretty much what she wants to say. I hope that is true.

I was driving toward town to pick up Barbara when I decided to go through Indian Camp. Mon-tse-no-pi'n was working in his cornfield that is near his home and I stopped and got out of the car.

Mon-tse-no-pi'n saw me and walked to a platform that was near the edge of the cornfield. Mon-tse-no-pi'n wore no shirt and his lower body was covered with a breech cloth and leggings made from trade cloth and tied with a yarn belt. He sat down on the platform and started putting tobacco into his pipe. It was an ordinary pipe and not a pipe one would use in ceremony. I also sat on the platform and our conversation went something like this.

"You have come to see me. That is good."

"If I am taking you away from something, I can come back at another time."

"You are not taking me away from anything that I do not want to be taken away from." He smiled about that. His wife brought a dipper full of water from the house and handed it to me.

"That is good," I told her.

"I want to talk to you," he said. *"That day you were here you said you would come back. I thought about sending for you."*

I waited and did not speak and he continued.

"I am troubled by what happened to your sister's family at Grayhorse. Big Hill People. It is her father's side of her family but it can bring you trouble. Somehow things work that way.

"I told you about times when your grandfather and I were boys. We went back that far. Because we went back that far we trusted each other. We looked after each other. Your grandfather is not here to help you. I believe I can help to look after you.

"Wah-she-u-tse told you and your cousins he would fight those people if he could see them. I feel that way. Back there in old days we fought hard and we lived. Many other men fought hard and did not live. I do not believe it will be necessary for old men to fight. There are many young men who would fight them if we could see them.

"Osages have died before their time to die. When that happens someone with a paper steps forward. They always have a paper. That paper can talk. It says that money and land belong to them with paper after Osage is dead.

"Horses and cars and houses. Even the things they cook with. All of that they say belongs to them that have the paper, after Osage is dead.

"I watched them. When Big Antlers died they came and they took all of those things. They treated those things like the things belonged to them. They would be angry and then they would smile and they would laugh and

be happy. Then they would be angry again. Maybe they thought something was missing that they could have.

"When Big Antlers died they took his dog, but the dog he came back." Mon-tse-no-pi'n smiled. *"That is true. The dog did not like those people.* *"It is not good for people to act like that. White people or Indians. Anyone. It is not good to act like that.*

"If you and your cousins must have that paper be careful. Make the paper say your money and your land will belong to someone that will not harm you. Someone that will not kill you."

After a moment I said, *"What you say is true. Paper that Osages put their mark on is in the middle of the trouble."*

"You have listened. That is good. There is one other thing I want to talk to you about."

Mon-tse-no-pi'n waited. He was deliberate in inhaling the smoke from his pipe, and he blew the smoke out into the air and waited.

"We will have I-lon-shka dance soon. Not many dancers, but it will be good. I want you to come here and dress for the dance. We can walk over there to arbor from here. I want you to eat here." He nodded toward his wife who was inside the house. *"She will cook. She will have her nieces helping her. They are good girls. Maybe you will be interested in one of them. They are like you. They went away to school. Maybe one of them and you will get along."*

I told Mon-tse-no-pi'n I would come to his house to dress and eat during I'n-lon-shka dance. Then I told him, *"I would like to paint a picture of you. I can do that. I can paint a picture that will look like you."*

He started with a serious look. *"It is not good to make a picture of me when I am working in my cornfield. People will not know if you have a picture of a man or a picture of a woman."* Mon-tse-no-pi'n smiled. *"Come back at another time. I will be ready for you to make my picture."*

"Would it be good if I come back tomorrow?" I was studying his face and his posture. I was trying to remember his features.

"That is good," he said.

I left to pick up Barbara. She carried a small gift wrapped in white paper with a white ribbon. She was cheerful and I think ready for a party. She wore a new yellow dress.

"Is that what they call a Flapper Dress?" I asked.

"Yes. You are late. Where have you been?" She pretended to be angry.

"I stopped by Mon-tse-no-pi'n's house in Indian Camp. We had a good talk. I am going to sketch him tomorrow."

"That is what you have been wanting, isn't it?"

"Yes. He also wants me to meet his wife's nieces. Cute little things."

"That is probably where I will miss out. My sister is married so I don't have any sisters as back up."

Grace Oak helped Doris cook and together they turned out a good dinner. I think Grace, like most Cherokees, is not interested in French cooking but she tried.

As I remember it, the purpose of the dinner party was to learn if there was something we could do for the wedding. I suppose there wasn't anything because we didn't discuss it. Molly probably discussed it with other people.

Thinking of Ted as married was something I had not thought about, and it logically led to the thought of a little Ted.

When no one was looking Walter Whitman reached into his inside coat pocket and handed me an envelope containing the surveillance picture. I went into the bedroom and opened the envelope. The picture was taken from Walter's office window looking down onto the street, and the man in the picture who was following Molly was Kenneth Carson.

By midnight everyone had gone home. I walked outside to the front lawn and sat on the platform. The sky was clear and the moon was just a day short of full. The star that Grandpa called the Male Star was setting. I suppose other people call it the Evening Star. Without concentrating I had learned about astronomy from Grandpa and Dad. At the university I once enrolled in an astronomy course and found I knew more about astronomy than other students. The names of Grandpa's stars were different from names the professor used, but the stars and the seasons were the same.

The three stars the Greeks called Orion's Belt are prominent in the winter and I learned them first. Those three stars are important to the Deer People. I once heard Whitedeer explain to some young Indian people the significance of the three stars. One of the young boys told Whitedeer about the Orion story. Whitedeer was interested to know people other than Osages found the three stars important.

I remember Grandpa's words clearly. *"We are Sky People and when we started to come down to earth we were stars."* Grandpa pointed toward the sky. *"Up there we knew where our place was and after those people came down here they had to find their place. The stars in the heavens will know their place forever. It is people down here that need order."*

After a few minutes Wolf ran to me and stood in front of me wagging his tail. Tom came and sat on the platform. "Been watchin you from over there. Don't think it's a good idea for you to be out here alone like this. Course, I been watchin, so I guess it's all right."

Photographers and artists have traveled through Osage country often and most of the older Osages know how to sit for a picture. At least they have the general idea. Actually getting them to sit for a picture is another matter, so I felt lucky I could paint Mon-tse-no-pi'n's portrait.

Mon-tse-no-pi'n sat in a chair near the cornfield and I sat facing him. He was dressed in buckskin leggings and shirt. He held his war club across his chest and his roached hair was mostly gray. Since the previous day his wife had shaved the sides of his head.

The ornamentation in Mon-tse-no-pi'n's dress was simple and was limited to a choker worn round his neck that was made of four rows of bone beads. His wife wanted him to wear his otter hat that would show him to be a man who had attained a certain degree of respect but he wanted his roached hair to show. I explained to them that it was only a drawing and that I could draw him with the otter hat and I could draw another picture of him without the otter hat.

I believe Mon-tse-no-pi'n to be eighty-two years old, maybe eighty-three. He is trim and lean and he looked splendid. Later, when he removed his shirt so I could draw the clan tattoos on his chest, I saw scars on his body. The scars were not clan markings but scars from buffalo hunts and war parties.

His face is weathered and his eyes squinted just a little. His whole face smiled when he smiled and whenever he asked me a question his whole face asked the question. Mostly, his eyes were insightful and told me he understood my need for drawing his image. That was more than I understood about my need for the sketch.

I sketched the narrow strips of beadwork of his moccasins and the small fringe on the top of his moccasins and the fringe that dragged from his heel. The hickory handle of his war club was marked with nicks and scratches. The metal head of the club was scratched and worn.

Mon-tse-no-pi'n noticed that I was sketching a scar on his left shoulder and he said, *"A Pawnee gave me that scar. The Pawnee was tough."*

Hu-ah-toin, his wife, came out and sat on the platform and watched. *"Do you want me to get the war club that is decorated?"*

"This club is good," he answered.

"That club is all beat up."

He did not answer and she dropped the subject of the war club.

I sketched the pattern made by the shoots of corn that had pushed through the earth's crust in the small hills where he had planted the corn seeds. Also, I sketched the big hill in the background that was where I met Walter Whitman to ask him to be an observer for me.

It was almost noon when I finished sketching. Both Mon-tse-no-pi'n and Hu-ah-toin were pleased with the work and that made me feel good.

One does not turn down the offer of food without offending the host and when Hu-ah-toin asked me to eat with them I was pleased. I was also hungry.

I thought of painting Hu-ah-toin but I would wait until I was ready to start on the portrait before asking her.

After we ate I drove home. The bluestem grass was turning and the hills were becoming a deep green. Blackjack trees leaf out late and their dark green clusters on the hills brought a good contrast. The variety of trees along Cedar Creek were different colors and I made mental notes of those colors.

Tom's car was gone and Doris was cleaning house. There was so little going on at our house during those days that I wondered what she found to clean.

I gathered the sketches of the cathedral and of the Rocky Mountains and leaned them against the wall in the corner of the room where they would be out of my way. I set the easel up in the southeast corner of the room near the east windows so the light from the afternoon sun could brighten the canvas. Not direct rays from the sun, just the brightness.

The canvas easily attached to the easel. Not quickly, just easily. I would not work fast nor would I purposely work slowly. I just wanted to paint well.

The canvas was ready but the pencils and charcoal sticks were not sharpened and I sharpened them with a knife and smoothed the lead with a piece of fine sand paper.

I began sketching the image of Mon-tse-no-pi'n onto the canvas and stopped. The pencils would not work. Then using a brush I mixed some light yellow ocher onto the palette so that the paint was thin. It would dry quickly and would not run.

Doris found a piece of cotton cloth for me and I tore the cloth into four small pieces and dipped one of the pieces of cloth into the thin paint. Using the cloth as a brush I rubbed the paint onto the canvas in the outline of the image of Mon-tse-no-pi'n's body and darkened the paint just a little to create the basic image of his head and his arms and his hands. I would start and complete the painting sitting face-to-face with Mon-tse-no-pi'n but this would be a good preliminary piece and I would learn from it.

I mixed titanium blue paint with paint thinner and took another clean cotton cloth and rubbed the blue sky on to the canvas with three or four spaces left white so that I could paint clouds.

I was working at a steady pace.

The earth color of the garden went on next, then the very light green that would be the trees and grass. All of the paints were still thin and went on quickly. This took only a few minutes and I stepped back and sat on the tall chair and looked at the canvas.

I closed the double French doors between the sunroom and living room to keep the paint fumes from the rest of the house. Then I opened the French door to the sunporch and all twelve windows to let the fumes escape to the outside.

Standing on the sunporch, I waited. The paint was thin and should dry soon. When I went back into the sunroom Doris was opening the French doors to the living room. "I like the smell of paint," she said. "The smell of paint makes me feel like something is happening around here."

In Grandpa's little rock house I opened one of the trunks and took out an eagle wing fan. It was a left wing. I took it back to the sunroom so I could study it but decided I would use Mon-tse-no-pi'n's fan as the model, so I returned the fan to the trunk and closed the trunk.

The canvas was dry enough so I could put on more paint. I mixed in some turpentine with the yellow ocher paint and added paint thinner to make it thin like before. With a wide brush I put thin yellow ocher onto the canvas. Mixing the turpentine with the other colors, I went over the canvas and added a layer of thin paint to the canvas that would hold the image of Mon-tse-no-pi'n.

I did not want to wait for the oils to dry, but I had no choice. The paint would control a certain amount of the process.

It turned out I would wait a full day before adding more paint. The paint and the canvas and the brushes did control a great deal of what happened from that point on and as always I hoped that I was an equal with those materials. I suppose the final picture would determine that.

CHAPTER
45

Molly called me on the telephone, she wanted to meet at the Bon Bon to discuss the dress she was considering for the wedding. I wanted to ask her to call Barbara who would know more about a dress, but I thought she probably just needed to talk. I said I would meet her and hung up the telephone and went to the sunroom to study the painting briefly.

I had an early meeting scheduled with Mr. Bartholomew at the Agency and the thought of that meeting drew my attention away from the painting.

At the agency Mr. Bartholomew was busy and I waited to see him. Mrs. Street, the secretary, offered me coffee. "No, thank you. I have had too much coffee already this morning." I don't know why I explained that to her. Maybe it was because drinking coffee may very well be the only thing federal agency employees and Indians have in common. It is a well-entrenched habit with both groups. After a few minutes Mr. Bartholomew, who always looks a little grim, came out into the hallway and shook my hand. "How are you, John?"

"I am fine, sir."

We went into his office and sat down. "John, I have some very good news for you." It was amazing to me that anyone could deliver good news with such a stern and grim look.

"What is that, sir?"

"Well, you are, no doubt, aware that you invested some of your surplus funds in the Grand Hotel here in town?"

"Yes. I am aware of that."

"Well, John. The hotel," and he looked thoughtful and stroked his dark beard, "while it may appear to be profitable, well, the hotel has been experiencing financial difficulties." He reached into his desk drawer and took a check from the drawer. He held it up for emphasis.

"John, I think we have made a very attractive settlement for you. This is a check for thirty-two thousand dollars. This afternoon we will deposit this into your account here at the Agency."

"What is the check for?"

"It is the settlement for the funds you advanced to the hotel corporation."

"Why do I need a settlement?"

"John, the hotel has experienced difficulties and we thought it best to agree to a settlement and let all parties continue on their separate ways."

"Is that the amount they owe me?"

"No, no, John," and he smiled. "In matters like this, John, you are lucky to get anything at all out of that investment."

"How much financial difficulty is the hotel experiencing?"

"I am afraid the hotel is in bankruptcy."

"How much money did I loan the hotel?"

"Three hundred twenty thousand dollars."

"And Mr. Baskins only paid interest, he never paid on the principal?"

"Yes, but that is not unusual in matters of this nature."

"And I am receiving 10 percent of what is owed?"

"Yes, 10 percent of what is owed on the account. But, John, you were in a bad investment. You can now take these funds and place them in something that is more stable. Something you don't have to keep an eye on."

"Has this been through the bankruptcy court?"

"Yes, John, it has. And the judge of the bankruptcy court did not blink an eye. He said you were to be paid a full 10 percent of all that is owed to you."

"Then it is over with and I can not go back and ask for more of what is owed me?"

Franklin Bartholomew was getting irritated. "John, this is as good a settlement as you are going to get. We had to argue very strongly to get you any money at all out of that deal." Mr. Bartholomew's eyebrows wrinkled and he stood to his full six foot five inches. "Now, the judge has ruled and the Agency has signed off on the agreement. The hotel has been sold. The deed to the property has been transferred to the new and rightful owner. I will deposit these funds into your account this afternoon and the deal is done. Over and done with, do I make myself clear?"

"Very clear, sir. Do you have any more good investments for me?"

He stared at me and his jaw tightened.

"John, you are very lucky to have the staff here at the Agency to look after your affairs. And, yes, we do have other investments that I suspect you would be very wise to look into. However, I have another meeting in a few minutes that I must prepare for. When you want to talk to me about other investments you make an appointment and we will talk about it."

Mr. Bartholomew left the room. He was angry, I am sure. He left the check lying on the desk. It was made payable to the United States of America for Mr. John Grayeagle. I folded the check once and was going to drop it into Mr. Bartholomew's wastebasket, but that would have been a foolish and silly thing to do. Maybe he would find the check and maybe he would not find it, so I left the check on his desk. It was nice to get out into the fresh outdoor air. I descended the stairs that led down to the Bon Bon. In my own way I had stood up to Mr. Bartholomew and the Agency and it was a good feeling.

I stopped on the stairs to the Bon Bon and looked out across the valley, beyond the rooftops of the brick and granite office buildings, and hotels, and the houses, and homes of the town, and I focused on a hill. The hill is perhaps five miles east of the Agency. The base of the hill is round and the hill reaches a peak in the middle of a valley. The hill is, of course, a work of nature, and I thought that some day I would climb to the top of the hill, and I would study the hill, and I would learn it. Then I would paint a portrait of the hill.

The three Whitedeer sisters were at one of the Bon Bon tables. They always dress well and are friendly. I had not seen them since Ted's party and I stopped to speak with them. They told me they were leaving for England on the following day and would miss the wedding. They were sorry about missing the wedding because their grandfather was going to handle part of the ceremony. I wished them a good trip and they assured me they would have a nice trip and one of them suggested that Ted might have another party when they returned from England.

Barbara asked, "What did you learn at the Agency?"

"As bad as your dad said it was."

"You don't want to talk about this, do you, John?"

"No, not really."

"You've told me all I wanted to know."

"I don't mind if you talk about the hotel," Molly said. "If you are going to handle your own affairs you must tend to your business."

"Thanks, Cuz, but we can talk about the hotel later. Did you guys find a suitable gift?"

"We did," Molly said and they both giggled.

"It's a secret," Barbara said. "You'll just have to wait."

Relaxed is a good way to describe how I felt and I would wait a day before continuing with the portrait. My train of thought had been disrupted and I was afraid the disruption might creep into the portrait. I would not really lose a day because I would study the canvas. I would just not add any paint to the canvas.

I thought about Mr. Bartholomew. I wondered if he has always been that grim or had life made him that way. If life made him that way, it did a good job of it.

CHAPTER

46

I was up early and studied the sketches of Mon-tse-no-pi'n. Spending a day away from the painting at a critical time was a risk I had not wanted to take. At mid-morning when the sun was fully up and I was emotionally back into the portrait I began putting oil paints onto the canvas. I wanted to do the portrait sitting face-to-face with Mon-tse-no-pi'n but this was going well and I would move to his home to complete the painting in a day or two.

I decided the portrait should be realistic and in detail. That would take a lot of time and it was a good decision.

The leggings he wore on the day I sketched him were made of elk hide and were old. He had worn the leggings on many buffalo hunts. His wife told me about the scars on the leggings. One scar in particular was important to her. The scar was made by a charging buffalo that knocked his horse to the ground and injured Mon-tse-no-pi'n. That was before they had children and Hu-ah-toin was a young bride and remembered the concern she had for her husband. He was able to finish the hunt by enduring pain and had a successful hunt. She did not try to hide her pride when telling about the incident.

His expression did not change during the telling of the story, but I think maybe Mon-tse-no-pi'n was pleased she related the story.

She said she wanted that mark on the leggings to be clear in the portrait and for me to tell people who saw the painting about the mark and I told her that I would do that.

Most of Tuesday morning and afternoon I worked on the detail of the picture. The insight I perceived in Mon-tse-no-pi'n's eyes that day when I sketched him was starting to come through in the painting.

I was absorbed in the process of the painting, and the intensity lasted for several hours, and I took only a short break for lunch. At mid-afternoon I was physically and mentally tired and I stopped. It was a good tired and I sat and looked at the canvas for a while, partly to study the canvas and partly to enjoy the painting. I knew then I would finish the portrait and it would be as good as any I have done.

The windows to the sunroom were open and the breeze coming through had a warmness that I enjoy during spring.

Doris came into the room. "John, there is a young man to see you. Do you want me to make some more coffee?" The young man followed her into the room.

"Do you want coffee?" Doris asked him.

"Yes, ma'am, thank you."

Doris left the room to make fresh coffee. I recognized the young man. We are about the same age. "Joseph, how are you?"

"*Ha-weh.* My Grandfather Gla-moin wants you to come and talk to him. Wants you to come to Hominy next week, Thursday 'bout noon. He wants you to eat with us."

"I will be there and listen to what your grandfather has to say."

"You know where his place is, don't you?"

"Yes. I remember when we were kids and we spent a day playing on the creek. Do you remember that?"

"Yep, I remember that. That was a lot of fun. I'll tell him you'll be there on Thursday." Having delivered his message, Joseph looked around the room. Then he said. "I kinda like your house. I've been thinkin 'bout buildin a house. Be okay if I look around?"

Joseph's family is a traditional Osage family whose family members follow much of the old social order. I know that Joseph's marriage was arranged and it was a full Osage wedding. I also know they have given each of their children clan names and I suspect he will build his new home near to his parents home.

"Sure, look around all you want. I'll go with you." I showed him the main house and we walked the lawn and looked at the barn. I pointed out Grandpa's little house and Joseph laughed and said his grandpa had a little house. We had just finished our tour and Joseph was nearing his car when Molly drove into the driveway and parked beside Joseph.

Molly got out of the car. "Hey, Joseph," and Molly waved to him. Joseph waved back. "Hi, Molly. I gotta be goin." Joseph nodded toward Molly and said, "John, would you tell her?"

"Sure."

"What does Joseph want you to tell me?"

"His grandfather asks us to come and see him on Thursday. About noon."

"What does he want to talk about?"

"Didn't say. Guess we will find that out on Thursday."

I knew I could leave the canvas for as much as a full day and return and pick up the painting without fear of losing my plan for putting the oil onto the canvas. That was good.

It was a lot like the old days. Molly stayed around the house all day. Doris was listening to New Orleans music on the Victrola. We had a snack on the sunporch and Molly helped Doris cook one of her new recipes and I worked at the portrait.

Later that evening when we were through eating, Molly and I sat at the dining room table for some time talking.

Doris read magazines and smoked. Occasionally Doris would change the music to another region of the country and she would dance alone for a moment before going back to the magazines.

"John, do you think Mavis coming into the family will change us?"

"I think it will. She and Ted see so much of each other. They already have changed us."

"You're right. I never thought of that. What about Will? What do you think of Will?" I could tell Molly was very interested in what my answer would be.

"I like Will. I have a great deal of respect for Will. I guess I like him, but I don't really know him."

"What about you and Barbara. How close are you two?"

"I am not sure. At times I feel extremely close to Barbara and I have even had thoughts of marriage."

"Really?" Molly smiled broadly.

"Well, yes. I think I will continue seeing her and wait to see if the part that is missing falls into place."

"What part is missing?"

"I don't have any idea, but I know something is missing."

"John, you and I have always been told to look at each other as brother and sister. That is what we have been told. Do you think a blood brother and sister could be closer than we are?"

"I don't have any way of knowing. I know I think of you as my sister."

"My mother and dad were serious when they told me that."

"Grandpa said he had not known a time when so many young people did not have parents. He said in earlier days we would have had relatives to take us and be our family. Grandpa did not look for anyone to see about me because he thought he could do that himself."

It was late when we finished talking. Molly decided to stay over and slept in my old bedroom where I slept before Grandpa died. It was nice to have one more person in the house.

CHAPTER

47

Tom was cleaning his rifle. Things important to Tom are that his gun is clean, his knife is sharp, he has plenty of Prince Albert tobacco, and his coffee is strong. With those things in place Tom is living life and enjoying it.

Tom leaned over to the table and smashed out his cigarette. Like most smokers he watched the cigarette until it was out. "I been trailin that Carson guy just 'bout every day. Well yeah, it has been every day."

"What have you learned?"

"I know where he hangs out and who he sees. He don't see many people. Monday he was out near Nelagony taking target practice with a high-powered rifle. A thirty ott six I think." Tom pulled his tobacco from his shirt pocket. "I'm sure he's been meetin somebody there. Tonight I'll find out who it is he sees over there."

"Are you sure he doesn't know you are following him?"

"There aint't no way he knows I'm tailin him. He ain't real smart." Tom worked at rolling a cigarette. "One day I followed him to that hill that overlooks Molly's place and one day to a spot near Ted's ranch. I know he's up to something."

"That doesn't sound good, Tom."

"It ain't good, that's for sure." Tom lit the cigarette. "The only good thing is we keep up with what he's doin."

"Well, be careful, Tom. This guy sounds kinda mean."

In my preoccupation with other things I forgot to ask Tom what he was doing that evening that might shed some light on Kenneth Carson and I wished I would have asked.

Superintendent Hugel is always congenial. He smiled and welcomed me into his office. There were several Osages conducting business and the Agency was crowded with people who work for the oil companies.

"John, we are still considering your request to handle your own affairs. Just be patient and within a few days we will know what we plan to tell the central office." He had his hands folded on his desk and was smiling. The picture of President Coolidge hung behind his desk.

"That is good, Mr. Hugel, just let me know when."

"Fine, John. We will do that."

"Sir, I wish to withdraw six hundred dollars to assist two Indian athletes who have made the United States Olympic team. They will be traveling to Paris this summer and I would like to assist them. The Olympic Committee will help with their basic expenses. I know the rules well and we will not break Olympic rules."

Mr. Hugel smiled and looked out the window at the trees and at some workers who were putting up a new net on the tennis court. "Six hundred dollars?" He was thoughtful.

"Yes. I spoke with Mr. Bartholomew on Monday. He deposited thirty-two thousand dollars in my surplus account. Mr. Bartholomew said the Agency staff is doing an excellent job of handling my affairs and I have nothing to worry about."

"When will you be needing these funds?" He did not mention the problem Jim Thorpe had for earning far less than three hundred dollars as a baseball player. He must have been thinking about it.

"I will see the athletes later today and I would like to hand them the money then."

Again, Mr. Hugel was thoughtful. I waited. Finally, he said, "Okay, John. If you will wait here a few minutes I will have your voucher."

"Thank you, sir. I figure we all must do our part for our national team, don't you think, sir?"

"Yes, yes, of course." But his thoughts were elsewhere.

I waited in the hall and within a few minutes Mr. Hugel returned and handed the voucher to the cashier in the teller's cage.

"Would you mind putting the funds into two separate envelopes? Three hundred in each envelope."

"Not at all." She carefully counted out the money into two stacks then placed each of the small stacks of bills into an envelope. "There you are, Mr. Grayeagle."

On one envelope I wrote the name of Mr. Will Chapman and on the other Mr. Joe Eagle. I placed the envelopes in my inside coat pocket and asked to use the telephone. I would give Ted some money from the checking account to help with training expenses. Ted does take on worthy projects. I called Barbara on the telephone and asked if she would have lunch with me.

"Sure, where do you want to eat?"

"Let's see. What about Ted's?"

"Ted's?"

"You have to agree it's better than most restaurants."

"As long as Mrs. Bigcreek doesn't mind."

During the drive to Ted's place, we talked. "Have you made any progress on your career?"

"Not really. I spoke with Walter Whitman one day. You know, I think he is cautious because of Daddy."

Neither of us spoke for a while. When Barbara spoke she was serious. "John, Daddy wants me to tell you that if you die intestate, the courts will determine who inherits your property."

"Does that mean if I die without signing a will?"

"That's what it means."

"Then your dad thinks I should have a will?"

"Yes, and so there is no question about it, I do not want to be included in any will you might sign. I was already thinking that, but Daddy told me to say it."

"What if Aunt Mary is unable to find a suitable mate for me and you and I should decide to get married?"

"Even if Aunt Mary never finds a suitable mate for you."

When we reached Ted's place, Molly was out near the track. A carpenter was building three rows of bleachers near the track. Three of the boys from Hominy were watching Will work out. Will was a good prospect for the football team in the fall. We all liked his speed.

Roper was helping time the run. Hank Bigcreek who ran track at Haskell was getting in shape to push Will and Joe.

Will and Joe were gracious in accepting the assistance along with some advice from Barbara about Olympic rules. Will told us the gift would allow them to compete on an even footing with the other contestants. Molly said she wished we could go to Paris and watch the games. I think we all were thinking that.

Mrs. Bigcreek prepared a large picnic lunch and when the runs were completed we sat on the ground in the middle of the oval of the track and we ate. It was a big lunch with fried chicken and mashed potatoes and gravy and lots of vegetables and we talked.

Later, Mrs. Bigcreek brought coffee out to us. Joe told us about an aged Cheyenne uncle who was in the Custer fight. The old warrior is his grandfather's brother. Joe was proud of him and it showed through even when he preferred the story to be subtle. Joe said he thinks about his uncle when he competes, particularly in football. It was nearly dark when we finished eating, and it was fully dark and the moon was up and bright by the time we finished talking.

CHAPTER
48

It was evening when Tom came into the sunroom. He was smoking a cigarette, and although he has had a lot of practice, I do not believe Tom has ever really got the hang of rolling a cigarette. I suppose they turn out the way he wants them and it is none of my business, but his cigarettes seem to be short and crinkled and fat and thin. Tom looked at the painting for a moment. "You know, Johnny. That kinda looks like old man Mon-tse-no-pi'n."

"You think so?"

"Yeah, it does." He kept looking at the painting. "Sure does. I wanta show you somethin and I need ya to go with me."

"Where are we going?"

Tom looked at me. "I just wanta show ya somethin. Ya might wanta take along a gun." Tom would sometimes hunt at night, but this was not a hunting trip.

We walked outside to the driveway. Tom shined a flashlight into the backseat of his Ford. There was a pistol and his shotgun and his .22 rifle. He looked at the guns for a moment.

I trust Tom. I know he would not put me in danger. Still, this did not look like a normal evening activity. "Do I really need a gun, Tom?"

"Wouldn't be a bad idea," he said, and he turned the flashlight off.

I went to the house and got the double-barrel twelve gauge and a pistol Dad left to me. "Tom, you know I am a member of the Peace Clan."

I could hear him laughing slightly in the darkness. "Yea. So was your grandpa an I know what he did with that war club of his."

We drove through town and then east to a place near Nelagony where Tom turned off the main dirt road onto a small two-track lane for a short distance. He turned the car into a thick growth of brush and trees and stopped. He turned his car lights off and turned off the engine.

Tom's voice was soft. "We'll walk from here, Johnny."

"What do I need to bring with me?"

I knew he was smiling in the darkness. "Bring that double-barrel and the pistol. I don't think we'll need em. If we do, the twelve gauge will scare the hell out of em and we'll start firin our pistols and they'll think there's a dozen of us."

"Okay, Tom. What are we doing?"

"I want you to see for yourself. Kenneth Carson has been meetin somebody out here. We'll walk for 'bout a half mile. We gotta go around that hill. There is a stand of tree not far from the creek. No one'll ever know we're there. I been out here bunch a times. I was out here today. We're all right." We took a few more steps. "He still don't know I'm followin him."

We walked the edge of the big hill following a creek. It was a steep hillside. The moon was only two days past full and gave as much light as we needed.

"I been clearin dead leaves from our path so we won't make much noise. I was out here today. Me'n Wolf was actin like we was huntin squirrels. We didn't see nobody so it didn't much matter." We walked slowly. Then Tom said, "If we talk now we better talk quiet. Probably better whisper."

Tom had cleared the dead leaves but the path was narrow and we had to be careful not to step on dead leaves beside the path. We turned up the hill and walked over part of the hill and I could smell coffee brewing and a fire. Then I saw the glow of a campfire on some of the taller trees.

Tom led me down the hillside to two dense cedar trees. He had cleared a small area inside the outer coverage of the trees. We were perhaps thirty yards from the campfire that was in the middle of a clearing in the woods.

There was nothing to do but wait. The coffee smelled good.

Tom whispered, "Have your guns layin on the ground and ready."

I nodded in the darkness. Then I whispered, "Okay." I was not about to lay my gun down.

Kenneth Carson, the man in the trees at the falls on Sand Creek and who asked me for a light in the café, was standing near the fire. He held a tin cup of coffee. He was talking to Otis Davis. Davis was squatted down near the fire and stoked the fire with a stick.

They spoke in low tones and we could hear only parts of what they said. Both of the men were smoking cigarettes. We were there for probably ten minutes when we heard the third car. Then we saw the lights of the car shine through the woods as the car bounced over the rough bumpy trail.

They both turned to watch the car drive into the clearing and stop. Alan Sanders got out of the car slowly. He was wearing a suit and a hat, as always.

Otis Davis called across the clearing to Sanders, "Good evening, Mr. Sanders."

Sanders gave him a small wave of his hand and said nothing. Sanders walked toward the fire and toward us, and his glasses reflected the flickering light of the fire. Carson did not acknowledge Sanders except to ask, "D'you want some coffee?"

I could not hear that well but I am pretty sure Sanders answered, "Yes. I'll take a cup." Davis squatted down near the fire and poured Sanders's coffee into a tin cup. He stood and handed it to him. Sanders nodded a thank you to him and sipped the coffee.

Otis Davis poured whiskey into his cup and seemed to offer the whiskey to the other two. Sanders shook his head no and Carson accepted the offer and extended his cup and Davis poured the whiskey.

The three men spoke in low voices. Sanders handed manila envelopes to both men and they opened the envelopes and took out some papers. I think the papers may have been pictures. They talked for about twenty minutes holding up the papers to the light occasionally. After a time Sanders removed an envelope from his inside coat pocket and counted out money to both Otis Davis and Kenneth Carson. The two men placed the money in their wallets.

They spoke for a few more minutes. Sanders walked toward his car. He was getting into the car when Davis called to him, "See you back here at eleven Friday night."

Sanders nodded and waved and got into the car. When he had the car turned around, Sanders drove away.

Otis Davis and Ken Carson spoke for maybe five minutes then poured the coffee onto the fire and kicked some dirt onto the coals, but not enough dirt to smother the embers. Then they both left in their black cars.

When we were certain they were gone Tom asked, "Does this help any?"

"Tom, it helps a lot."

"Thought it might." Tom rolled a cigarette. "Wish they hadn't poured out that coffee."

"I'll make you some coffee when we get home."

Tom laughed a little. "I'll make the coffee."

"You don't like my coffee?"

"You never enrolled in coffee makin."

Returning to the car we walked faster. When we reached home, I called Molly. I missed her at the apartment but she was at the ranch and she was still up. I told her I would explain everything in the morning but that she should be careful and that I would see her early, first thing.

Tom made coffee. I kept thinking about those two thugs and they bothered me. Partly because Otis Davis was Mavis's uncle and Ted was going to marry Mavis, and partly because my parents and Grandpa had taught me to stay away from people like that.

I was seeing more and more the wisdom of their teaching.

The window near my bed was open and the cool air felt good.

I thought again of the two thugs, but Mr. Sanders was another matter. I had trusted him most of my life and now I learn that he is clearly not trustworthy.

All of those thoughts about people I would deal with were mixed in with Tom's coffee and I could not sleep for a long time.

I knew I had to go to Hominy around noon the next day to see Gla-moin and I wondered what he wanted to discuss and that also kept me awake.

After a while a flock of geese flew over going north. The geese were honking loudly and flying low. I remembered a late September day when Dad told me that the geese were gathering to select their leaders for the trip south and my child's mind could imagine those geese huddling to pick leaders for the trip south. A few weeks after that when a flock of geese were flying over Dad pointed out to me how the leaders of the flock will change in midair and a different goose will take the point position in the large vee formation in the sky. After a while another flock of geese flew over going south and I thought again about those geese selecting their leaders then flying south, following their leaders in the dark night and soon I fell asleep.

CHAPTER

49

With her troubled expression Madame Richarde explained
she had not seen Molly since early morning when Molly
dropped by for coffee and a roll. I walked along Kihekah
Avenue thinking I would see Molly before I reached Main Street and
the Triangle Building. When I reached the Triangle Building I saw
the red vase in Walter's office window. I went into the newsstand of
the bank building and purchased a newpaper. Outside I climbed to
the middle landing of the courthouse stairs and pretended to read
the newspaper while I pulled the message from its secret place.

april 21
to the goat
ass paid fb money
also
ass met with wwb
also
on other matter I met with fb in his office
fb said you are an ingrate
said you have never worked for
anything in your life
I told him
that is nature of inherited wealth
fb did not like my answer
the osprey

I interpreted the note to mean Alan S Sanders paid money to Franklin Bartholomew of the Agency. Mr. Sanders had also met with W. W. Baskins. The last part of the note was clear that Franklin Bartholomew held the attitude of many federal employees who represent Osages and resent Osage oil. That was no surprise.

I drove slowly along Kihekah and I saw Molly looking at the window display of the Ole London Shoppe. I honked the car horn and she saw me.

"Are you ready to go to Hominy?" I asked.

"Be ready in five minutes. I need to go to the bank."

"I have money."

"Then I'm ready."

Walter's note caused me some anxiety and on the road to Hominy I checked the rearview mirror often, looking for Kenneth Carson, but I did not see him.

When we reached Gla-moin's home I relaxed.

Gla-moin's wife is Wah-kon-se-moin and she is of the Deer People, and most people call her Aunt Annie. She asked us to come in. Mi-keh-wa-ti-an-kah was in the living room with Gla-moin. Molly and I shook hands with the two older men and with Joseph, the grandson.

The rugs the Navajos make were scattered around the living room floor and sofas and chairs were covered with striped Pendleton blankets. There were photographs on the walls and Wah-kon-sa-moin, Aunt Annie, was weaving a yarn belt that was tied to the back of a chair.

Gla-moin waited until we were seated then he said, "*I have wondered about you since your grandfather died.*"

I answered, "*Living without Grandfather is hard but I am trying to go on.*"

It was relaxing to be in circumstances that reminded me of our home when I was very young and my parents were alive. The grandchildren and the great-grandchildren added to the relaxed atmosphere.

The dinner was hominy and beef and pork and Aunt Annie had lily roots and dried pawpaws. There was also what Joseph called white man's food and those foods were well prepared and were good. While we ate there was talk of peyote meetings and birthday hand games and dice games.

When we finished eating Gla-moin said he thought it would be good for us to go outside and sit under the trees. The afternoon was warm for April and the air in the low-lying area was still.

Gla-moin spoke. *"There is something I wish to say. The old people said we should include those who have no parents. My mother died when I was a baby. My aunt took me, she raised me. No natural mother could have been a better mother to me than she was. So, I want to tell you that if there is something you want of me, then come and tell me and if I can help you I will.*

"Today only a few people follow the old teachings. The old people said to follow those ways would prepare our children for a world that will not be. Looking after the children who have no parents is part of the old way we should keep.

"Many of our people follow Moon Head and his teachings of Jesus and Peyote. Moon Head's teachings are good and have power. The churches of Jesus are good. Those churches have power.

"You attended white man's school that prepare our children for the world they will live in. Government people say that and I see that can be true.

"Years from now when people say who were people called Osages I want you to tell them about the old way where the stars and the sun and the moon are in place. Tell them about our four-legged brothers and the birds who gave our people courage and skill from their courage and skill so we could make a way for ourselves on earth. The willow tree made us well, and the thunder and lightning and stars taught us the seasons.

"We put those old teachings away and our world changed. Now people smile at us and they shake our hand. People want to help us. Sometimes it makes me think of February. This world we see is not what we think it is."

We sat for a few moments and no one spoke. The stillness of the warm spring day was good. Then Mi-keh-wa-ti-an-kah spoke.

"Wah-ni-un-tah, on that day when you drove your grandfather and me to cut cedar for a Pipe, your grandfather told you he would tell you why we needed a Pipe but he became ill and he went away. Now I will tell you. We

will hold a ritual to bring a man into the Non-hon-zhin-ga. Your grand-father wanted to have the ceremony at his old camp on Cedar Creek.

"You are here today so we can tell you it is time to prepare the camp on Cedar Creek for that ceremony. Your grandfather, Xui-tha-ho-tse, his camp place is hidden and no one goes there. The camp has good springwater and a good stream. We can hold ceremony and no one will bother us.

"Your Grandfather Xui-tha-ho-tse was planning to help in the cere-mony. His teachings went way back there, he was qualified to do that, he knew those old ways.

"Lightning came down from the sky and went into that tree. I think it is strong. Now, I have finished making the Pipe. Wa-tsa-moin of the Bear Clan is keeping the Pipe. His wife has woven a sheath for the Pipe.

"Grandson and Granddaughter, not all of our people have put away the old way, there are those who follow those old teachings. A man west of Grayhorse and west of Fairfax town is ready for the ceremony to be a Non-hon-zhin-ga. Sometime when buffalo rut we will hold his ceremony.

"The time came when we could not do the ceremonies in the right way, so we put them away. Buried them. We did not bury all of them. Now, we need some of those old ways and we have gathered what is necessary to do it the old way. To do it in the right way. If you do not want this ceremony to be at Cedar Creek tell me and we will find another place."

I waited. What was happening made me feel good. I spent another moment putting my thoughts together then I spoke.

"The dinner Grandmother Wah-kon-se-moin prepared was good. It made us feel good and we feel welcome in your home.

"My grandfather believed the old way. There is much about the ceremony I do not know, still, I want you to use the camp on Cedar Creek. If there is something I can do to help, tell me. If I am able I will do it."

"That is good," Mi-keh-wa-ti-an-kah said.

"That is good," Gla-moin said. *"Granddaughter, you look like you want to speak. Go ahead. Speak."*

"Yes, there is something I want to say," Molly said. *"I remember once when we were children. My cousin Wa-tsa-ka-wa and my cousin Wah-ni-un-tah and I, we huddled next to one of those bark lodges and we listened while the grown people talked about burying a Pipe.*

"The Non-hon-zhin-ga said we children would be taught by white people and we would speak like white people. He said we would not know Osage ways. I remember that. It is clear in my mind.

"The man who spoke was a good man and I respect him. Still, one thing he said was not right. It will take more than white teachers to make us think like white people.

"There is much we do not know about the teachings of the clans. Still, when the people buried the Pipe, they did not bury our thoughts. We still have those thoughts and we remember those things our parents taught us.

"It is true we are different from the generation of Osages before us, just as the generation after us will be different from us. Generation after generation we have changed some things to make a way for ourselves on earth. Still, the things that are important have remained the same.

"It is true we sound like white people when we speak their language, and yet before we learned the language of the white people, we spoke Osage and our thoughts are Osage thoughts.

"Things in the mind and things in the heart make people what they are, and I know we were born with hearts that are Osage. That does not change."

There was a silence that lasted for several moments. Not an awkward silence but a good silence. Then Gla-moin spoke.

"Granddaughter, what you say is true. One of my own children. He has gone in different directions. Wrong directions. A wrong path, but I see in that one an Indian. I see in that one an Osage. Now he is finding who he is. I think of him when I work on this ritual."

Molly spoke again. *"The thoughts in my heart are important but the things I do are important too. If there is a place for me, I want to help with the camp. If there is a place for me, I want to help cook for the ceremony."*

Gla-moin spoke. *"Granddaughter, there is a place for you. Someone will come to you and tell you what you will do."*

Cousin Molly is the closest thing I will ever have to a sister. I understand her well and on the drive back to Pawhuska that day I knew that she felt good about herself and she felt strong and I was happy for her.

Things were not as settled in my mind as they were in Molly's mind, and that bothered me.

CHAPTER
50

That evening the Richardes had a Black Forest dessert they said was very good. I do not eat many desserts but they always look good to me. Barbara and Molly tried it and they agreed it was good.

"John, I don't want to disturb this pleasant evening," Barbara said, "but I have to tell you something. Daddy learned that W. W. Baskins has purchased the hotel from his brother."

"So, Baskins owns the hotel again and everything is the same, except this time he doesn't owe anything on it," I said. "Does your dad know how much it cost him?"

"Thirty-two thousand bucks. The same amount his brother paid the bankruptcy court."

"There's more," Barbara said. "The brother left town and no one expects him to come back. Oh yes. Baskins's brother is rumored to be a shady character."

"You know, I was starting to suspect that his brother may be a shady character."

"Holy cow, John," Barbara said. "How can you joke about this?"

"As I understand it, there is little else I can do. Besides," I said, "at this point, I am more interested in keeping people from having car accidents and being poisoned than I am in people stealing from me."

"I'm worried about Ted," Molly said. "I like Mavis all right, but when they get married won't Mavis be his heir?"

"Sure," Barbara said.

I said, "Let's call this the bright side. If Ted dies before Molly and I, then Mavis would not inherit from us."

"Yes, the bright side," Molly said. "I don't like the bright side any more than I like the dark side."

"More on the bright side," I said. "Mr. Sanders has scheduled us to sign our wills tomorrow. I suppose we are certainly safe until then. After that, I doubt there is a bright side unless we go along with Tom and just shoot it out with Sanders and whoever."

Molly asked, "Is Tom still keeping an eye on the guy named Carson?"

"Yes. I know for sure that Carson and Otis Davis are in with Sanders. I learned that last night." I waited a moment. "I am still not sure if Mavis and Lucky are a part of the deal."

Barbara said, "But, it probably isn't a good idea to trust her."

No one picked up on the comment.

"You know," Molly said. "I don't like this. It seems that we are nothing but targets. It's like Wah-she-u-tse said. If I could just see those people."

Roper was climbing the stairs and he looked tired. "Well," he said, "has your source told you any more about this Carson character?"

"No, he hasn't and I apologize for being unable to tell you my source, but I gave my word."

"Your word is your word," Roper said.

It was dark when Molly and I drove through the gate at my place and Tom was sitting on the platform. He walked to the garage where Molly and I parked the car.

"Did you find out anything?" Tom asked.

"No. I just went to Hominy and ate and talked with Gla-moin for a while. Did you learn anything?"

"No. Carson went back to his apartment about six and picked up a sack of something. He drove south of town but I don't know where he went. Maybe Hominy or maybe Wynona or he mighta gone to

Big Heart. I followed him 'bout five miles and decided he probably won't hurt nobody tonight so I turned off the road. Can't follow too much longer than that without him gettin suspicious."

"Good," I said. "I think I'll go inside and take a break. Want some coffee?"

"Yeah."

Doris was playing a Leadbelly Leadbetter record on the Victrola when we got there, and Tom made coffee, and Molly and I sat in the living room. Doris started to take the Leadbelly record off the turntable. "I'll put on a Maurice Chevalier," Doris said.

"Why don't you just turn Leadbelly over?" Molly said. "I like Leadbelly."

"I didn't know that. Want some tea, Molly?"

"Sure."

"I met Leadbelly once, down in New Orleans. I was in some dingy little club down there and he came in about midnight and sat in with the locals til about five in the morning."

"How does a white girl get into places like that?"

"Color don't matter nearly as much as music."

I was half listening to Doris and Molly talk about musicians and the conversation was interesting but my listening was interrupted by a car that turned into the driveway.

"I don't recognize them lights," Tom said. "I'll see who it is."

Tom and I stood near the door that leads toward the garage and watched the car approach. He had his rifle leaning against the post. In the semidarkness I saw Barbara and T.E. Williams get out of the car.

"Just us," Barbara yelled. "Daddy and me."

They came into the house through the backdoor and Mr. Williams was carrying a typewriter and he set it on the kitchen table.

"We have something to discuss," Barbara said.

Without saying anything Doris brought out a cake and some coffee and sodas.

"John, I am deeply troubled by all of the unscrupulous business dealings you have faced," T.E. said. "I frankly believe you have recovered all that you are going to on the Grand Hotel transaction. I would not even call it a transaction, it is really just a swindle. That is all you can call it."

Doris started to leave the room. I asked her to stay. I pretty well knew at that point who could be trusted and she could be trusted.

T.E. continued, "John, you asked if I could write a will for you that is different from the one Sanders recommended?"

"I remember that. I still think it is a good idea."

"So do I. At the time you asked, I told you it would be unethical for me to write the will without Sanders's approval. Lawyer's ethics and so on."

"Well, can you write it?"

"Yes. Based on what Barbara told me, I believe a different will may very well save your life. None of us like to think about things like that, but it is true." T.E. turned to Molly and said, "Molly, I can also write a will for you. The only thing I need to know is who you wish to leave your estate to."

T.E. thought a moment. "There is one catch. I will write a will for each of you. However, you must carry the will into the Agency in the morning and file it yourselves. You should hand the paper to Mr. Hugel, the superintendent. He cannot accept it from me because Sanders is Molly's guardian. Sanders could still challenge the will, but chances are he won't. In fact, I am pretty sure that he will not."

"I want to leave my estate to Mon-tse-no-pi'n," I told T.E. "He is an older man that lives in Indian Camp." I thought a moment. "Would I be placing him in danger? I guess what I am asking is do you think anyone would kill him for my estate?"

"I don't know that," T.E. said. "It would be much more difficult for a criminal to get your money from him if there is no tie between them."

"Okay. Then let's leave my estate to Mon-tse-no-pi'n."

Molly said, "Could I leave my estate to Saint Louis School? There were times when Mother Superior felt like killing me, but she would never ever do it for money. Maybe to save my soul but not for money."

"Okay," I said. "That still leaves Ted."

T.E. said, "We can get this out of the way and then worry about Ted. He should be safe until after the wedding."

Molly and I looked at each other and I had seen her expression all my life. She and I were agreeing that it was somehow good to have T.E. confirm what we suspected.

T.E. sat at the kitchen table with a pencil and paper and wrote a last will and testament for my signature. We were all quiet and I answered a few questions for T.E. It took about thirty minutes. He handed the draft to Barbara to type. While she typed, T.E. wrote out a last will and testament for Molly's signature.

The process took perhaps three hours. Doris kept us in refreshments and replaced the jazz music with Maurice Chevalier and other slower, more familiar music. Tom and Wolf sat outside watching.

T.E. suggested we sign the wills in the morning so his secretary could notarize them.

Molly again slept in my old room. I thought I would have trouble sleeping but I did not. My bedroom windows were open and there was good moonlight and before I fell asleep I heard a small pack of hunting hounds chasing a coyote near the ridge of the hill. I listened and could tell that the coyote was circling and then I could tell that a fresh coyote had switched places with the one being chased. The hounds never knew the difference.

CHAPTER

51

We met in T.E. Williams's third-floor office. Signing the wills and having them notarized took just a few minutes. T.E. placed a telephone call to the Agency and handed me the telephone receiver and speaker. I asked to speak to Superintendent Hugel and when he came onto the line I told him we wanted to see him for five minutes. Mr. Hugel said that if we could get to his office within fifteen minutes he would see us.

We took the elevator down to the news and tobacco stand and went out onto the street. The sidewalk was more crowded than usual. We felt confident we were safe until eleven o'clock and I kept telling myself I was overreacting. We climbed the stairs to the Bon Bon. T.E. waited there and Molly and I climbed the stairs to the Agency.

Mr. Henry Hugel was waiting in his office. He stood while we shook hands.

Mr. Hugel said, "John, I have just a few minutes to talk, but let me tell you this. We have been having quite a discussion about you handling your own affairs."

"I hope I am not causing the staff too much trouble."

"No, no, nothing like that. It's just that the government takes a lot of time to do just about anything. What you asked us to do is a serious step and we are taking a little time on it is all. Don't want to make any mistakes, you see."

"Mr. Hugel, I have written my will. I have signed it and it is duly notarized." I handed him the document.

Molly said, "Mr. Hugel. I have also written my own will. Mine is also notarized." She smiled and handed him the document.

Mr. Hugel held both documents and studied them briefly. "This is a little unusual for someone with a guardian, Molly, to write her own will." He thumbed through the document a little more. "However, it does seem to be well put together. You wrote this yourself, did you?"

"Well, I got some advice on format," Molly said, "but it says what I want it to say."

We waited while he studied the documents. Finally Mr. Hugel called to his secretary and instructed her to stamp the documents as having been received and to stamp the copies that we would keep.

"I would like to spend more time with you, but like I said on the phone, I have another meeting. Mr. Bartholomew is out at the moment and I will give these papers to him as soon as he comes in." We walked out into the main hallway of the Agency.

"When do you think he will give the papers to Mr. Bartholomew?" Molly asked.

"When we are at least across the street, I hope."

We descended the stairs to the Bon Bon. Barbara and T.E. were waiting.

"How did it go?" T.E. asked.

"Like clockwork," Molly said, and she smiled and handed our stamped copies of the wills to him.

T.E. placed the copies into his briefcase and closed it. Then he smiled, "I am starting to enjoy the Bon Bon's coffee," and he turned and went down the stairs to return to his office.

"Molly, we may have taken most of the profit out of shooting us."

Madame Richarde brought out the tea and coffee and said, "I think you will like this new tea, Molly." We thanked her and she went back inside.

Molly said, "You know when Ted built the house he bought all that silverware and dishes and stuff and it is really hard to buy them a wedding gift. But I think I may have found something. I couldn't help myself. I got them another gift and it is a good one."

"Okay. What is it?"

"I guess I can tell, after all, I didn't promise myself to keep it a secret." She sipped her tea and waited just a moment. "I got them a baby grand piano. It is beautiful. It is supposed to be delivered this morning."

"What time this morning?" Barbara asked.

"At eleven. I know that was the time we were scheduled to sign the wills in Mr. Sanders's office, but I just got through signing a will. I know when he sees me he is going to talk to me real stern, but I am not going to change my mind. So, what is the point in going to see him?"

"Good point," I said. "You go on and see about the piano. I will meet with Mr. Sanders. I am certain he knows by now we have signed other wills."

"You think so?" Molly asked.

"You can bet on it," Barbara said. "I think I should go with you, Molly."

Molly and Barbara left to see about the piano. I had twenty minutes before the eleven o'clock appointment. I went to Bander's Mercantile Store and had been there for a short time when Alan Sanders came into the store. He was walking fast toward me.

"John," he said, and he looked serious. "I just learned that you have signed another will that leaves your estate to some old man out at Indian Camp."

"Yes. I was planning to come in at eleven o'clock and tell you about that."

"And did Molly sign a will that left her estate to Saint Louis?"

"Yes. I believe she did. Well, not really to the saint himself. I believe she left it to the school that is named for Saint Louis." I remember thinking if this is going to get me shot I may as well enjoy it. "You know. I suppose the Church would look at it as if she really is leaving her estate directly to Saint Louis. You know, I am sure the church will look at it that way."

"John. You two cannot do that."

"I think we can, Mr. Sanders." It was surprisingly easy for me to say. "I would rather leave anything I might have to that old man. There isn't anything wrong with that, is there? Molly and Ted certainly have all the money they need."

"John, that old man has all the money he needs, but that is not the point. Let's go up to my office and discuss this. Where is Molly?" He looked around as if he might see her. "I need to talk to her too."

"She went to see about a musical instrument. A grand something or another. Maybe a grand saxophone, no, it was a grand piano."

We crossed the street and took the elevator to Mr. Sanders's office. We discussed the matter from his point of view and from mine. He was visibly angry and my point of view did not impress him much, if at all. He kept telling me I could not do that. He pointed out all that he had done for Molly and for me. He said he was Molly's guardian and he would fight her will based on her incompetence.

Mr. Sanders had always been a courteous and kind gentleman. Even that day last week in the long house he was only arrogant and not really mean. I had never seen his mean side, but on this visit he suddenly showed me that mean side of his personality. He told me I could not get away with what I was doing and that he would get me.

He added that he had a stack of IOUs from Ted this high, and he held his hand about a foot above his desk. Hopefully, that was an exaggeration. I was courteous to Mr. Sanders and I left his office and took the stairs down to the street.

I was pleased to think I held my own with Sanders. However, I was concerned about Ted.

I went back to the Mercantile Store and made a pretense of looking at blankets and stood near the front window. Very soon Mr. Sanders left the Triangle Building and crossed the street walking fast to the parking lot behind the bank. Then he reappeared driving his car and turned the corner and drove east on Main Street.

With Sanders out of his office and not watching I wanted to drop by and thank Walter Whitman for his assistance and to catch up on what he had been doing. I did not feel too threatened at the moment but I also knew Mr. Alan S. Sanders did not appear to be giving up on any plans he may have.

• ◆ •

When I reached Ted's place the workmen were finished with the piano and Molly was doing her best to play a Scott Joplin ragtime piece. The tune is familiar but I do not remember the title. I think Molly has something of an ear for music.

I had a feeling Mavis was pretty much on the level, but the thought that Ted may still be in danger would not go away. Mavis would not turn down anything that came her way, of course, but she is also not a murderer. Not that I knew what a murderer might look like, or act like, or think like. At least I was not aware of any murderer acquaintances. I was exhilarated and silly thoughts kept coming into my head.

I kept remembering that first day we met Mavis at the railroad station restaurant. She did seem to know who Ted was and that was the only unsettling thing about her. The rest I could explain to myself.

Getting ready for the rehearsal was a pleasant time. Just as we were getting started, Roper received a telephone call and had to go out to the ranch. A fence was down and cattle were out and in the next pasture.

Barbara played classical pieces she learned for piano recitals and then Molly tried to show Barbara how to play ragtime piano. It was clear Mavis enjoyed the last-minute details of the wedding. Aunt Mary and Mrs. Bigcreek and Grace Oak were busy in the kitchen and Hank was outside keeping the fire going under a kettle of hominy. It was a pleasant time but I could not relax.

Our plan was for a brief wedding rehearsal and some food. Later, around seven, Ted wanted our little group to meet at the Bon Bon.

CHAPTER

52

The Bon Bon was crowded. Mavis and Ted were early and they sat at the large table in the middle of the terrace. A band was performing a concert at the bandstand on Sixth Street. It was John Phillip Sousa March music that could easily be heard from the Bon Bon on that still spring evening and was a nice addition to the atmosphere.

Roper showed up and he was dressed like a working cowboy, sweat and dirt and something on his boots.

Molly said, "Roper, were you actually working at the ranch?"

"Bring me some coffee. Some exotic coffee," he added, "with a little, you know," and he tipped an imaginary bottle to his lips. Madame Richarde assumed a more formal stance as she always does when she is serving an illegal drink, even when the entire country is drinking illegally.

Walter Whitman joined us. It was good to see him. I have a respect and a new appreciation for Walter. There were many things about the evening that were going well.

Molly tried calling Sonny to invite him, but he wasn't at home, and Barbara like the rest of us was in good spirits.

Ted and Mavis told us about their plans for a wedding trip to Colorado Springs. They had reservations at the Antlers Hotel. Mavis had never seen the Antlers and was looking forward to staying there and they were excited and we listened. The staff people at the Antlers know Ted as a good guest and I am sure they will have a good trip.

Walter told me that he wished to pursue our conversation concerning the old people and our rituals. He compared the old men's recitation of the prayers with learning the *Canterbury Tales* word for word. I told him that was a good analogy and when we had some time we should plan a dinner and discuss the subject. I told Walter I would speak with Mon-tse-no-pi'n to see how much of the rituals I can discuss and Walter agreed that was a good idea.

Mavis told us about the trip into town to pick up Ted's new suit. The suit fit him perfectly. Ted added that Harry had acquired the knack of tailoring a suit with a western cut. Mavis and Molly began a conversation about Mavis's dress and Molly's dress. Ted and Roper and Walter were discussing the differences of English horsemanship and western horsemanship.

I more or less drifted, thinking about the picture of Mon-tse-no-pi'n. Creating a picture with that much emotion was something new to me. It gave me a deeper understanding of the intense feelings the impressionist painters had for their art. I knew they were intense, they had to be. I sensed it when I looked at their work, but that was their work and their time to live and to paint. Painting Mon-tse-no-pi'n is my life and my time. That was the source of the emotion I was experiencing on that day when I first sketched him.

That thought also had to have something to do with why I believed the painting to be a quality work of art. It occurred to me how little it mattered what anyone else thought of the painting and that, too, was new for me.

Monsieur Richarde told us that later when the crowd thinned out he would play a French betrothal song on his accordion for Mavis and Ted.

Madame Richarde brought a tray of champagne glasses to our table and Monsieur Richarde brought an ice bucket with a bottle of champagne.

Molly said, "I want to make a toast."

Monsieur Richarde opened the champagne and poured the champagne into the glasses with a bit of style.

We took the glasses and Molly stood and continued, "There are so many things I want to say and so many toasts I would like to make."

"We have til Saturday," Ted said.

"I may need it. First, I think we would like to welcome Mavis to our family." Molly turned to Roper and said, "And we include you as a part of our family, Roper."

Roper nodded and raised his glass slightly.

So Molly raised her glass and said, "Here's welcoming you, Mavis, to our little family." We drank from the champagne glasses and I was relaxed and a part of a special group.

"We have gone through a difficult time during the past few months," Molly said. "We have had to call on our elders for guidance and we have had to lean on each other for strength. I think it is in times like these that we . . ."

It was then, in the middle of Molly's sentence that I heard the shots that were so close together and were yet so distinguishable and separate. The first was the crack of a .22-caliber rifle. The second was a high-powered rifle. Just as I heard the shots Molly spun and crashed onto the table and then to the floor of the terrace and I could see small drops of her blood fly past me in an a rounded pattern.

Walter and I both moved to cover Molly. Mavis instantly plowed into Ted knocking him to the floor and she shielded him with her body.

In little more than an instant Roper turned the table to shield Molly.

It was chaotic with people yelling to each other and some people screaming. Some ran down the stairs to the street and some lay flat on the floor. One man jumped across to the terrace of the apartments next to the Bon Bon.

The shots came from the hillside west of the Bon Bon, I was sure. The sound of the shots seemed to be to the right of the stairs.

"Get a torch, mate," I heard Walter say. He was trying to help Molly. "Get me a torch." He thought of the right word. "A bloody flashlight," Walter yelled.

Madame Richarde was on her hands and knees looking at Molly lying on the floor of the terrace. She said calmly, "I will get the light." She got to her feet and while keeping low she ran to the inside dining room.

People were frantic, and they were yelling and screaming. Some people followed Madame Richarde to the inside dining room, scrambling for a safer place.

Monsieur Richarde came out of the inside dining room carrying a double-barreled shotgun and he ran to the corner next to the hill and crouched behind the wall at the corner lamppost looking northwest up the hill in the direction the shots seemed to have come from.

"She's still breathing," I heard Walter say. "Get me a tablecloth, John." I grabbed two tablecloths and handed them to Walter.

"Tear one in strips," Walter said. "Hurry, old boy."

Madame Richarde held the flashlight so Walter could see to work on Molly.

Someone yelled, "Call an ambulance." It was a man's voice.

"Where did the shot come from?" Ted yelled.

"Up there," Roper said and pointed in the direction of the hillside, "to the right."

I was looking down at Molly and she very slowly opened her eyes. She was stunned but conscious. "What happened?" she asked.

"You're going to be all right," I told her. "You've been shot."

"Was anyone else shot?"

"No, just you."

"Don't try to talk, Molly," Walter said. "I think we have about stopped the bleeding."

We heard a siren.

Those people who had not left began hurrying down the stairs. One man was trying to pay his tab to Monsieur Richarde who was still crouched behind the railing. "Hide! go away!" Monsieur Richarde shouted to the man.

A man that I recognized as Dr. Raymond Wallace came running up the stairs. "What happened, John?"

"Boy, am I glad to see you. Someone shot Molly."

"I was having a sandwich across the street," Dr. Wallace said. He knelt down and looked at Molly and inspected the wound. "Good job," he said to Walter. "Did anyone call an ambulance?"

"I did," Madame Richarde said.

The sheriff came up the stairs. "What in hell happened here?" he yelled.

"Somebody shot Molly," Ted said. "Came from up that way." "You boys take your flashlights and cover them other stairs down the street." He pointed north. "Probably too late, but we can try. Don't ask too many questions, just find the son of a bitch." The two deputies started down the stairs. "Call the city police tell them we need help to comb that damned hill."

An ambulance arrived and quickly they were readying Molly to move her down the stairs on a stretcher. Dr. Wallace was with her.

"She's going to make it," Dr. Wallace said. "She'll be laid up for a while, but she'll make it."

Monsieur Richarde stood up and relaxed for a moment. Ted looked down at Molly and he became furious, uncontrollably furious. He grabbed the shotgun from Monsieur Richarde and started up the stairs.

"Where you goin with that thing?" Mavis said.

"Going after him. The police are going round to stop him so I'll go straight at him. One of us ought to get him."

"He might shoot you. If he don't shoot you the police might shoot you, Ted."

"Can I have that flashlight?" he asked. Madame Richarde handed him the flashlight and Ted ran up the stairs about three steps and turned to his right and went into the brush along the hillside.

I was walking beside Molly and she asked softly, "Why are people yelling at Ted?"

"He is going after the guy that shot you and I think I better go with him."

"Yes, you go with Ted. Look after him and I'll be all right. I heard Dr. Wallace say I would be."

"I'll stay with Molly," Roper said.

"Good," I turned and went to see what Ted was up to.

There could be more shooting, I knew that. There were more sirens down on the street and on Grandview Avenue on the hill.

I heard Ted yell, "Over here." Ted was about forty yards up on the hillside waving the flashlight. "Over here, Sheriff." Then he fired off a round from the shotgun. I could see the fire from the bore of the gun blast into the air. "I found him. He's been shot too," Ted yelled.

"Damn!" The sheriff said. "Who in hell shot him?" Then he yelled, "Don't do no more shootin, Ted."

"I think he's dead," Ted yelled. "I'm sure of it. He's dead. I won't do any more shooting, Sheriff."

I walked quickly up the hillside with the sheriff who showed the way with his flashlight and his pistol drawn. Ted had moved quickly through the thick brush.

The sheriff shined his light onto the gunman lying on the ground. It was difficult to see because the sheriff kept moving the light, but it was Kenneth Carson. His brown hat was on the ground beside him. He was lying on a high-powered rifle. The part of the rifle I saw was a high-powered bolt action rifle but I could not be sure.

"Whoever did it got him clean through the head," Ted said.

"Well, what do you know about that," the sheriff said. It was a rather absent-minded comment not a real question.

After a moment the sheriff said, "I doubt that we will catch the guy who did this. I think we already got the guy that shot Molly." He pointed the flashlight at the dead body of Kenneth Carson. "I'm pretty sure this is our man."

"That's what it looks like to me," I said.

"You know him?" The sheriff asked.

"I've seen him around, but I don't know him."

"I'd like to know who in hell shot him." The sheriff hesitated, then said, "At least, I think I'd like to know who shot him. Don't much matter. I'll bet if we test that bullet it'll show this here's the bird that shot Molly."

"I would bet on it," I said.

"How many shots did you hear, John?"

"I heard two. I am pretty sure the big gun fired first and then the .22 fired next. Yes, I am sure of it."

"That makes sense. Whoever shot him was probably tailin him and let him shoot Molly, then the big boss shot him to keep him quiet."

I waited around for a few minutes to see if anything else would happen. Ted was still holding Monsieur Richarde's gun and flashlight. We hurried back down to the Bon Bon and Ted returned the gun and flashlight.

"I am sorry about all of this," I told Monsieur Richarde.

"You go," Monsieur Richarde said. "Go see about Molly."

"You're right," I said. "Ted, I'll see you at the hospital."

It took a few minutes to get to my car and drive to the hospital. The ambulance was backed up the emergency ramp to the entrance on the west side of the building and Molly was already inside.

Roper was in the waiting room. "Dr. Wallace took her right in to surgery," Roper said. "Dr. Wallace said he was pretty sure she will be all right."

Marvin, the sheriff's deputy, was with Roper. "Sheriff said for me to stay here with Molly," Marvin said. "Sheriff said you never know. One of them might come looking to finish the job."

"I need to get out to the house and check on things there," I told the deputy. "If they shot Molly they may go out there and Doris and Tom would not know what was going on."

"Do you think there are more of em?" Marvin asked.

"I have no way of knowing," I said. "I'm just going out there as a precaution. Thanks for staying here."

"Good idea," Roper said. "I'll stay too."

Ted and Mavis came into the hospital just as I was leaving. "It looks to me like the big boss got away," Ted said. "Looks like that Carson shot Molly then his boss probably shot him to keep him quiet."

"That makes sense," Marvin said.

"Sounds right to me," I added.

CHAPTER

53

I drove fast toward home. Tom's car was in the driveway and I walked by and touched the hood of his car and the motor was still hot. The light was on in Tom's apartment that connected with the garage.

I opened the door to the apartment. Tom was sitting on the bed and stuffing his things into a canvas bag, and I asked him, "What are you doing?"

"Did I get him?"

"You nailed him, Tom."

"Did he hit anybody?"

"He hit Molly but she is going to be okay."

"Damn, I shoulda shot quicker."

"You did all right, Tom. You saved Molly's life." He kept packing. "You can't leave now."

"I sure as hell can't stay."

"Nobody knows it was you? Until this moment even I didn't know for sure."

Tom had very few things to pack, but he began packing things more carefully and it was taking a little while.

"The sheriff is not even looking for you. He told the boys to look around and see if they could find anything. I'm sure he is happy to see a character like Carson dead."

"He's dead, huh?"

"Real dead, Tom."

"Good."

"I've seen you hit squirrels in the head at that range."

"That was a man, not a squirrel. I hate stuff like this. I had all I needed in the war," and Tom looked at me. I know him as well as I know anyone and he wanted to believe me. "You really think I can stay?"

"You have to stay. If you run now they'll have no choice but to think you did it and they will come looking for you."

"Good," he said, then he stopped putting things into the bag and sat still for a moment before he laid his bag down and started rolling a cigarette.

"Ya probably right, Johnny," Tom said as he finished making the cigarette. He took a match from the box and lit the cigarette. "I ain't got no place to go no how. The Thunders and the Grayeagles is the only family I got. I ain't had another family since I was a kid."

"Tom, we need to get out to Nelagony to see if Sanders and those guys are meeting. We need to be there before eleven o'clock."

"I plum forgot 'bout that." Tom picked up his cigarette papers and tobacco. "Let me get somethin to shoot with."

"I'll check on Doris and tell Cloud what we're doing."

"Johnny, ya think Cloud will wanna go?"

"Probably, but he needs to stay here because of Doris."

"Good idea," Tom said.

"I'll meet you at the cars in a minute or two." I walked toward the backdoor of the main house. Doris would probably be in her bedroom and it would take only a minute to tell her. When I rounded the corner of the main house I saw a small light in Grandpa's little rock house.

The light startled me and I stopped. If someone wanted to harm me they probably would not light the lamp.

I took the few steps toward the little house with caution and opened the door slowly. The kerosene lamp in the little house was dim. I thought it was Grandpa standing near the fireplace looking at his war club. It was a dread excitement and my heart was racing.

He was holding something and he turned toward me but his face was still in the shadows.

"*Wah-ni-un-tah,*" he said.

"*Wi-tsi-ko?*"

"*No. I am Wa-tsa-moin.*" It was Star That Travels, and he held a Pipe in front of him.

"*You looked like Grandfather standing in this house.*"

"*I am a Hun-gah, I am of the earth. We made ourselves of the bear. He has courage and is quick and strong and he fights with his whole heart to protect his home.*"

"*I have been told that by my grandfather.*"

"*You are a Tzi-zhu, you are of the sky. When you were a child, Gla-moin gave you the name Wah-ni-un-tah, the Giver of Life. You are here so that people in trouble will find safety and protection.*"

"*I was told that and I have tried to live that way.*"

"*That is good. You helped Mi-keh-wa-ti-an-kah and your grandfather cut a stem for a Pipe. This is that Pipe.*"

He handed the Pipe to me. "*Did your grandfather tell you about the Pipe?*"

"*He told me the Pipe would give me courage. He did not tell me all he knew about the Pipe.*"

Star That Travels said, "*We have put aside most of those old ways. Maybe we put them away too early and it is that maybe we should have kept the Pipe. Maybe we did the right thing in putting certain pipes away. Moon Head and his teachings of Grandfather Peyote and Jesus, and the Blackrobes and their teachings of Jesus. There is much power in those ways and that is good. I have taken up those ways. It is true I have kept some of the old ways. This Pipe.*

"*Keep this Pipe with you, Wah-ni-un-tah. You will need courage because you must face your enemy. This Pipe will tell you what to do about your enemy.*

"*You are from the Sky Clan. You are of the Peace People. Still, you must face the enemy and you must destroy your enemy, the enemy of the Osage People and you must do it quietly. Your grandfather was a peacemaker and he protected the people. That is every man's obligation.*"

Wa-tsa-moin walked past me and his quick and smooth movement caused me to think of his clan name of a shooting star as he
moved out into the night where his driver was waiting, parked near
the summerhouse, and the driver opened the car door for him and
Wa-tsa-moin got into the car and the driver drove the long car down
the drive way and out onto the main road.

I took Grandpa's war club from the wall and stood in the middle
of the rock house holding the Pipe and the club. Star That Travels
was right. That is every man's obligation as it is my obligation.

I stood still for a moment surrounded by Grandpa's things. I
waited.

"Who was that?" I heard Tom say. "I thought it was your Grandpa."

"So did I. Kind of scared me."

"Scared the hell out of me," Tom said.

"It was Wa-tsa-moin. He was a friend of Dad and Grandpa."

Tom waited a moment, then said, "If we're gonna go to Nelogony
we better get movin."

"You're right. I'll tell Doris and I'll be right out."

Doris was in the living room reading. I told her to leave all of the
lights on in the house and Cloud said he would stay close to her.

We drove Tom's Ford to Nelagony. We reached the trees where
Tom hid the car at about 10:40. We did not have much time, so we
walked as fast as we could walk, without making noise. There was
moonlight to make the path easy to follow. When we were near we
could see the glow of the campfire reaching some of the tall trees.

Otis Davis was sitting on a log near the fire with a shotgun beside
him leaning against the log. He took a bottle from his hip pocket and
poured some whiskey into a tin cup and took a drink.

Within minutes the lights of a car came into the clearing. Alan
Sanders got out of the car. He was in a hurry. "Where's Carson?" he
called to Davis.

"Haven't seen him," Davis called back.

"Did you ever tell him to hold up on getting rid of Molly Thunder and John Grayeagle?"

"No," Davis called back. "I never could find him."

"Neither could I," Sanders said. He was walking toward Davis. Sanders was excited and kept talking loudly.

Sanders said, "I heard Molly Thunder was shot. You know anything about that?"

"Not a thing. I thought we were gonna wait til her an that Grayeagle boy signed them wills," Davis said. "Were'nt that the plan?"

"Well, that was the plan, but we never told Carson. I looked for him, I just couldn't find him," Sanders said.

Sanders was still talking loud and in a bit of a rush, "I heard somebody got killed over there where Molly Thunder got shot."

"That son of a bitch," Davis said. "If he messed this deal up, I'll kill him myself."

"It may be too late for that," Sanders said.

Tom whispered to me, "I'll shoot em both."

I placed my hand on his arm that was holding the gun. "No," I whispered.

"Why not?" Tom whispered.

My heart was racing. "I don't know, Tom. We're not like them. At least I hope we are not like them."

"There ain't nobody but dead people gonna be like them when I get through," Tom whispered.

"Wait a minute, Tom. Let's listen to what they have to say."

Otis Davis's voice was still loud and we heard all that he said.

He handed Sanders a tin cup. "You think that little bitch is dead, Mr. Sanders?"

"Looks that way."

Davis poured coffee into the tin cup. "Then that only leaves John Grayeagle, for now."

"Tell you what, Davis. We'll wait a few days then we'll go ahead and kill John Grayeagle. Then we'll wait til the Thunder and Grayeagle wills are probated. Bearsky will end up with everything they have, I can see to that, and I can do it in a hurry." Davis held up the bottle of whiskey and Sanders nodded and Davis poured the whiskey into the cup. "They both signed wills but I can get those wills declared void. Later, when all of that is done, we'll kill Bearsky.

"They will have signed those wills right before they were killed so it'll look like somebody killed them so that old man out in Indian Camp could inherit their money," Sanders laughed and took a sip from the cup. "That's what I'm going to argue and the people at the Agency will go along with it."

"You ain't been wrong yet, Mr. Sanders."

"I been right about every damned one of them and I'm right this time." And he took another drink of the coffee and whiskey he held.

My stomach began to churn, and when I thought of my parents and their car wreck I thought I would throw up. I thought about Molly's parents, Uncle Silas and Aunt Anna, and their car wreck. I thought of the days and nights without my parents, and of Grandpa, and him trying to take their place, and I briefly felt a rage inside me, but only for a moment. Then my heart stopped pounding and I was calm. I knew what I had to do.

Sanders said, "We sure can't be seen together." He was thoughtful, "I'll contact you when it's time to finish the job. Probably day after tomorrow before we kill Grayeagle."

"Wait here," I said to Tom.

"What are you doin?" Tom whispered.

"If they kill me, then shoot both of them," I said, not whispering. "I am going to face them."

They must have heard me, because when I stepped from the thick cedar branches and into the clearing, they were facing me. I held the Pipe in my left hand and the war club in my right hand. Sanders was startled for a moment, then he extended his hand to me.

"John, what are you doing here?"

"I came to see you, Mr. Sanders. You too, Mr. Davis."

"I'm glad you're here, John. Did you hear about Molly being shot?"

"Yes. I was there. Your boy Carson is dead."

"Carson? I don't know any Carson."

"I know the son of a bitch," Davis said. "And maybe he couldn't kill you but I sure as hell can." Davis dropped to the ground on one knee and reached for the shotgun leaning against the log.

I moved toward him quickly and slung the war club in a high arching motion and I felt the weapon drive deep into the back of his right shoulder

Davis screamed and I pulled the war club from him and Davis rolled on the ground near the log still screaming in pain.

"My God, you almost cut his arm off!" Sanders yelled. "For God's sake, John. We can talk this out."

I looked again at Davis writhing in pain and quickly looked back at Sanders. I thought he might attack me but he did not move.

"Okay, Mr. Sanders. Talk this out."

"Things just got a little out of hand, John. That's all. I never had any notion of Molly getting killed or of anybody getting hurt."

I remember looking at Davis on the ground and thinking that Grandpa's teachings and beliefs toughened him so that he could handle this kind of confrontation. "You're lying, Mr. Sanders."

"I swear to God, John. I'm not lying."

I knew I should kill Sanders but I also knew I did not have Grandpa's temperament.

"For God's sake will you help me?" Davis was crying. "I'll tell the police Sanders is the brains behind this whole deal."

"The police are no longer involved in this."

Davis was crying. "Please get me to a doctor." He struggled and sat up against the log, propping up his damaged arm with his good arm. "Please."

I knew Davis would soon lose consciousness and I turned to face Sanders.

"Listen, John," Sanders pleaded. "Please, John. I am an old man. I have helped your family . . ." He stopped and stood staring at me. He was still holding the tin cup. "Please, don't kill me."

"Before I do anything I want you to know that in my way of thinking, killing you is not murder."

Sanders was whimpering, and with his left hand he removed a watch from his vest pocket. "Here, John. This belonged to your father," and he held the watch out to me. I did not take the watch, and he laid it on the ground, and he still held the tin cup.

Davis was still crying and I heard the crack of Tom's .22 rifle and the tin cup flew from Sanders's hand and Sanders doubled up in pain holding his hand. "What in the hell are you doing? What do you want me to do?"

"If you want your partner to live take him to a doctor. Otherwise he will die. That is up to you."

"I will take him."

"Never tell anyone about what happened here tonight. If you tell anyone, I will find you and I will kill you with this war club. If I see you again, I will kill you. If you kill me, then that man out there in the trees will kill you."

"You will never see me again, I promise," Sanders said.

When I turned to leave, the fire was still burning and neither of the two men moved but I could hear Otis Davis crying.

We walked the trail in the moonlight and my body was numb. Somehow it hurt to acknowledge that Sanders had a hand in my parents' deaths but it was a fact I could not escape. Again, I thought of my parents. I had mental images of their funeral during the freezing cold weather and the snow and ice and wiping the tears from my eyes and Grandpa standing next to me and mostly of me being alone as a child and I was grateful for Grandpa and Molly and Ted.

I had never felt hatred before but I felt hatred for Sanders and Davis. Then my hatred started to spread like the ripples caused by a rock thrown into still water, spreading to the lawyers and the judges and the people who sell things and I then thought of Grandpa and the words of Wa-tsa-moin and I gripped the Pipe and managed to regain a sense of calmness.

I am Tzi-zhu-wah-shta-gi. I have made myself of gentleness. A gentleness that is not weak but a gentleness that is fair and strong. As all men must, I had met my obligation and I will meet it again if necessary.

CHAPTER

54

I did not sleep Friday night, all of Saturday, and most of Sunday. During that time I visited Molly several times. On those visits she was sleeping but Dr. Wallace told me she was doing well. On the third visit she woke up for a short time and began talking. She asked me to make a list of people who sent flowers and cards but she became tired and went back to sleep before she could finish expressing her thoughts.

Cloud stayed around the house and reported nothing unusual happening, and I did not see Tom.

Saturday's newspaper had a large picture of Molly on the front page. I did not look at the photographs and did not read the article. Roper told me the article speculated that Carson mistakenly thought Molly was someone else and shot her by accident. The paper also had a picture of Carson's dead body. Roper said it was a grizzly photograph. He said the article did not connect Molly's attack with the deaths of Martha and Evelyn Thunder.

Sunday evening I fell asleep and awoke a little after noon on Tuesday. I was experiencing a calmness I had never known. It was not a good calmness. I went to the hospital and learned that Molly was recovering nicely.

Dr. Wallace dropped by to check on Molly. We stood in the hallway of the hospital outside of Molly's room and he told me Walter's military training saved Molly's life. I seemed to know that, but it was good to talk to the doctor, and to hear it from him. I was starting to revive a little.

When I left the hospital Barbara was parking her car next to mine. She had just missed me at home and had been looking for me. Seeing her seemed to fill a void and for a moment everything seemed alright. She said, "John," and we embraced. "How do you feel?"

"I'm beat. I'm not thinking that well and I don't seem to care. It's good to see you."

We drove out into the country and neither of us spoke for some time. Barbara turned to me, "Daddy said that on Monday the agency received a letter from Sanders. He resigned as guardian for Molly and Ted. According to Daddy's source, in the letter Sanders claimed to have brought them to a point where they could handle their own affairs, and he was no longer needed."

"Ted may very well need a guardian, but not one like Sanders."

"That's what Daddy said. Daddy also said no one has seen nor heard from Sanders. His office is closed and you can't see in."

"I suppose instead of eighty-seven lawyers in Pawhuska there are now only eighty-six."

"Daddy will like that comment. Daddy also said that people around town are starting to connect Sanders with the shooting and he said a lot of people around town are starting to get nervous, but nobody is talking openly."

"Smart bunch of people. Have you seen Ted?"

"No. I heard he and Mavis had quite a fight. Not a swinging fight but a word fight. Roper thinks Mavis told Ted she knew Sanders before she came here, but she wasn't in on any criminal stuff."

"That's kind of what I think," I said.

"I don't know how Roper knew about the fight, though."

"Roper always knows both the Indian side and the white side of things around Osage country."

"Roper said they are going ahead with the funeral. I mean wedding." Barbara laughed a little at her slip of the tongue. "Roper thinks Ted is crazy. Said he is not sure if he will attend."

"He'll be there," I said. "He can't help himself. I think that Mavis telling Ted the truth probably saved their relationship in the long run when it could have ended it."

"Should have ended it according to Daddy. Roper thinks that way too. I guess just about everybody, including me."

"Any serious questions I may have had about Mavis were pretty much answered when the shooting started and she knocked him to the floor and shielded him."

"Really? I thought that was too much of a show," Barbara said. "She knew nobody was going to shoot Ted."

"I never thought of that."

"When I was telling Daddy about the shooting the other night he said it sounded like the sheriff put on quite a show."

I said, "That was a pretty bold shooting. It was out in the open. It sure wasn't like one of those made-up car wrecks or whiskey poisonings."

"Daddy said someone is controlling the sheriff but he doesn't know who it might be."

"I suppose I should drop by the Bon Bon and apologize to the Richardes."

"Yeah, sure. Business at the Bon Bon is booming."

"Are you kidding me?"

"Nope, I'm not kidding and ours is the table people ask for."

CHAPTER

55

The wedding was delayed for a week and it was a more simple ceremony than Mavis and Ted had planned. Because of the chaos on that Friday night, I thought few people would attend, but I was wrong.

Tom, who always sat on the back row when he occasionally attended church, sat in the back row of chairs on the lawn. He asked if it was okay if he rolled a cigarette and Ted laughed a little and told him it was okay and patted Tom on the shoulder.

Molly was in a wheelchair, and her shoulder in a cast. Will Chapman pushed the wheelchair and a nurse dressed in white walked with them. Molly hid it well but she was in pain. It was when she smiled that the pain showed.

"Are you all right?" I asked.

"Wouldn't miss it, Cousin."

"I mean is it wise for you to move around?"

"It's not a question of wisdom, it is a matter of loyalty."

"You don't learn very fast, do you?"

Molly laughed and then held her shoulder because laughter brought pain. "I guess not. Maybe I don't learn at all."

Mr. Johnson, the Justice of the Peace, and Whitedeer stood on the patio, waiting.

I was best man and waited with Ted in the main house. At three o'clock we walked out onto the patio and down the steps to the lawn to wait for Mavis. When we were in place a lady began playing the wedding march. Mavis held Lucky's arm, and she walked slowly and regally down the aisle on the lawn. Lucky was stiff and his smile was nervous.

When the Justice of the Peace asked if anyone had a reason why the couple should not be joined in holy matrimony, I looked at Molly and she smiled and she signaled with her head for me to stand up and say something. Roper raised his hand slightly and moved forward as if he was going to stand and protest. Aunt Mary saw us and she came as close to a laugh as she will get. I believe no one but Aunt Mary noticed our juvenile behavior.

They recited their vows and exchanged rings and the Justice of the Peace pronounced them husband and wife.

Whitedeer's vast knowledge of the clans and his new knowledge of Christianity as a Road Man of the Native Church gave him a special insight into the marriage of Mavis and Ted.

"Creator, Father and Son of the Creator. You have given us a day that is beautiful. There is gratitude in our hearts." Whitedeer moved his eagle wing fan to bless Mavis and Ted and continued his prayer, *"Creator, the world has changed. Your prophet Moon Head told us we must make a prayer from our hearts, so I will do the best I can.*

"This young man, Wa-tsa-ka-wa, Bright and Radiant Star, who is from the Black Bear Clan. He is a good man. He comes from a good family. All Osage People knew his father and mother.

"I do not know a prayer for this young White Woman. I do not know all of Moon Head prayers. I will do the best I can. I believe you created her and she is one of your children.

"Creator, your prophet Moon Head. He told us there are good White People and there are bad White People as there are good Indian People and bad Indian People. I believe this young woman is a good White Woman.

"She and Wa-tsa-ka-wa, they want to be husband and wife. I believe it is good. Several nights ago an evil white man tried to kill Me-tsa-he. I think that evil man also wanted to kill Wa-tsa-ka-wa. This young White Woman tried to protect Wa-tsa-ka-wa with herself. She is a brave woman. When

they have children I believe she will protect those children as a good mother would. I believe they will be good parents for their children. She will be a good wife for Wa-tsa-ka-wa who is from the Bear Clan.

"*Creator, I ask you to give these young people the wisdom and courage to enjoy the lives you have given them together.*"

Ted was married.

The guests slowly drifted from the chairs and altar toward the patio and the main house and the summerhouse. Several older Osages stopped and shook hands with Tom on their way to the main house. Tom remained slumped in his chair and removed his green plaid hat and shook their hands and said nothing.

Later, Barbara and I were sitting on one of the platforms and I watched Tom. He had been leaning on the fence facing the track and he was smoking and he looked to be in thought. He walked toward us and he said, "You know, Johnny. I kinda like them old Osage weddings. All them fancy clothes and foot races and horse races and eating and singing."

"So do I, Tom."

"Now that was a good time."

Aunt Mary was getting ready to leave and Barbara and I walked over to speak with her. She acknowledged times were changing. She was very cordial to Mavis and had made her feel a part of the family. "She's a nice girl," Aunt Mary said.

"I believe she is."

"*I have seen many changes in my lifetime. I have adjusted to all of them. I think I can adjust to Wa-tsa-ka-wa's wife.*"

I laughed and said, "*I know you will adjust.*"

"*What about the girl you are with? Are you serious about her?*"

"*I do not know.*"

"*She is beautiful and I have heard she is a good woman.*"

"*She is a good woman. That makes it hard to make a decision.*"

"*I want you to find an Osage, but do what will be best for you.*"

"*It is good you say that. I will do what is best for me.*"

Everyone had eaten and the older people were preparing to leave.

The band was from Tulsa and they were setting up on the patio. A lot of people began arriving and the sun was setting and Molly caught my eye and she waved for us to come to her.

We said goodbye to Aunt Mary and were walking away when Barbara said, "Okay, what did Aunt Mary say? Did she ask about me?"

"Well, not really a question. She said you were kind of ugly, but that she thinks that is good. She also thinks you are probably lazy, but you can probably learn to grow corn."

"What did she really say?"

I was going to tell her what Aunt Mary said when I saw the sheriff's car turn the corner and drive through the gate. He was driving slowly and stopped at the front sidewalk. I was not much in the mood for a party, but I was sure not in the mood for bad news.

All of the people on the patio and in the yard and those getting out of their cars stopped and faced the sheriff, and the whole place was quiet. The sheriff looked serious when he opened the car door, and got one leg out, and stood up with one leg still in the car. Then he took his hat off and held it in the air. His whole face turned into a smile and he yelled, "Hey, everybody. Black Gold won the Kentucky Derby!"

The crowd of friends and visitors and relatives cheered and the leader of the band showed he was on his toes by starting a ragtime song.

The sheriff was still yelling, "I knew I wanted to celebrate and by-damn I figured this was the place to do it."

The first one I saw on the floor was Willie Gore doing his version of a dance. It was a good way to start a party.

Later, our little group of friends sat in the study where we had given Molly and Evelyn the gifts at Ted's last party. We could hear the music from outside and we could hear the people shooting at the bell near the track. It was quite a party even by Ted's standards.

CHAPTER
56

Tom stayed around for a few days after the wedding. He went to town and made sure he was seen by a lot of people so he would not appear to be running away. Then he left town, "for a month or two. Think I'll go fishing," he said. "I gotta pull myself together. This is like what I went through after the war." Tom is a good man. He is a loyal man.

The painting of Mon-tse-no-pi'n is finished. It isn't exactly what I wanted, but Mon-tse-no-pi'n is pleased with it, and I suppose it turned out better than I thought it would. I came out of the experience with some new points of view as far as painting is concerned, realizing I have a lot to learn, and a ways to go before I am the artist I want to be.

After gathering my fishing tackle and preparing a lunch I drove out to the campsite to fish and to see what I needed to do to the site for the meeting Mi-keh-wa-ti-an-kah was planning.

Walking through the campsite, I stopped at the cedar tree. It looked the same and I reached out and touched one of the branches and the tree was still strong. I noticed several small sprouts had pushed through the ground. Sprouts of cedar trees that would be like the tree they came from, and somehow that made me feel good.

The day was perfect and I set up for fishing. I thought about the events of the past few weeks. A lot had happened, I recognized that, and thought I would just let it go at that. In time I would sort things out but I needed to do some fishing before I started sorting.

After half an hour of casting and not catching anything, I got out the cork, and the hook, and the sinker, and I found a worm under a rock, and put the worm onto the hook, and dropped it into the water, and waited. I was thinking it was nice to be relaxed and interested in something like fishing when I heard a car. The car came to a stop on the ledge over the great boulders that formed the wall behind Grandpa's camp. Then I heard Barbara calling me from the edge of the boulders above.

"Down here," I called back. "I'll meet you at the crossing to your right."

I thought maybe the meeting she planned with her father had gone well and she needed someone to congratulate her. I walked downstream the short distance to meet her and realized it was something more serious.

"What's wrong?"

"John, I have some distressing news."

"What is it?"

"It's Mr. Baskins. A little while ago he jumped from the third-floor window of the hotel and he is dead."

"Baskins? Are you sure he jumped? It wasn't an accident, and he fell or something?"

"No. He jumped." She walked over to me and I held her. "It was awful, John."

"Did you see him fall?"

"No, but I had just left Daddy's office and was in front of Bander's Mercantile Store, and I heard people screaming, and looked over there. He was all crumpled on the sidewalk where he landed." She began crying. "I went back up to Daddy's office and he said I should come and tell you. It was awful, John."

There is a large rock that juts out into the stream and Barbara and I sat on that rock and talked.

"John, I thought of you instantly when I saw Mr. Baskins lying there."

"I really didn't know him that well. He was always cordial to me, except lately when he knew I knew about his swindle. After that I sensed an anger toward me. A real hostility in his eyes the last time I saw him."

"Daddy said you never know how people like that will react to being found out. The word around town is that he was somehow swindled out of the hotel that he swindled you out of. His brother swindled him is the story. Daddy also heard that his financial holdings are worthless and he had a pile of debt. Enormous debt, and rumors of criminal activity."

At that moment, however ill-gotten his temporary wealth, I felt a great pity for Mr. Baskins.

"You could look at it as self-inflicted justice," I said. "Although, I doubt he did it for justice or any other noble reason. Probably, he just could not face certain people."

"Like who, John?"

The thought had not occurred to me and I wondered.

"Daddy thinks if we knew that, we would know a lot more about that sham bankruptcy. We would probably know more about the Agency too. Daddy said someone at the Agency had to sign off on the deal." Barbara's tears were dry. "Daddy said Sanders is probably somewhere in another town scheming to commit more thefts and murders."

"Your dad is probably right. I doubt he will ever be punished for the crimes he committed and I doubt that he would choose the path of Mr. Baskins."

"John, do you know more about Sanders than you are telling me?"

I thought about the question for a moment then answered, "Grandpa said to let sleeping dogs lie."

"That is probably a good idea," Barbara said. "Maybe I don't want to, now, but some day I probably will want to know."

"Some day, ask me."

CHAPTER
57

Moonlight is shining through the south windows and onto the floor of Grandpa's little rock house. Barbara and Molly left around ten. I am alone, trying to conceive a way of painting a series of pictures that will explain the Osage experience.

The concept must include the clans, and the ancient philosophy, and the newfound wealth. That would include the many good things that have come from oil.

It is a difficult undertaking. An enormous, complex undertaking.

No doubt part of the Osage experience includes people like Sanders and Baskins. People who will commit murder, or anything else, to get an interest in an Osage headright that allows them to share in the oil. They will do anything to get an illegal deed to land that belongs to Osages.

There are others, like the people at the Agency, and lawyers, and business people, who may once have been good people, but their greed made them do evil things. I have no interest in painting them, or in painting experiences like theirs. I doubt that I will ever have that interest.

My thoughts go to the many good people I know, like Barbara and her family, who are good, honest people who make up the town, and thinking of them places my thoughts back on a good track.

I have been searching to find that moment in time to start painting the Osage history. What will the subject of that first painting be? Will it be a life symbol, like the elk or an eagle or a star? Will it be a group picture like those photographs at an I'n-lon-shka dance, or could it be a portrait of a person I know, like Molly?

Molly is a good person. Like this evening when she got us all together to look at pictures she received from Mavis and Ted in Colorado Springs. She brought Will with her. I do not know what is going on between Molly and Will, but I and everyone else suspects there is something. I know Aunt Mary is disappointed, she hoped Molly would find an Osage. Anyway, it was good to have our group of friends together.

Barbara came early, before the others. I have not had much time to think about it, but she and I have a lot to talk about. I looked forward all day to seeing her. I suppose I think about her more than I am willing to admit, even to myself.

As turbulent as it has been I am grateful for the events of recent weeks. I somehow have more feeling for Grandpa and the challenges of his generation, and for my parents' time. Every generation loses something as it moves toward a new era, and we as Osages have taken on a lot that is new during recent times. It may be that we must be prepared to give up something. I suppose choosing what we give up and what we keep will determine our future, as individuals and as a tribe.

Grandpa and Mi-keh-wa-ti-an-kah and those Osages before them were well equipped to face life. Those Osages of the past had the sky and the sun and the stars and the earth and the water and they had the seasons and the earth creatures like the buffalo and deer of which they had symbolically made themselves.

They were the universe. They had war clans to lead in war, and peace clans to follow in peace, and very often those ancient Osages called upon Wah-kon-tah, and asked Wah-kon-tah to let them find courage. Courage, one of us earth creatures' intangibles.

There are mysteries in life that we try to understand and sometimes we make a little progress in that search. I think I saw that in Mon-tse-no-pi'n's eyes on that day I first sketched him.

Some day I will find a way to make my brushes and oil paints and canvas express what it was I saw in Mon-tse-no-pi'n's eyes on that day when I first sketched him and began work on painting his portrait. I plan to work to see if I cannot acquire for myself at least some of those qualities that allowed him to look so deeply into my soul. I do not know what those things are but I will try to find them.

Mon-tse-no-pi'n and those other Old People acquired those qualities in a world that is not available to my generation. They buried some of those teachings with the Medicine Bundles and the Sacred Pipes. They buried those things with dignity and then they went on with their lives.

I am grateful the Old People did not bury all of our teachings and all of our rituals. I will search for those qualities within Indian People and in those teachings the Old People did leave us.

It is good that Mi-keh-wa-ti-an-kah and others are going ahead with making a new Non-hon-zhin-ga. I believe he was right when he said this may be the last time we will do this ritual. I am grateful to be a part of it.

I try to make mental pictures of the ceremony as Grandpa described it. Grandpa said it was powerful. On the final day the candidate would be recognized as a man of knowledge, a Non-hon-zhin-ga, and his family would be proud. But this time it will not be like the old days when word would be sent to other villages by runners to tell them of the new man of knowledge. Still, the family will be proud.

Grandpa said over eighty clan representatives and firemen and cooks would be needed to fulfill the requirements of the ritual. In the old days it would have been a big lodge full of people, not at the beginning, but it would be crowded before the ritual was complete. The people would come into the lodge in an order and Grandpa said the drum would get loud at times and the fire builders would keep the fire burning evenly. The ceremony we were planning would be in the fall of the year in what we now call October and the fires would light and warm the lodge.

In the old days staves were stuck into the ground near the candidate and headsmen. The staves would seem full of life as well as wonderful works of craftsmanship, but mostly they were powerful. Through the night those old prayer songs were sung, repeating perfectly the words and phrases from past centuries and sometimes there would be a drum barely beating and then there would be no drum, but a single voice singing the prayer. The voice would sing clearly and with emotion. At one place in the ritual a single voice would sing softly and evenly for a while, and then that voice would become stronger and would be joined by other voices. Then there would be many voices and the women would join the singing of those deep and meaningful words until everyone was singing the ancient prayer. Grandpa said that was when it was powerful.

It was the people, and the earth creatures, that created the clans that gave insight and courage and those other qualities to individuals like Mon-tse-no-pi'n. But, he was not the only one to have qualities like the ability to look through my eyes and into my soul and to know why I wanted to paint him. Many of them had those qualities.

Qualities like that I suspect are not limited to a single group of people, such as Osages, nor are such traits limited to a race, such as Indians. Still, I must begin my search somewhere and I will begin with Osages. Those are good qualities that I want as a guide to live by, and I want to paint them so that others may use and enjoy them.

That may be a lot to ask of some pencils and brushes and tubes of paint and linen canvas, but those things may very well be all I have to work with.

Then, some day when I know I am a capable artist, I will paint Grandpa.

CPSIA information can be obtained
at www.ICGtesting.com
Printed in the USA
LVHW111914230920
666903LV00002B/247